THE MAN
WHO FELL FROM
THE SUN

RICHARD VALANGA

Copyright – Richard Valanga 2023

First Edition 2023

The author asserts the moral rights under the Copyright, Designs and Patents Act 1988 to be identified as the author of this work.

All Rights reserved, No part of this publication may be reproduced, stored in a retrieval system or transmitted, in any form or by any means without prior consent of the author, nor be otherwise circulated in any form of binding or cover other than which it is published and without a similar condition being imposed on the subsequent purchaser.

Author's Notes

This is an alternative version of Lucifer.
 Maybe an alternate reality.
 Possibly.
 Lucif-er Heylel is one of my favourite characters who made his debut appearance in my novel The Last Angel and I knew straight away that I had to write his story. Maybe this novel should have been called The Life And Loves Of Lucif-er. Possibly?
 And his story continues in my novels Bloodlust and the sequel Lust For Life with the possibility of a reborn lost love.
 But there is an alternate Lucif-er from another reality that will threaten his sanity and his very soul, this story may be found in the memoirs of The First Angel Alphar.
 Possibly.
 The Blue Ripple can affect everyone.

Contents

THEN

1 - LUCIF

2 - LUCIFER

3 - SHALEIL

4 - DESIRE

5 - CARESS

6 - LANAR

7 - YESHUA

8 - CANDIDA LUX / LU'NA

9 - JACK

NOW

10 - THE FALLEN ANGEL

11 - THE FIRST ANGEL

12 - NAMELESS

13 - A NEW REALITY?

14 - ALPHAR

For

Linda Ann Wrout

*To get to Heaven
You have to go through Hell*

THEN

LUCIF

CHOSEN

"He will be called Lucif-er, Son of Lucif."

    The young father's heart was full of pride, it pounded hard in his muscular breast like it would burst open with joy at any moment. This was the happiest Lucif had felt since he had first met his beautiful wife Shaleil. Tears actually filled his eyes as he looked at the newborn baby that was ever so gently moving in the flickering shadows.

The bedroom's crude oil lamp was burning low, Lucif knew that he would have to get more oil after his day's work. But what little light there was shone on his exhausted wife and her baby who seemed to be already aware of his new surroundings.

"He sees us, his eyes sparkle like the heavens above, praise be to the Great One!" declared Lucif.

The young Lucif-er could see.

He could see the moving blue light in the corner of the bedroom.

A light that his young parents could not see.

"And look Lucif, his eyes are blue!" Shaleil declared with pride.

"By Amon, you are right my love. Look mother, look at Lucif-er's bright blue eyes."

The old woman was as exhausted as the young Shaleil after helping with the long childbirth but she did look at her grandson's eyes.

"He is one of The Chosen, he sees those who watch, he sees the Neteru… and I fear that Duma is here."

Her words made Lucif's blood run cold through his veins, he shivered nervously in the heat of the Meccus night.

"You think that he can see the Angelic mother?"

Lucif's mother looked to the corner of the room where the newborn child was still looking.

"His eyes shine blue because they can see the Neteru, soon they will be brown again as when they first opened."

"But why would Duma the Angel of Death be here mother, Shaleil and our baby are fine now?"

Lucif's mother did not reply, she looked deep into her son's eyes and he saw how tired and old she now looked. He suddenly realised that she thought that Duma was there for her.

"No Angel of Death is here this night mother, you just need to rest. Go to your room and I will tend to Shaleil and Lucif-er."

That night Lucif's mother died in her sleep.

Lucif-er's eyes became brown.

SHAKAS

Lucif and Shaleil Heylel were Annonites, people from the country of Annon, a relatively small country whose shape was that of an inverted triangle, the top of Annon embracing the Mediterranean sea. To the left of Annon was Tjehenu (ancient Libya) and to the right was the north of Egypt.

Lucif and Shaleil lived in the capital city of Meccus which was surrounded by a mountain range that was full of diamonds and gold, this was what made Annon a very rich and prosperous country. Annon's wealth meant that it could afford a fearsome army which for many years repelled the constant threat of the Egyptian expanse.

But Lucif and Shaleil were not wealthy people by Meccus standards, Lucif was a building labourer and Shaleil was a seamstress who made what money she could by sewing what needed to be sewn by her immediate neighbours. They lived in the working class district of Shakas which bordered the poorest and most dangerous part of Meccus, an undesirable area known as Khamit. Here was where the most poor of Meccus lived; beggars, thieves, homeless people, petty criminals and prostitutes, it was a proverbial den of iniquity from which there seemed to be no escape for the unfortunate who lived there, a blot on the overall magnificence of Meccus. But some did prosper there; the gang leaders who exploited the weak.

Lucif did own his own home though, a house he had built himself which had three rooms, two of which were for sleeping and the large main room which was the kitchen and living room combined. The house also had a vast rear garden which was surrounded and protected by a high wall. In this area was a makeshift stable for Lucif's black horse, a standard retirement gift for service in the Annon Army. It was always Lucif's plan to extend his house into this spacious area, something he had not got round to yet because his labouring work always took priority; hard tiring work which involved long hours and little recreational time. However Lucif and Shaleil lived a decent and happy life and were well respected by their neighbours, it was only the constant threat of the nearby Khamit that posed any sort of worry for them. But Lucif was a strong man, a feared man and only on a few occasions did the people of Khamit trouble him.

KHAMIT

Lucif-er was one year old and was known to the majority of people as simply Lucifer. It was not long after Lucifer's first birthday that Lucif returned as normal from his hard day's work to find Shaleil crying uncontrollably on her bed.

"What… has happened my love?" Lucif asked as he gently held her trembling hand.

Shaleil looked up at Lucif, her tear-filled eyes dark in the flickering lamp light.

"Robbers Lucif… they took our savings… and…"

Shaleil broke down, shaking with fear.

"And?" demanded Lucif.

"And… Lucifer!"

"What! And… you, did they…?"

"No… no, they did not touch me, they wanted to, they were going to but then they heard people outside."

"But… why take our son?"

But Lucif thought that he knew the answer, child abduction was on the increase, a slave child was worth a lot of money in certain countries. His blood began to boil with anger.

At that moment, three of Lucif's friends rushed into his house, exhausted from chasing the intruders.

"Lucif, we rode after them into Khamit… but we could not find them" said Omar and his voice full of disappointment.

"I… heard him say Abrax" Shaleil mumbled quietly with fear.

"I know of him; Abrax is a gang leader, the owner of Khamit's biggest brothel" growled Lucif, his voice now full of venom.

Lucif went to his room and returned with his two gleaming army swords which were sheathed in a cross on his back.

"I go to Khamit now my friends."

"And we will come with you."

ABRAX

The sun was beginning to set when Lucif and his three companions entered Khamit, the lights from the centre of the distant Meccus were quickly obscured by the dark narrow streets and overcrowded tall buildings that housed the poor that dwelled there.

"I hate this place" said Ahmed and he spat on the dirty ground below him, "Poverty and disease is rife here, can the wealth of Meccus not help these lost souls?"

"Are we wealthy?" asked Lucif immediately but Ahmed did not reply immediately.

They had stopped beside the Khamit market place, every small stall was shut and empty and closed down for the night.

"No… not wealthy Lucif but we work honestly for a living, there is not much hope for the people here" Ahmed eventually replied.

"I have heard talk that Khamit is to be cleared and torn down" added Alix thoughtfully.

Omar interrupted him, "They have been saying that for years, every great city has a slum area, it is the way of things."

Lucif looked around the square from his horse, he knew that they were being watched by dark eyes in the shadows.

"They will take our horses if we let them" said Alix who sounded a bit wary of the silence that surrounded them.

"But we will not let them" Lucif said, his voice bold and authoritative, "I do not leave this dark place without Lucifer."

From the corner of the market square an elderly man emerged from the darkness.

"You are not from Khamit are you?"

"No old man, we look for the house of Abrax."

"Ah, you seek the pleasures of his house then?"

Omar was about to slap the old man but Lucif held his arm.

"If you have horses then you have money" continued the old man whose appearance was shabby and neglected, his bodily odour offensive to Lucif and his friends.

"Yes we have money and if you tell us where the place we seek is then you can have a silver deben."

The old man's eyes instantly lit up.

"Continue on the road out of the square, it is the main route to Meccus. The house of Abrax is not far for you now, it is a large building with tall palm trees either side of it."

"That could be any building you old fool" barked Omar.

The old man smiled.

"The door and window boards are painted red, a black scorpion on the door is the sign of Abrax."

Lucif threw the deben down to the man and again he smiled, his brown broken teeth showing his appreciation, a silver deben was worth much in Khamit.

"I hope you find what you are looking for."

The four men from Shakas rode on.

"He knows" said Abrix, "He knows about Lucifer."

"How could he, he's just an old beggar, he meant women you idiot."

The four of them laughed but then their expressions became grim again as the building with the red door and windows came into view.

"This is it, the house of Abrax" said Lucif and he noticed that his heart was pounding hard.

If they have harmed Lucifer then I will kill all within this damned red house.

To the side of the house of Abrax was a large stable that was obviously used for the clients within. The stable was guarded by two men and Lucif paid them to leave their horses there pretending that their intention was a night of drinking and debauchery.

"Your weapons will be taken from you once you are inside" one of the guards stated and Lucif nodded in agreement and when the four friends entered the red scorpion door, they were stopped by two large muscular men.

"Your swords are not allowed inside, we will keep them and return them to you when you leave."

Lucif withdrew his curved swords from his back and with one swift move he sliced both ways on one of the men's neck which sent his head instantly down to the floor, his puzzled eyes looking blankly to the ceiling. The other man stared in disbelief as he watched the bloody head roll towards the open door, the blood from the neck looking like small red snakes in the dust.

"Wha.."

But before he could say anything or shout a warning to anybody, his head was beside the foot of the door too. Omar had been as swift as Lucif.

"Some security guards they were, they will watch that door for all eternity now" said Omar and a wide grin filled his face.

Lucif looked around the small hallway that they were in, there was nobody else about but music and laughter and the sound of erotic moaning could be heard throughout the building.

There were six rooms in the hallway, three on either side of them, this was where the sounds of sex were coming from. Ahead of the four men were two sets of wide stairs and in-between these stairways was a double doorway that was covered by thin red vertical drapes. This was where the music and raucous merriment was coming from but Alix wanted to look inside the nearby rooms.

"No you fool, they just fuck in there. Behind the red drapes is where Abrax will be."

"I think that you are right Omar" added Lucif, "We go quietly inside and we stick to the darkness of the sides."

The music hall was large and wide and dimly lit by standing oil lamps and wall lamps. Round tables surrounded the room and on the open dance floor women danced, some in the act of removing their clothes and veils from themselves in a sexual way. It was an enticing sight but the four men took little notice of it.

On the opposite side of this smoky hall was a long table which was draped in a red cloth which was decorated with many intricate black scorpions. At the centre of this table sat a large man with a protruding well-fed stomach and a thick black beard. This man was surrounded by scantily clad women who were eagerly vying for his immediate attention.

"That is him, it has to be, Abrax the Black Scorpion" whispered Lucif, "Come with me Omar, down the side of the tables, keep to the shadows so that they do not notice our weapons. Alix and Ahmed, you go down the other side and do the same."

"What is your plan Lucif?" asked Omar.

"My plan is to kill Abrax if he dos not return my son to me."

Omar smiled, "The simplest plans are the best."

The four warriors did what Lucif suggested, nobody noticed them as the guards of Abrax were more concerned with their wine, shishas and the dancing women. The music was intoxicating, neys, ouds and darboukas stirring up the frenzy of those in the hall.

As soon as Alix and and Ahmed had managed to get behind Abrax without attracting any sort of attention, Lucif and Omar walked casually to the front of the table.

Abrax was wildly kissing the women around him oblivious to the two men standing in front of him but some of his bodyguards at the front of his table were not and immediately they confronted Lucif and Omar. Lucif withdrew his swords and told the men that were now threatening him, "I would not if I were you."

At that moment Abrax felt the sharp steel of Alix and Ahmed's swords in his back, his women fled immediately from him leaving the Black Scorpion alone and obviously surprised.

"What is this, who the fuck are you?"

"You have something of mine Scorpion, something I want back."

Abrax guards wanted to attack Lucif but Abrax stopped them.

"No you fucking idiots, I have swords at my back!"

Abrax was angry that he could be so easily threatened in his own house. He turned to Lucif.

"I do not know what you mean, what could I possibly have of yours?"

"Do not play with me Black Leech, yes for that is what you truly are, not a scorpion but a leech that feeds off the helpless and vulnerable here, making money from their weaknesses."

"I… provide a service here, that is all, see that all here are enjoying themselves."

"But not me, I want what is mine!"

"And what is yours?"

"The son you took from me and do not try to deny it."

"Why would I take your son, how could I profit from that?"

In an instant, Lucif's two swords were at the throat of Abrax, small trickles of blood began to drop down from below his beard. This time Abrax looked truly scared.

"You tell me. One wrong word and I will throw your head to the leeches that inhabit this room."

Abrax began to tremble, never had he ever shown fear to those that served him, his guards looked confused as they had never seen him like this before. Then Abtax noticed the branding scar on Lucif's left arm.

"You are ex-army like me; the Sigil of Annon - the inverted triangle of our country, the X for no surrender, the two crossed swords and the V for the upheld arms of victory."

"I am ex-army but not like you dark heart. Why did you take my son?"

Lucif squeezed the blades of his sword harder on Abrax's throat.

"They…wanted him."

"Who did?"

"People in Meccus, rich people."

"Why?"

"They heard of his glowing blue eyes, they heard that he had the 'Blue Vision' and that he could see the Neteru."

"His eyes are brown like mine, that is just a rumour, just an old woman's tale, it was a trick of the lamplight when he was born. Do you all hear that!" Lucif shouted to all that were listening.

"But those that want your son do not believe that it was a trick of the light."

"Who are they?" Lucif asked again and he knew that his patience was running out.

"They will kill me, kill you and your friends too if I tell you who they are."

"I will kill you now if you do not bring my son to me, I will slice off your head and my two friends behind you will stab you in the back."

"No, no please.."

Abrax's shaking hands snapped his fingers and within minutes a white bundle of soft cloth with Lucifer in it was brought to Lucif, the child was unharmed and safe and smiled with glee when he saw the face of his father.

"Your child is fine, no harm has been done to him, it was only business."

"And my business is complete here but if you ever try to steal my son again, I will find you and kill you, you can be sure of that. Now come with us and if your pathetic guards try anything then that will be the end of you, understand?"

Alix and Ahmed forced Abrax out of his brothel, their swords still tight at his back. His guards did not dare try to stop them and remained inside. When Lucifer was safe with his father on his horse and the other three were mounted, one of Lucif's swords was still at Abrax's throat.

"We go now Black Leech, do not ever darken my door again."

The four triumphant men rode swiftly away towards the safety of Shakas and looked forward to seeing everyone's faces light up when they saw the infant Lucifer and as they headed home in the still of the night, Alix had to say, "You're a wanted man now Lucif, they will come again for your son one day."

"I think Alix is right Lucif" added Ahmed, "I think that they will send Abrax again to abduct Lucifer."

"I think not" replied Lucif and his smile was one of triumph, " I think that Abrax's gang-leader days are over because of how easily we beat him."

"But there is always someone who will take his place though, why did you not take his head off?" asked Omar.

"I did not want to be looking over my shoulder for the rest of my life, retrieving something from a gang-leader is one thing, killing one is another. And you are right, there is always someone waiting in the wings, there are always other leeches out there, you just have to try and avoid them but also you have to let them know that you will exterminate them if you have to."

Omar smiled.

LUCIFER

NETERU

Abrax did not threaten the house of Lucif again. Lucif felt that he had adequately squashed the rumour of his son's 'Blue Vision' that night but he was never certain and was always over-protective of his son during the following days and years. Lucifer quickly grew strong and clever though and it was not long before he was stealing from the nearby wealthy markets to help out at home because his mother Shaleil had fallen into persistent ill-health after his abduction, she found it hard to work and concentrate and every day she seemed to become weaker and evermore frail.

One day when Lucifer was six years old, he was once again pilfering in one of the market places. He had stolen what fruit he could - apples, date palms, a small coconut even… his wide pockets were so full of nuts that they were leaving an unwanted trail for the fat overweight fruitier that was hastily trying to follow him.

"Come back you little thief, I will have your guts made into headbands you young scoundrel you!" he growled but the young boy was too fast, too knowledgeable of his environment, he knew all the quick escape routes and soon he evaporated amongst the packed crowd like a needle that had fell into a haystack.

The exhausted sweating man quickly gave up the chase, wiping his forehead and shaking his fist frantically in the air at the little phantom who was now nowhere to be seen, "Next time I will be ready for you and your fingers will be cut from your little thieving hands!" but the boy did not hear him, he was already heading for his house with his much needed ill-gotten gains.

The narrow streets on this part of the perimeter of Meccus were vast and intertwining like a giant compact maze or maybe an unearthly mythical snake that was in the process of encircling the city so that it could crush its heart then feast on all within it.

Lucifer was heading back to Shakas, a place that had now unfortunately become known as a poor area, a home with two parents who were both now struggling but for different reasons – his mother's serious health issue was taking a strangle hold on her and every day her condition deteriorated. His father remained an honest and strong man and resisted the temptation to turn to crime and to become a gang-leader. He continued to work as a building labourer but those long hours and the poorest of wages meant that the family was constantly struggling to survive, Lucifer had become a small thief due to necessity.

As Lucifer neared his neglected home, the decline in prosperity of the area became abundantly clear; beggars, homeless people, petty criminals and prostitutes filled the cramped streets. Khamit had overlapped into Shakas, it was now part of the proverbial den of iniquity from which there seemed to be no escape for the unfortunate that lived there, a now bigger blot on the magnificence of Meccus.

As Lucifer turned a corner into a narrow alleyway he came to an abrupt stop, standing of him was a tall man who looked wealthy, Lucifer knew this simply by the way he was dressed… but there seemed to be something different about him by the way he looked and sounded.

"What is the rush little one?" the tall man asked in a voice that sounded deep and menacing. Lucifer was immediately alert to what this man wanted.

"I... just on my way home sir."

"Sir? I like that... and it seems that you are in a rush because I think that you have stolen something?"

"I... am not a thief sir, believe me."

The man laughed and it seemed to echo in the deserted alleyway.

"So you bought all that fruit that is stuffed everywhere on you?"

More laughter.

Lucifer was scared now and as he instinctively pulled out his small sharp knife that he kept hidden in his back pocket, one of the stolen apples fell to the ground

"So the young thief knows how to defend himself, that is good."

The man picked up the apple and stared at it and as he did Lucifer noticed that his eyes seemed to be black.

The man slowly offered the apple back to Lucifer...

"Eat it now young thief and I will let you go on your way."

Lucifer was shaking as he took the apple from the man.

"You want me to eat it?"

"Yes, now and I will not tell the fruit merchant where you live."

"You... know where I live?"

Lucifer was shaking now.

"Yes Lucky I do..."

He knows my name!

"Eat it... now!"

Lucifer felt that he had no option, it was no use running because the scary man said he knew where he lived. Reluctantly he bit into the apple...

"Good... good little Lucky... enjoy the taste, the apple juice... in your stomach..."

Suddenly Lucifer felt sick...

It felt as if something was happening to him

As if something was squirming inside of him

Something alive

And then it felt as if his skin was darkening

Like it was cracking open

Like small snakes were

Crawling all over him

Coming out of him...

Lucifer wanted his father suddenly, to help and protect him.

"Father, father..." he muttered...

Then he felt something strange happen, something in his eyes.

They had turned blue and were glowing like bright jewels.

The tall man with the dark eyes stepped back…

And Lucifer felt suddenly stronger and better. He threw the apple to the ground and turned away from the man and began to run…

The man began to laugh again.

"Yes, go home little Lucky… but I will return one day and claim what is mine now."

The man stood on the apple and squashed it… black juice squirted out from it like thick oil.

Lucifer ran as fast as he could, his heart beating loudly from the terror he had just experienced and as he turned into the dusty street on which he lived, he paused for breath and began to try and forget the scary man… then he noticed another man sitting beside the door to his house, a man he had never seen before and somebody who immediately seemed to be not of Meccus. The man was wearing a long robe with a hood that covered most of his face. This man did not seem like a beggar because the robe was made of the finest cloth and yet Lucifer sensed a sadness about him. Lucifer did not enter his house straight away and the hooded man spoke to him with a gentle voice, "You do well for your family little Lucifer, your parents are very proud of you."

"You… you know my name too?" replied young Lucifer and suddenly he was scared again, was this man an agent of the fruit merchant that had chased him, was he a friend of the scary man? But if he was, why was he sitting so placidly and calm before him?

"Yes I do, I am here for your mother, and sadly she has not long left in this world. Go to her Lucifer and lovingly say your goodbyes because tonight she will be with The One God in Heaven."

Tears suddenly filled Lucifer's eyes, he did not know that they were still blue; "No… no, you lie!" he cried, "You know nothing of our Gods or of our Heaven" and he sprinted into his home, straight to his mother's room where she lay on the bed, gasping pitifully for her breath...

"Lu… cifer… I am so glad that you are home now."

"Mother, I saw a man, he said…"

"Said what my dear son?"

"No… nothing… look, I have fresh fruit and nuts for you, even a juicy coconut."

"Oh that is lovely my son but you must be careful, you know what they do to young thieves these days."

Lucifer held up both hands and opened them out, "Look, ten fingers mother, count them. They do not call me 'Lucky' for nothing."

Lucifer's mother tried to laugh but this was cut short by a vicious rasping cough that seemed to drain what little colour there was from her thin cheeks. Lucifer had never seen his mother look so pale and frail and this worried him greatly.

"I need to sleep now son" she said weakly, "I do not know what time your father will be back from his work but he will really enjoy the fruit that you have brought home."

It was late when Lucifer's father returned from his work and the first thing he heard was the sound of his son crying at the side of his mother's bed, his mother had died peacefully in her sleep.

"It… is fine my father; the man said she would be with the gods in Heaven this night."

Lucifer's father stood as still as a statue, a statue that was stained and unclean, exhausted from the long day of work, his head slumped as he muttered, "Anubis has claimed her then… she… struggled so hard for us…"

Then finally he began to sob and Lucifer went to him, they held each other tight in their grief and their small home in Shakus seemed to fade away.

THE BLUE VISION

As soon as Lucifer was tall and old enough, he joined his father on the building sites of Meccus, it was hard tasking work that made his young body physically stronger and he kept their bellies well-fed with his highly developed art of thievery. Lucifer knew that to survive he had to remain strong; his eternally grieving father was now struggling to keep up his work load and regularly received the studded strap from the taskmaster which usually resulted in Lucifer receiving the same for intervening. But his father did not react to the cruelty he received because he knew that killing the taskmaster would not benefit the future of his son. And that immediate future meant time in the Annon Army.

At the age of sixteen years, Lucifer was conscripted into the army, five years was the minimum time for a new recruit, after which they would receive a horse and be allowed to retain their two swords. It was a rite of passage for the young Lucifer and something he would never forget.

The Annon army was powerful and feared by both of it's neighbours, it was also an intelligent army, one that did not send young trainee soldiers into any sort of serious conflict. Lucifer was sent to the town of Ramiton which was near to the city of Khnumar on the Mediterranean coast. It was here that Lucifer was trained in the art of hand to hand combat, here that he was given his first two swords which like his father he sheathed on his back and it was here in a seedy seaside whorehouse that Lucifer lost his virginity.

The woman was much older than Lucifer and well experienced in the art of lovemaking. She was large breasted with a full shapely figure that many men and women desired and she was still attractive despite her years. Lucifer spent the whole of his first night with her having virtually non-stop sex which both fulfilled and surprised the woman because most of her clients usually left her as soon as the act of copulation had been completed. But Lucifer's sex drive was insatiable and he went back to the woman as many times as he could and confessed to the woman who was called Meryt that he was in love with her; Meryt just laughed. Lucifer's nickname of 'Lucky' had stuck with him and the told Meryt that he had been lucky to have met her.

"Lucifer 'Lucky' Heylel eh? I think they're wrong, you should be called 'Fucky' Heylel."

Meryt laughed even louder and the cheap red wine that she was drinking dribbled down from her mouth. Lucifer laughed too, he loved being in the army, he loved being able to see Meryt regularly but he knew that after five years he would return home to help his father.

When Lucifer reached the age of twenty years he felt like a grown man, a man that was immortal, no soldier in his regiment could beat him at fist fighting or swordsmanship and he had caught the eye of his commanders who suggested to him that he should make a career of the army as he had the necessary skills and the strength and guile to quickly rise through the ranks. Lucifer was surely tempted by their suggestion but it was his first taste of death in combat that made him realise the implications of mortality and that he could not leave his father to die a lonely old man.

Lucifer's regiment had been sent on tactical manoeuvres to part of the north Egyptian border and it was here that they came into contact with a large band of Egyptian rebels. The Egyptian leaders had given Annon their full approval for the eradication of any rebel forces and the Annon army always wholeheartedly complied with this request.

The battle which spilled into Annon territory was fierce and when one of Lucifer's swords pierced his first victim's heart he stopped suddenly: he stopped because he realised that he had enjoyed it so much which was not what he was expecting, the rebel would have most certainly killed Lucifer but he was the one that was in Amenti with Anubis.

A bloodlust consumed Lucifer and he lost count of how many rebels he killed, he became covered in the blood of his victims as his rage increased, "You will never cross our borders to rape and pillage again!" he shouted and his surrounding comrades cheered and were motivated by his stirring words. Then Lucifer felt a strange change come over him, it was as if there was an unknown energy surging through his body, he did not know it but his eyes had turned blue.

On the battlefield, men in hooded cloaks were silently attending to the dead, some were kneeling before the fallen as if they were praying for them...

Suddenly a swirling blue light surrounded them and the cloaked men vanished.

"They are the Neteru" a deep voice said behind Lucifer but it sounded like the voice was in his head.

Lucifer turned but it was as if he was moving in slow motion and time had stopped still. In front of him stood an Egyptian rebel who was most surely dead because of the deep bloody wounds that had been inflicted on his body. The rebel's sunken eyes were not white and brown or even bloodshot, they were dark and solid black, like two ebony pearls that were glowing unnaturally on the battlefield.

"They take the pure ones, the nice ones, the ones who love and care but I am only interested in those that have a dark heart and do not care, they are the ones that I need for my army."

"No... get away for me spirit, you are dead, you are not Anubis, this is some sort of vision that I surely see."

"You see it because you have the Blue Vision, it is in your sparkling blue eyes."

The dead man reached out with his bloody hands and touched Lucifer as if he wanted his soul; he penetrated Lucifer's mind in an instant.

"Ah, you liked killing here this day and you liked fucking that whore back in Ramiton, you want to do more sordid things with her, you want to explore the erotic realm with her and you can Lucifer with me, now and in your afterlife. A warrior with the Blue Vision can be very useful to me."

"No, never... I love my father, my home in Shakas, I will never turn to the evil ways of life."

"I think you will one day Lucif-er, I can feel it in your bones and I am rarely wrong about such matters."

"Never dark one, go back to your fiery pit in Amanti from whence you came..."

But then Lucifer had to know,"Who are you?"

"I... am Nameless and I am Many and you will be One with Me one day."

"Never Black Eyes!" Lucifer screamed this at the top of his voice and the dead rebel suddenly vanished in a dark swirling mist that was not blue. Time seemed to return to normal and Lucifer rubbed his arm where the one who was Nameless had touched him, he felt violated but he knew that was safe and unharmed and the battle with the rebels had been won.

The dead one was a vision, an imagination of the mind, the result of battle probably, I cannot dwell upon this thought Lucifer immediately and somehow the dead man called Nameless faded in Lucifer's mind and the priorities of life became his main concern.

When Lucifer was twenty one years of age he left the Annon army and returned home with two medals of service, two swords and his white Arabian steed. He did not work at first and he spent part of his army savings on his father's house as he had always planned to do. This made his father Lucif so proud, his son had returned a battle hero just as he had and he had shown complete loyalty to his family's humble beginnings.

During this time of leisure, Lucifer built three extra rooms on the back of the house just as his father always wanted and it was during these days that Lucifer found his first true love.

LILITH

There had been a delayed formal welcome home party for Lucifer, delayed until the housing work had been completed. Lucif used what little savings he had to fund it which caused an argument between him and his son because Lucifer was not bothered about such a gathering just for him; but his father had insisted and he was still the head of the house. Sadly his closest friends Omar, Ahmed and Alix could not attend as the three of them had re-enlisted in the Annon army, the deterioration of Shakas being one of the main reasons, the hardships of daily life being another. Lucif had remained in Shakas even though he had been sorely tempted to pick up his swords again and go with his friends but he wanted a home for Lucifer to return to. Other friends of Lucif attended the gathering though and one in particular brought his daughter with him, she was called Lilith and she was someone that Lucifer did not recognise immediately.

The welcome back gathering was held in Lucif's rear garden and Lilith used the excuse of offering party food to the tall handsome young man with the shining brown hair and the piercing deep brown eyes that seemed to burn right through her.

"Would you like some fruit Lucky? You used to steal it for me."

Lilith smiled and her beautiful long black hair moved softly on the gentle warm breeze.

"You know that I was called Lucky?"

"Of course silly, do you not recognise me?"

Lucifer looked at the vision of beauty before him and her hair was now shining like black steel under the high Meccus sun. Her face was thin, her cheeks sharp like a marble bust and her full red lips seemed to pout at Lucifer as he studied her. She was wearing a scented flowing white dress which was daringly short for the time and it easily revealed Lilith's shapely figure.

She is absolutely gorgeous thought Lucifer and suddenly he realised who she was.

"You cannot be Lilith surely, the little girl who used to follow me and my friends everywhere?"

"I am Lilith and yes, I did follow you and your friends, we stole many things didn't we?"

Lilith and Lucifer both laughed.

"Yes, we did indeed… and I am thinking that you are stealing something right now."

Lilith looked puzzled, her brown eyes mystified in the bright gleaming sunlight.

"What am I stealing from you?"

"Meet me beside my father's stables when the moon is new and high and I will tell you, dare you do that little Lilith?"

"I dare and I am no longer little, you are not that much older than me remember Lucky."

"I can see that you are not little" Lucifer laughed as he looked at Lilith's full breasts and pointed nipples which were now hard and erect as Lucifer's gaze passed over them.

"I think that the army has made a man of you" Lilith said and a mischievous sensual grin filled her face.

"I will meet you tonight, I will go home first with my parents then I will return."

"They will not mind that?"

"They will not know."

This time the mischievous grin was Lucifer's.

The celebrations finished at midnight and when Lucifer had finished clearing and tidying the garden, Lilith returned as she had promised.

"You father, will he not hear or see us?"

"I have checked, he is in a deep sleep, snoring like the great god Shu himself. He has drank much wine, tomorrow is his one day of rest from the building sites of Meccus."

"He works hard doesn't he?"

"He always has, he misses my mother so much as I do but I guess life goes on doesn't it?"

"It does Lucky and your life plans, what are they?"

Lucifer looked towards his house and the results of all the hard work he had recently completed.

"Those extra rooms I built, I will furnish them with the most modern of furniture and decoration and I have other development plans for this house that will be the envy of all of Shakas, it will be a house worthy for my future wife and family."

"And who will be your future wife Lucky?"

"I think that luck has already smiled down upon us, don't you?"

"So that is what I was stealing from you?"

Lucifer looked lovingly into Lilith's eyes that glowed magnificently in the moonlight like two searchlights.

"Yes Lilith, you have stolen my heart."

Lucifer and Lilith kissed, a long sensuous kiss that did not stop, a kiss that made them drift slowly into the stables behind them and then down onto the soft warm hay beside the two black and white horses who seemed to smile as they looked down upon the intimate young lovers.

Lucifer made slow passionate love to Lilith, it was not like the one-sided uncaring sex that he used to have with Meryt. This felt like real love and Lucifer knew that it was real love because of how Lilith responded to his experienced lovemaking. The night felt like it was the most important time of their lives and when they were finished and tired, they held each tight hoping that the night would not end.

As daylight broke slowly over the mountains that surrounded Meccus, Lilith whispered to Lucifer, "We will have a bed though Lucifer?" as she picked the thin pieces of straw from her tussled black hair.

"Of course little Lilith, I will steal one for you."

The two lovers laughed

The very next day, Lucifer made his wedding plans and a list of all the things he wanted completed before they married, he knew that it would take some time because he would have to save up what earnings he could and that meant returning to work with his father as a builder. The strange thing was that he was never tempted to steal as he had done when he was younger, Lucifer was now as honest as his father… but Lucifer knew that those skills of the thief that he possessed were always there if he ever needed them.

So the future now looked bright for Lucifer and Lilith… but as it turned out, Lucifer was not quite as lucky as he thought he was.

SHALEIL

WEDDING PLANS

So Lucifer went back to work on the building sites of Meccus with his father but immediately Lucifer noticed a change in how the workers were treated by their so-called superiors, there were now stricter taskmasters who seemed to be constantly using their heavy leather studded straps to make sure that the work was completed on time or if any worker made some kind of a minor mistake.

"How has this happened father, where has this new cruelty sprung from, it was not as bad as this when I worked with you before?" Lucifer asked Lucif.

"The rich want to be richer, Meccus is developing and growing at a much greater rate now and this is breeding greed."

"But I saw a man whipped today, because he had simply used the wrong wood?"

"To replace that wood meant extra time on the build…"

"But physical punishment like that, is that necessary, they could have easily deducted his pay?"

"It all depends on what taskmaster you have, some are fair just like before but most do seem to be cruel these days. I keep my head down now and concentrate on my work and do a good job like I have always done and I suggest that you do the same because I know you…"

Lucifer interrupted his father, "I would not let anyone whip me now."

"That is what I thought" and his father smiled, "but let us not dwell on such a thing, we will work hard and when we have the money required you can marry Lilith."

Time rolled by deathly slow for Lucifer, the monotonous daily grind of the building work he did with his father could not compare with the excitement and exhilaration of his time spent in the army. But Lucifer gritted his teeth because he knew it was what he had to do if he was to wed Lilith but he did reveal his feelings to her, he knew that a long happy marriage had to be a truthful one."

"I do not know how long I can do this work Lilith, the different taskmasters we get now seem to want more from us every day and I know it is now beginning to take it's toll on my father."

"But your father is strong and well respected by all in Shakas?"

"He was strong but he is much older now remember and I have seen him struggle to keep up with his workload which was not the case before I went into the army."

"But you are there to help him are you not?"

"I am but I have my own work to do… I really think that this work is now killing him, sending him to an early grave and it is not right."

"But it is what he knows, what he has always done, what else would he do?"

"I… don't know but it all boils down to money, how much deben you have and we don't have much. We skimp and save for your dowry but it never seems to be enough, we will both be old before we marry at this rate."

Lucifer managed an ironic smile and Lilith noticed it, she wanted to laugh but thought better of it.

"My parents don't expect anything from you Lucifer, they would let us marry tomorrow if we wanted to."

"No, I have my principles, we will marry how I planned and we will honeymoon on the coast of the Uat-Ur in beautiful Khnumar."

"Khnumar sounds wonderful my love but it is not necessary, if we can not afford it then…"

"We will afford it" interrupted Lucifer and Lilith knew that he was angered now, "I am determined that it will happen."

"But how or when if you cannot save up enough? My work pays well Lucifer, we can use some of my savings?"

Lilith worked in a rich suburb of Meccus which actually was not that far from Shakas even though at times it seemed a completely different world. She worked for a large and successful fashion stall and acted as a model to display the various dresses and coats that were new. Lilith was attractive and desirable and attracted the attention of many a young Meccus suitor but she only had eyes for her one and only Lucky. Lucifer did not like the work she did but he knew that it did pay well and he did trust Lilith despite the constant attention she received from everyone, it did add to his frustration though, much more than Lilith realised.

Lilith became sad and warm tears began to fill her eyes, "How.. can it happen? It will never happen will it…"

Lucifer kissed Lilith gently on the cheek, "It will happen my love, I am making plans."

Lilith looked into Lucifer's eyes and saw that mischievous look that was always so appealing to her.

"What plans?"

Lucifer smiled.

"What would Lucky do?"

Lilith's eyes opened wide.

"No Lucky, you cannot do that, what if you get caught?"

"Did the young Lucky ever get caught?"

"But that was just fruit from the market, do you intend to steal food for us?"

Lucifer laughed.

"Not food little Lilith… diamonds and gold!"

"Do you intend to work in the mines then, that is harder than the work you do now and to try and steal there would be so tempting, you know what happens to miners who attempt to steal don't you?"

"I do know what happens to them, a prison life sentence that includes hard labour until they can work no more."

"There are rumours that heads will be chopped off soon for such crimes."

"I do not intend to work in the mines, stealing there would be too risky."

"Who do you intend to steal from then?"

"The rich, the rich who pay us such a measly wage, I know that some keep their silver and gold in their houses."

"But it will be guarded surely?"

"Yes, most likely but that is why I am making plans, it will be like an army manoeuvre and I am sure that some of my old comrades will be interesting in helping me out, just like me they are disillusioned with this rich country of ours."

It was as if Lilith was trembling now.

"Oh Lucifer, I am so worried now."

Lucifer held Lilith tightly.

"Now, now there, do not be scared little Lilith, there is no fear for steady men, Lucky Heylel will be rich one day."

"And what will your father say of this?"

"He will not know, he will never have to work hard again though, he can remarry and maybe live how he should live."

"And where will you say that you got the money?"

Lucifer thought about this.

"Gambling, a gambling night in Meccus perhaps?"

"And do you think he will believe that?"

"Yes because he will want to believe it, my father is not stupid, he knows that his days of working hard are nearly over."

Lilith hugged Lucifer tighter than he was holding her.

"Please do not do this Lucifer, please…"

But Lucifer's answer was simple.

"I have to, the plan will work."

But fate had other plans for Lucifer.

THE BLACK LEECH

Not long after Lucifer had confessed to Lilith what he intended to do he was once again working with his father. Lucif had felt ill that morning, pains had seared through his chest all night but he had still gone to work despite Lucifer's advice that he stay at home. Lucifer begged his father to stay in his bed, finally admitting that he would steal if it was necessary to supplement their income but his father declined.

"If I have to die then it will be with dignity, I will die paying my way in life. You will not steal like I knew you did my little Lucky" he said.

Like Lucifer, his father was stubborn and proud and this was the first time he had ever mentioned that he knew what his young son had done in the market places all those years ago. But Lucifer's father was to pay the price for his stubbornness.

Both men were working at a construction site that was busy building yet another temple to the king and queen of Meccus, they had been given the task of carrying buckets of hot black oil into the temple for the immense roof inside. This black tar-like substance was poured into two metal buckets and was carried by a heavy wooden beam across the shoulder. Lucifer was glad that he had been given the same task as Lucif as this meant that he could keep an eye on his ill father.

As the day drew on, Lucif became visibly weaker and slower and Lucifer knew that the taskmaster had noticed this. The taskmaster was a cruel brute of a man who looked more like an ex-warrior than a labour supervisor and Lucif had not recognised who it was.

Near the end of their lengthy shift, Lucifer's father slipped, causing the oil from one of his buckets to splatter onto the wooden platform to the temple door. Lucifer was directly behind him with his load of boiling tar.

"You bloody old fool" shouted the taskmaster as he wiped small spots of hot black oil from his leather sandals. Then he looked intently at Lucif and then said, "I know you…"

Lucif looked at the man, his eyesight blurry from his illness. The man had a thick grey beard and a large round stomach, Lucif focussed his eyes as hard as he could then a cold shiver crawled down his spine as he realised who it was. Hate was pouring from the man's eyes.

"I lost my business because of you, I was overthrown and cast out, all because of a peasant labourer from Shakas."

"Abrax" said Lucif, "You are older but you look the same, fat and ugly and you found the right job didn't you, watching others do all the hard work while all you do is beat them, you're still the Black Leech in my eyes."

Lucifer was astounded by his father's words, by his boldness in front of the taskmaster and he wondered who this 'Black Leech' was and as he looked at Abrax's hateful face he saw the anger building there.

"Now I am going to give you what you deserve, something I should have done years ago."

The enraged Abrax reached for his studded leather strap.

But Lucifer was not going to let this man beat his father. Just as Abrax was about to lash out at his father, Lucifer swung his bucket, sending the hot tar all over Abrax's wide body. Smouldering oil from the other bucket splashed onto Lucifer's legs and feet but he was not bothered, he was enjoying the sight of this evil man screaming in pain…

Abrax now looked like a living lump of molten tar and as he screamed louder, Lucifer smiled, he knew that this vile man would never beat his father or another worker again. Lucifer's excuse would be that he had tripped on the long leather strap of the taskmaster so it was in fact the taskmaster's own fault for what had happened, he knew that the building security leader would not believe this but at least it would be some form of defence for his actions.

Shock and silence apart from the cries of the taskmaster surrounded the entrance to the temple... and in the vacuum of that stillness, Lucifer noticed a hooded man watching from the shadows of the temple. Unbelievably it was the same man that Lucifer had spoken to the night his mother had died; the man had the same shining blue eyes, the same beard, the same cloak. And the man smiled and nodded... and as Lucifer looked down to his stomach, a sharp wide blade had cut through it from his back and blood was gushing before him like a cruel red fountain. They had not waited for Lucifer's excuse, an armed security guard had seen what Lucifer had done to Abrax and had decided to take immediate lethal action.

Lucifer dropped to his knees and the buckets of black oil merged with the sand and his blood. The last thing Lucifer saw was his father coming toward him, eyes full of tears, shaking like he was about to collapse from exhaustion, like his heart was about stop beating.

HOTEP

A blinding blue light suddenly surrounded Lucifer and his father and as they stood up together they looked around and noticed that the temple and Meccus had disappeared.

"What... where are we father, where has the taskmaster and the temple gone?"

"I do not know my son" replied his father and his voice sounded as if it was echoing in a dream.

Lucifer looked at his hands and his skin and he was puzzled by the blue glow that surrounded them.

"Our skin, see how it glows...have we... entered another realm father?" Lucifer stuttered as his mind struggled with the memory of what had just happened and Lucif knew what his son was thinking but he did not say anything but a gentle voice behind them did.

"Do not think of your death Lucifer, your mind will reject it, think only of your new life, the new world that your souls now inhabit. Walk with me, they call me Hotep."

It was the hooded man with the blue eyes.

"We are to go to the great god of death then?" asked Lucifer's bewildered father.

"There are no gods, there is only one God who is known by many different names in the world of mortals; Aenor, Elohim, Yahweh… but come now, someone is waiting for you."

The three men began to walk slowly through the pulsating vein of the portal and Lucifer marvelled at the living beauty and colour of it, he had just died but he had never felt more alive.

Lucifer noticed that time seemed suddenly different, as if the turning of the world had stopped, it was as if they had entered a dream world that was completely safe from all the dangers of life and it was a strange sensation but a supremely calming one. Lucifer liked this feeling but what he did not realise was that his thoughts of the living and Lilith had begun to fade as if life had been nothing but a dream. He was consumed with the 'now' because that was all there was.

As the end of the glowing portal approached Lucifer and Lucif noticed a transparent shadow in the distance and as they neared this small slim figure they were astounded when they realised it was Lucifer's mother. Both Lucifer and his father ran to her and the light in the portal seemed to change as if by magic, a bright sky full of coloured clouds and birds appeared magnificently above them.

"I have waited so long for you, so so long. Come with me now to rejoice and love as we once did" said Lucifer's mother Shaleil who was now youthful and beautiful again. Lucifer was sure that he could hear joyous music playing somewhere but then he thought that surely he was imagining it.

Tears fell like waterfalls from both Lucif and Lucifer, this was the mother Lucifer remembered and the love that consumed both he and his father was instant and immense. Lucif actually dropped to his knees and held onto Shaleil's hands.

"Are… you Neteru now my love, you look so young, so beautiful as you once were?"

"No, am not one of the Angelic, but we can be what we want to be here, exist how we want to for all eternity now."

Lucif kissed her hands and Lucifer held his father's shoulders.

This is a dream come true surely? thought Lucifer because he had never really considered what the afterlife would be like… but somehow there were small seeds of doubt in his mind which he knew he had to dismiss immediately. He did begin to think about Lilith even though the memory of her was still hard to access; he wondered what would happen to her now that he was no longer there to protect and marry her but he knew that he had to banish this from his mind too as there was no going back now…

Is there?

AKHET

Lucif, Shaleil and their son lived as a family again in a habitat that constantly filled Lucifer with wonder and love. Their plight and grim circumstances in Meccus was now a thing of the past, a memory that they no longer needed to endure. The three of them now led a serene and joyful afterlife but deep inside, Lucifer still yearned for Lilith as she was a memory that he would never let go of, he even began to secretly look forward to the day that she joined him in the afterlife. But this yearning increased Lucifer restlessness, the young roguish scamp that terrorised shops and the markets of Meccus began to yearn for the excitement he had known as a soldier and eventually he was given the chance to fulfil this desire.

"Join us Lucifer, become one of us and work for Yahweh and the Akhet" said Hotep to him one day.

"Work for Yahweh? I have felt His love in this wondrous land but I and all that I know have never seen Him. And what is the Akhet, you have never mentioned it before?"

"The Akhet is the Angelic Light, the Holy Ghost, the Clear Conscious that controls the portals of life and death. Come with me Lucifer, the Akhet awaits you because you have been chosen."

"Chosen, but for what?"

"To do the endless work of the Akhet my young friend, you are soon to be a great thief of souls."

The hooded man laughed at this then opened his arms and a great sparkling light burst from behind him, a bright blue light that formed the shape of large wings.

"You... can fly?" gasped Lucifer.

"Yes and you will be able to do the same soon, the power of the Akhet is great and mighty and only those that deserve it will receive it."

Hotep took Lucifer to that glorious place in Heaven where the Akhet was known to reside and for once the garrulous mischievous Lucifer was struck dumb as the consciousness known as The Akhet appeared before him as a living mass of light...

A light that moved slowly as if in a dream.
WELCOME LUCIFER
A great voice boomed throughout the gigantic gleaming hall...
A hall that moved as if it had a life of its own
Like it could change into whatever habitat it wanted to
And to Lucifer the voice sounded like many voices
As it echoed around the glorious place of the Akhet

THE ANGELIC HAVE NEED OF YOU

That is all that the Akhet said to Lucifer and it was certainly not the long drawn out ceremony that Lucifer was almost expecting… then he was hit and surrounded by a warm blinding blue light that consumed him completely. There was absolutely no pain whatsoever from this sudden energy burst, only a feeling of becoming something else, a realisation that he was ascending to another level of existence. Immediately he understood the true power of love and compassion and before he was totally overcome by this new revelation, Hotep took hold of Lucifer and flew out of the Hall of the Akhet with him and then on to Angelica, the place of the angels where he could rest and recuperate before his work as an Angelic began.

THE ANGELIC

For years, Lucifer worked tirelessly for the Angelic and the people he guided safely through the portals had usually lived in similar circumstances to him… gradually though, Lucifer began to question why cruelty and evil still existed in the land of the living, why you had to endure the hardship of mortal life before your soul finally ascended to a better plane of existence. *Surely there is no need for this?* he began to think regularly and he knew that this train of thought would not be welcomed by the Akhet

And he always wanted to go back to Meccus to see his love Lilith but he knew that this was not allowed by the Akhet as he once did try to go and see her. After a guiding a dead soul into the portal he remained in the realm of the living and began to fly to Meccus but he had been stopped in mid-flight and promptly returned to the portal, almost as if he had been a naughty child that had been attempting to run away.

The consciousness of the Akhet had read his mind and knew his intentions…

THIS IS NOT ALLOWED LUCIFER
YOU MUST NEVER LEAVE A NEW SOUL
YOU MUST GUIDE AND GUARD THEM
THROUGH THE PORTAL
THE DARK CONSCIOUS ARE AN EVER PRESENT THREAT
EVEN IN THE SAFETY OF OUR PORTALS

"So that is why I was chosen to be one of the Angelic, that you may need my skills as a warrior?"

YES

"I… can understand that but why am I not allowed to see the one that I loved?"

ARE YOU A GHOST

THAT WALKS THE LAND OF THE LIVING?
"No… I just want to see my Lilith."
YOU WILL SEE HER
IF SHE WANTS TO SEE YOU EVENTUALLY
SHE WILL HAVE A NEW MORTAL LIFE NOW
ONE YOU CANNOT INTERFERE WITH
"I just wanted to…"

Lucifer knew that it was not worth arguing with the Akhet and he became even more angrier now that it seemed that someone was ruling his life and his decisions, almost like he was working for a taskmaster again and that thought was incredible for him.

Lucifer continued his Angelic work but a deep resentment began to grow within him… then on one Angelic assignment he was sent to the field of a battle.

Suddenly he heard a voice that seemed vaguely familiar.

"It seems that we meet again Lucif-er, I thought we would."

Lucifer turned to look at the face of a dead warrior and he knew in an instant that it was the one who was known to him as Nameless.

"You again?"

"Yes, we do seem to meet in unfortunate circumstances don't we, blood and guts everywhere, horrible is it not?"

"Why are you here?"

"Oh probably the same reason as you, a bit of new recruiting you could say but how are you Lucif-er, you do not seem so happy, not like when I saw you killing on that Annon battlefield when we last met."

"I… do my work, I take these to a better place, that is all."

"Is it a better place? And why is this place not better, if I had my way it would be… join with me son of Lucif and you can be happy again, there is no reason why you cannot see little Lilith whose sensual body you so sorely miss."

This was a mistake by Nameless, he had referred to Lilith in a sexual way.

"No, you tempt me Nameless one, you are the Dark Conscious, the ancient entity that the Akhet told me about."

"They have a name for me? That is so nice of them don't you think."

"What I think is that you should leave so that I can do my work."

"Ah the ever conscientious Lucif-er, whatever happened to that mischievous young spirit called Lucky?"

"He… no longer exists now."

"I think he does, I think he is still in there somewhere, waiting to break free from his Akhet chains of slavery… so I will wait patiently my dear Lucky because I know that one day I will need your strength and your

help, not so much now but in the future when you are even more powerful. But remember, my offer to you is always there."

The dead man collapsed to the bloody ground, the one known as Nameless had instantly departed.

Lucifer was left alone on the grim battlefield to ponder the discussion he had just had, *Is it really true what Nameless had said that he could make the world of the living a better place? That I could be with Lilith even though I am dead to her or is Nameless the father of all lies?*

Lucifer continued his work as an Angelic but those early seeds of doubt were now beginning grow and bear fruit, sour fruit that was poisonous for the soul.

DESIRE

LILITH

Lucifer was seated in front of his large open window looking out across the wide expanse of Angelica. He watched in wonder as Angelic flew out of the shining Portals of the Clear Conscious, their work completed until next task. Lucifer noticed though that some had obviously come into contact with nefarious forces and the blue light that surrounded them was tainted with moving dark patches. He himself had never experienced any real danger in the portals and he now often wished that he would, he knew that it would be a way to expel the frustrated anger that was constantly building within him.

Lucifer drank from his large goblet of blue Angelic wine and continued to gaze at this wondrous realm that he lived in, a place that seemed to constantly change as more and more Angelic joined the fold. He was actually feeling rather drunk he realised and this always amazed him that wine could actually have the same effect upon him as it had in the world of the living; he knew though that it was because he wanted the numbing effect of the wine like he wanted the taste of food, he did not need any of these sustenance's now but he ate and drank because he wanted to remember.

And each Angelic day and night he did remember, a life that now seemed a lifetime ago, these were now constant thoughts of Lucifer and he was thinking of Lilith again when a soft voice in the doorway behind him broke his hazy nostalgia.

Lucifer turned to see the most beautiful Angelic he had ever seen, her light blue flowing dress was almost completely transparent which easily revealed her perfect figure. She had long flowing blonde hair which seemed to move as she spoke and her voice was dreamlike and seductive, almost hypnotic.

"I hope that you do not mind me coming here uninvited like this Lucifer?"

Lucifer looked momentarily puzzled.

""You know my name? But who… are you?"

"My name is Yarghab, Desire if you prefer."

Lucifer smiled, "Desire I think and it does seem a very appropriate name."

Is she blushing? I think she is…

I have heard much about you Lucifer and I have long desired to meet with you."

Lucifer smiled, "I am most pleased to her this."

Desire continued, "But I have someone with me who has wanted to see you for some time now."

Another vision of beauty entered the room and it took Lucifer's breath away.

It was Lilith, a young Lilith, the Lilith that Lucifer had always remembered, not the woman that had died aged eighty seven.

Lucifer suddenly felt weak, he thought that he was actually shaking which was an unusual feeling for him, it was as if his heart had come alive again as it began to beat at a much faster rate. He felt nervous, excited, exhilarated and for once he did not know what to say.

"Are you lost for words Lucky, I cannot believe that."

"Lilith… my love, I have thought about you for a lifetime, but… but are you one of the Angelic now?"

"No, I am not Angelic, it was the Angel Desire who granted me this wish of mine."

Lucifer slowly went to Lilith and gently kissed her on the cheek, tears filled both of their eyes."

"I have wished for this moment for so long" he whispered.

"So have I Lucifer… I had to see you again."

Lucifer twirled around, "Then I will leave the Angelic now, I am just one of many and can be easily replaced, we can be together again for all eternity."

Lucifer smiled but Lilith's head was bowed low.

"That… is why I have come to see you Lucifer, so that maybe our story can be completed?"

"Yes… it can, it can!"

"I think that you misunderstand me Lucky."

At that moment, a man appeared behind Lilith, a man that was as handsome as Lucifer.

"This is the man I eventually married Lucifer, after you died I wanted to die too, I tried to die but this man saved me; he is a doctor and we became close, we eventually…"

Suddenly Lucifer felt an immense rage burn within him, one that was easily ignited by the Angelic wine he had been drinking.

"Then I am not so Lucky after all am I? You come here to tell me that you love another man, why?"

"Because I still love you Lucifer, I was worried that you had stopped living, stopped loving because of your love for me; I was told that it could happen, that souls could cease to exist through heartbreak and sadness, that is why I eventually asked the Angel Desire to find you."

Tears rolled down Lucifer's face but he tried to remain strong, he felt as if a sudden hammer had just crushed his heart.

"Then our story is complete little Lilith… and I do understand why you came here but now I have Angelic wine I must drink so I think you and your husband should both leave now" Lucifer said abruptly with venom.

The young doctor began to speak but Lucifer stopped him, "Do not say anything, you might inflame the wrath of an old Annon warrior and I do not want that, I just want to be left alone."

The man looked away.

"Is that it then?" said Lilith sadly, her heart beating as fast as the heart of Lucifer.

"Of course my little Lilith, you stole my heart once and now you have given it back to me and I thank you for that."

Tears now streamed down Lilith's face, her husband put his arms around her shoulder and they both left the room of Lucifer, the crying of Lilith echoing around him.

"You do understand why she did this, don't you Lucifer?" said Desire and her face was also full of sadness.

"Yes, no… I suppose I do, Lucky Lucifer Heylel understands everything now."

After this sad and unexpected meeting with Lilith there was a definite change in Lucifer and a change in attitude to what he was actually doing as an Angelic. All he wanted now was to be the young Lucifer from his mortal army days, the Lucky Lucifer who had spent most of his time in a whorehouse.

A NEW DESIRE

Lucifer began to lose track of time, at times he felt like he was losing his mind such was the heart-wrenching blow that Lilith had delivered to him.

How is time measured here? he had often wondered but there was the equivalent of day and night, of light and dark but it was only the dark that appealed to him now, it seemed to match the darkness in his heart. He did not know for how long but he neglected his Angelic duties, portals had opened from him but he had not entered them so the portal sought out another Angelic; eventually this was noticed by the Akhet.

Desire came to visit him again.

"We are worried about you Lucifer."

"We, who are we? All I know since I became one of the Angelic are the Blue Portals that take me like a thief in the night to do their bidding whether I want to or not; they open before me like a carriage I did not order which wants to take me to some miserable abode or some Godforsaken battlefield or some other Hell-hole just so that I can see the suffering of the living. I have had enough of it I tell you, I will do it no more!"

"You hurt now Lucifer, your heart aches; we, they, understand that, that is why they have waited before sending me to you."

"Of course my heart aches, I… always thought that one day I would be with Lilith again, that is why I continued with my Angelic work and did not question it… work? We are no more than morgue assistants."

"You know that is not true Lucifer."

"All I know is that men and women should not suffer like they do, what is the point of that?"

"Only the Akhet knows the answer to that and it is something we cannot question."

"Well I can, I am sick of stealing souls from Nameless for Him or Her or whatever It is."

"You know of Nameless then?"

"Yes of course I do, am I the only one? Sometimes I think that what he said to me makes a lot of sense now."

"And what did he say to you Lucifer?"

"Many things, he said that the living would not suffer if he had his way, that they would constantly enjoy all the pleasures of the flesh and soul."

"You do know that he is the father of all lies?"

"Is he, maybe he should be given the chance to prove himself, have you ever thought about that?"

"And would there be love in this world of Nameless, the love that we know that is born out of hurt and suffering?"

Lucifer shrugged his shoulders indifferently.

"How can I know that, I do not even know what love is anymore."

"I think that you need someone to love you Lucifer."

"Love me… I need someone to fuck, do you understand that? Have you even had sex before?"

Desire went silent, Lucifer knew that he had been cruel to Desire saying this and that she was now thinking, trying to remember.

"I have known love Lucifer, just like you."

"I'm talking about sex, not love."

And there was still a bitterness to Lucifer's words.

"Then if that is what you want, then that is what you shall have."

"What?"

With a single thought, Desire's clothes disappeared.

"It has been an eternity for me" she purred as she walked sensually towards Lucifer.

A Lucifer who actually did not know what to do for once in a situation like this.

Then a young man called Lucky entered his mind.

THE VAAGEN

Desire did help comfort Lucifer's broken heart, a bleeding heart that he thought had been crushed forever. But Desire had shown him that life and death goes on and that eventually there would be someone else that Lucifer could love, He realised this but it did not change his mind about his work as an Angelic and the suffering of mankind and he began to realise that he was not the only Angelic who thought this.

The next time the Akhet came for him he was sent to a village that had just been butchered by the invading cruelty of the Vaagen, seafaring cannibals who terrorised coastal dwellers on many shores.

A young infant of maybe three years had been killed and was standing alone and confused, she was watching the Vaagen strip the flesh from her parents, human meat to be cooked on their vile fires.

This made Lucifer feel sick, he almost vomited then the rage built up within him again, he gently held the young girl.

"Do… not worry young one you are safe with me now, I am going take you somewhere safe, safe from the horrendous evil that you have witnessed here."

The blinding light of the portal opened and Lucifer and the child fled the bloodsoaked village and ascended to Angelica but instead of taking the child to her relatives of the past, he took her to the great hall of the Akhet were he was instantly joined by other Angelic that agreed with the action of Lucifer. It was instantly made clear to him that he had broken a rule.

WHY HAVE YOU BROUGHT A HUMAN CHILD HERE LUCIFER?
IT IS NOT ALLOWED

Lucifer's face was stern, he was determined to have his say, he was now the mischievous boy from Meccus who was not afraid of confrontation and being reprimanded.

"Why is it not allowed? I think it is because you do not want to know what this child has just suffered. Look at this poor infant, look at the confusion and pain in her eyes, mortal eyes that have just seen her parents cooked alive on a fire… if I had arrived moments later then she would have witnessed herself being eaten, this would have surely have sent the poor thing mad for all eternity, how can you justify that!"

THE CHILD IS HERE
THAT IS ALL THAT MATTERS
YOU HAVE DONE YOU WORK

"Then hear this Akhet, or maybe you are Yahweh or maybe you are both one like some holy ghost, I will do the work of the Angelic no more."

Lucifer then stated that he and his Angelic followers of a similar mind would take up residence in the land of the living and work to eradicate evil and suffering permanently.

But the Akhet was in no mood for a debate.

The great hall began to shake as the immense anger of the Akhet increased…

YOU ARE NOT PERMITTED TO DO THIS

were the last ear-splitting words that Lucifer and his like-minded band of rebels heard in the place of Angelica.

A light of imaginable force burst forth from the Akhet and hit Lucifer and his companions throughout the Angelic realm… within an instant they were expelled to the vastness of the surrounding universe, each heading in separate directions…

And Lucifer's mind-boggling hurtling trajectory sent him directly towards the Earth's burning sun.

The ethereal body of Lucifer was travelling at a speed he could never imagine, his mind was in a state of shock but instinctively he knew that he had to harden his Angelic skin or the unimaginable heat of the approaching lethal sun would devour his body and soul totally.

The diamond like body of Lucifer eventually slowed down and became part of a vortex that orbited the sun. Heat as intense as the deepest depths of Hell began to melt Lucifer's hardened skin and for the first time since he had ascended to the place he knew as Heaven, Lucifer felt pain and fear. Lucifer's hard skin became black and charred and his features melted and changed, he did not know it but he now looked deformed and demonesque like some creature from the darkest of nightmares.

Lucifer tried to open the light of his Angelic wings but like his skin they were burnt and scarred and could not help him escape from the mighty clutch of the all powerful sun. In that instant Lucifer realised that he could not bear an eternity of so much mental and physical pain, he knew that he had to go catatonic, a form of suspended animation that would prevent him from going mad but before he did he shouted his final goodbyes to his parents and his fellow Angelic exiles and hoped that his words would travel on the strange winds of outer space to them.

THE SUN

Time and existence became immaterial for Lucifer in his catatonic state; strange dreams came and went, reality came and went and then there was only nothing but darkness and numbness. The great yellow giant burned before him with contempt and total disregard for the living entity that flew around it like an irritating fly.

Vicious solar flares burst and spat persistently on the surface of the sun as the years of Lucifer became a blur then as Lucifer neared one such violent flare it suddenly and inexplicitly exploded with such force and venom that the body of Lucifer was freed from its incarcerating orbit. The power of this massive solar flare sent the black body of Lucifer hurtling through the vast emptiness of space again. Lucifer's body flew past Mercury; then Venus and the catatonic Lucifer had no idea of what was happening to him. As luck would have it for the man once nicknamed Lucky, Lucifer's speeding body began to slow down.

His body was nearing the planet known as Earth.

As Lucifer entered the blue world's atmosphere, gravity grabbed hold of him like a greedy monster and increased the speed of his inevitable descent. Lucifer hurtled like a speeding comet towards a landmass that was unknown to him, his white hot body crashed through a canopy of tall trees causing an instant forest fire then it smashed along the ground until it came to a sudden standstill near the edge of a quiet jungle stream. Hot steam hissed all around Lucifer's now still body but he was still totally oblivious to what had happened and where he now was and it was to be some time before Lucifer became aware of his new surroundings.

It was the start of a monsoon that eventually awakened Lucifer from his death-like slumber, the feel of cool life revitalising water on his ebony battered skin. Lucifer's red eyes opened like long-shut trapdoors and surveyed the tropical scenery that surrounded him…

Where am I?
Who am I?

Initially Lucifer could not remember who he was; his mind instinctively knew that it would be too traumatic for him so it had shut down its memory banks because it knew that he probably would go instantly insane. Lucifer felt no pain but the muscles in his body felt weak and stiff and awkward like a machine that had severely rusted from years of neglect.

Lucifer crawled slowly toward the nearby stream to taste the enticing and much needed cool water but when he saw his distorted darkened reflection in the rain splattered stream, he recoiled away in sheer abject horror…

What… what am I? Who is this red eyed black demon that stares back at me?

Lucifer rolled away then staggered to his feet, stepping slowly backwards in confusion, his mind reeling from what he had just seen and when he came to the stump of a tall thick tree, he sat down against it and tried to remember who or what he was.

Lucifer closed his eyes and went into a forced dream-like state and eventually after many days, images began to flash through his mind like the photographic snapshots of a vaguely familiar existence… gradually his life returned to him like an intricate giant jigsaw puzzle, piece by piece…

I am Angelic.
The angel who had argued…
The giant sun burned through his mind
And he remembered the pain
I am Lucifer, the fallen angel.

DIALO

Lucifer lost count of the weeks he sat beneath the rump of that tree; existence was a strange nostalgic blur for him as memories just kept constantly flowing through his mind like the illustrations of a book that were taking him to some sort of conclusion and then one day when the rain of the monsoon finally stopped, he suddenly stood up and decided to walk into the jungle behind him to explore and find out exactly where he was. Lucifer had now remembered that he had the power of flight but he was frightened to open the light, worried that the sun had burnt this most precious gift of his like it had his appearance.

Stumbling through the dense jungle foliage, Lucifer eventually came to a clearing that suggested the evidence of human life… crude wooden huts and mud habitats that indicated a primitive culture but nobody was to be seen. Looking through the sprawling village, Lucifer saw a large wooden building in the distance that seemed big enough to hold all that lived in this crude village and here a disgusting and gruesome sight greeted his red eyes, this place was surrounded by decapitated and decaying heads that were crudely stuck on sharpened wooden spikes, dead eyes still open in horror as if they were looking for someone to save them.

As Lucifer neared this sickly building, he heard a slow dull mortal chant inside that made a cold deep chill creep throughout his body. Whatever was happening inside this wooden structure, Lucifer sensed that it was most likely evil and primitive and an almost forgotten instinctive urge compelled him to go inside.

Lucifer stood quietly in one of the corners next to the doorway, his charred black skin made him virtually unseen; he had forgotten in that moment that he had the ability to bend his Angelic light and turn invisible.

It seemed like all the residents of the village were inside this giant hut which Lucifer now definitely thought of as some kind of central temple. Men women and children were sitting quietly chanting and swaying on the straw covered floor oblivious to the dark entity behind them in the shadows. These people had straight black hair and a dark brown skin and wore little in the way of clothing; in fact the women were virtually fully naked. They wore beads and bracelets made from small coloured stones and necklaces made of small bones that included human teeth.

At the far end of this crude temple, two torches burned behind a deep pit with a thick wooden pole across it. Inside this pit a fire was burning, the smoke circling around the top of the hut and escaping through whatever airway it could find. The sound of the chant increased and from a side entrance two of the tribesmen entered holding a very frightened small girl who did not look of the same tribe. Lucifer guessed that she had been captured from a rival tribe and that this girl was going to be roasted on top of the open fire.

The fearful young girl struggled and screamed but to no avail, the two men holding her were far too big and strong for her. As they neared the burning pit, Lucifer instantly began to feel angry, an anger fuelled by his pity for the hysterical girl.

I cannot allow this.

I cannot watch such a thing.

And as Lucifer thought this, a dark light opened from his back giving the impression of large black spiky wings. Lucifer flew across the surprised seated villagers until he stood before the two men and the girl. The villagers stood up instantly in terror and backed away toward the temple doorway.

The two men immediately began to shake and released their grip on the girl; their mouths open wide in fear and shock.

"Dialo!" they stuttered but they did not dare move.

"What are you doing?" bellowed Lucifer, "Do you intend to cook and eat this poor girl? This is something I will not allow… be gone from me you vile things, be gone or face my wrath!"

The men and the villagers did obviously not understand the tongue of Lucifer but their fear made them all react, they sped from the temple as fast as they could all shouting "Dialo… Dialo!"

Like the two men had done, the girl stood before Lucifer in frozen terror.

"Come with me young one" said Lucifer quietly and he grabbed the girl gently and flew out of the temple, far up above the tightly knit canopy of tall trees where he spotted small plumes of smoke miles away in the distance. Lucifer remembered that with his Angelic touch he could access the girl's mind but her thoughts were confused and erratic, jumbled with fear.

"Is that where your village is?" he asked the girl but she did not understand or react, she was now in some kind of surreal shock, in awe of being in the sky with the birds in the arms of a black winged demon. Lucifer flew to the distant smoke and encircled the village from a great height. Like an eagle he noted that the markings on the bodies of the tribe below were similar to that of the markings on the girl.

It has to be her people he thought and he then flew swiftly down to the centre of the village and the reaction to the sight of him was the same as the other tribe, the people recoiled away from him in spontaneous terror.

Lucifer released the girl gently on the ground and looked around at the stunned frightened faces… the girl ran to them shouting "Dialo, Dialo!" and this immediately angered Lucifer as obviously his kind deed had not been recognised by her or her kin.

"Yes, look at Dialo whoever that is… but I am not evil, I am not a monster!" he called out to them, then he took to the air again, straight up into the clear blue sky and as he did he suddenly thought of home, of Meccus, *a place where he would feel safe, a place where I will surely not receive the same reaction?* Lucifer had no idea of the location of Annon and Meccus from where he was but he closed his eyes and envisaged the great city and suddenly a direction came to him, the instinct of a bird which all Angelic had would guide him there.

MECCUS

Lucifer soared over land and sea until he came to Annon and the great deserts and then to the great mountains of diamonds and gold that surrounded Meccus. In the distance the city glowed like a beautiful mirage, like a tropical island surrounded by miles and miles of flat golden sand that eventually reached the feet of the tall jagged rich mountains.

As Lucifer approached Meccus, it was apparent just how much it had changed, it now seemed to be much bigger, larger statues and temples in a similar vein to the one's he and his father had helped construct dominated the city.

The curious Lucifer flew around the new metropolis from a great height and surveyed the changes below with much intrigue; to any casual observer he must have looked like a large black eagle or vulture that circling for prey.

How long was I held by the cruel grip of that giant sun? Lucifer pondered, *it must have taken hundreds of years to make these changes to Meccus.*

Then as Lucifer glided in the hot still air, he noticed a large crowd below in one of the open public spaces. Three men with their hands tied were kneeling on a sturdy wooden platform; their heads were bowed in front of three strong muscular men who held heavy curved swords that reflected the light of the sun like ominous beacons.

Execution! Lucifer thought at once, *have my people have not outgrown their primitive laws yet?* and again he became instantly agitated and angry.

"So you still do the work of a devil, then if that is so then I will show you a living devil, the demon of wrath and rage!" Lucifer cried out then he descended with great speed widening the dark light from his back as he alighted on the execution platform which created a greater vision of the image he wanted to portray.

The expectant crowd that was there to witness executions gasped at the unexpected unholy sight of Lucifer calling out immediately "Devilah, Devilah!"

Some the crowd ran but stayed out of sheer curiosity of this unbelievable sight that they were now witnessing.

The three executioners tightened their grip on their swords but it was with instinctive fear rather than courage.

"Yes look at me swordsmen, I am the Devil, and you will fear me this day!" Lucifer called out and as he did his skin hardened and sharpened making his appearance even more demonesque, he then flew at the three executioners with great speed and with his diamond sharp hands he cut and ripped their heads from their bodies before they could jump to escape from the platform. The remaining crowd screamed and panicked and ran in any direction that they could, dust rising frantically behind them as they went.

Lucifer then went to the three captive men who instinctively backed away from him in terror. Lucifer freed their tied hands then said to them,"Yes, you need to fear me. I do not know for what crime you are here for but if you follow any sort of evil path again, I will find you and I will execute you myself!"

The three shocked men ran for their lives as fast as their stunned legs could take them, confused as to why they had been saved and Lucifer looked down at the heads of those that he had just decapitated. He knew not why the men were being executed, perhaps he had been wrong saving them but the memory of what had happened to him in Meccus when he had been so cruelly killed while building the temple had prompted his action. He knew that evil was still prevalent in the land of the living and he vowed that he would seek it out and destroy it; the passive uncaring love of the Akhet had no place in his heart now.

Lucifer flew to the sparkling mountains in the distance and took shelter in the first open cave he came to. He looked at his hard black hands that were now covered in the fresh blood of mortals, at his black body that was gnarled and molten and grotesque… and he realised that he had forgotten that he had the Angelic ability to change his appearance, the magical light that could also conjure up whatever clothing he desired. Lucifer thought about what he had looked like before the ravenous flames of the sun had forged him into a demon and his appearance changed, he became the handsome Lucky Lucifer again, the man he was before his cruel banishment.

Lucifer stood naked at the mouth of the cave and shouted out to the world below with a voice that thundered on the wind…

"I will be the Devil… and when the Devil's work is needed, I will do it!"

A red hooded cloak formed in the air and covered his smooth muscular body, a sudden wind seemed to dance around him as if it were somehow alive and aware of the what was happening in that cave.

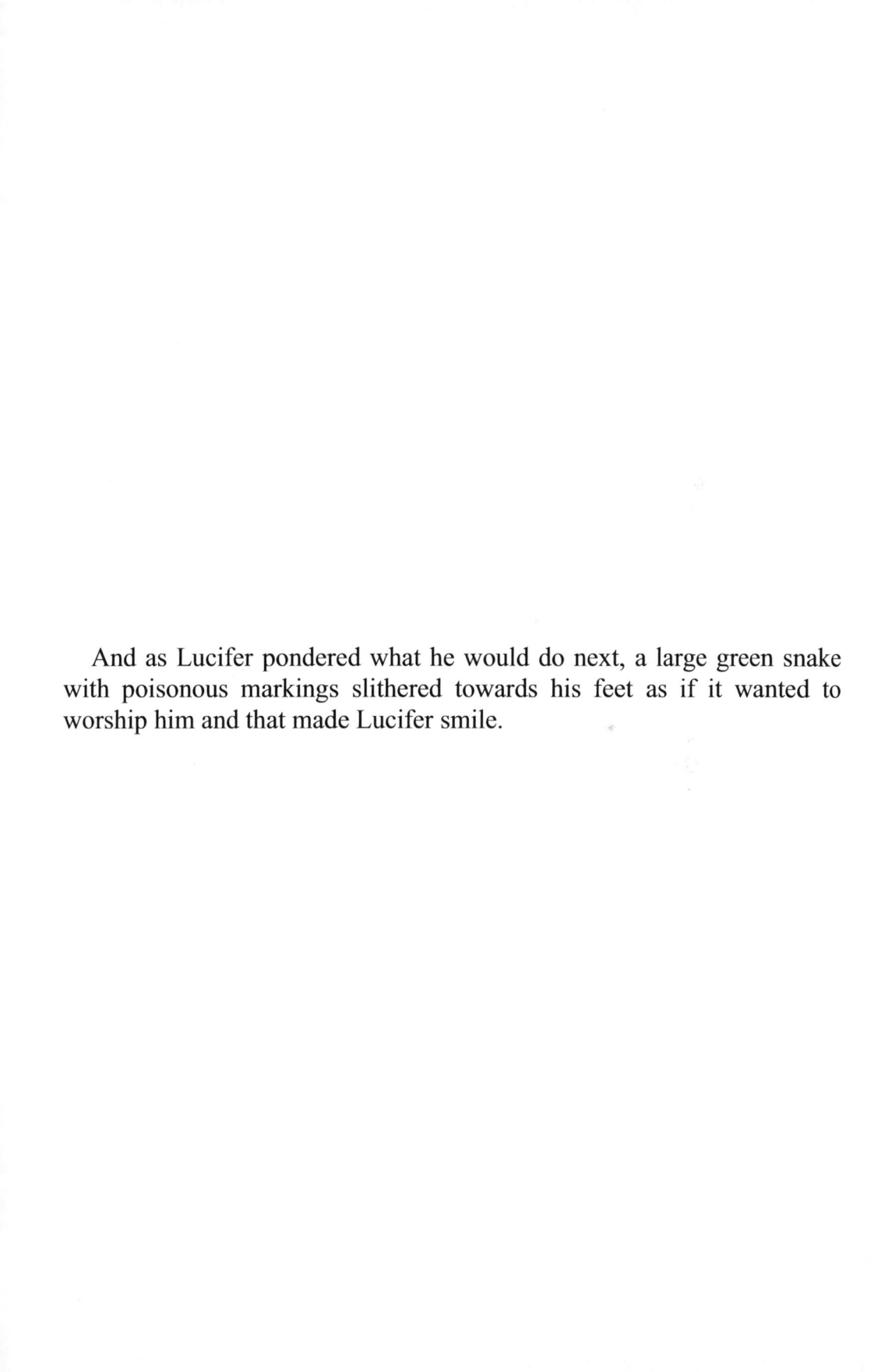

And as Lucifer pondered what he would do next, a large green snake with poisonous markings slithered towards his feet as if it wanted to worship him and that made Lucifer smile.

CARESS

REBORN

Lucifer's first thought in the high windswept cave was *I will need gold and silver deben in the land of the living. I will live in the luxury that was denied my family and I will satisfy my every needs because you never do know what the next sunrise will bring. I will do as I promised the Akhet, I will seek out and destroy evil and I will enjoy it. I will constantly enjoy the pleasures of the flesh but I will guard my heart so that it will never be stolen from me and cruelly crushed again, Lucifer Heylel has been reborn and this time I will control the pattern of my life, I will do what I want to do!*

ANUBIS

Lucifer realised that he could hear the dull thud of heavy metal on rock not far from where he was standing, the diamond and gold mines were still constantly at work increasing the wealth of Meccus and Annon. This would be where he would get what all the living desired.

Lucifer flew down from the cave to where he saw a long line of small horses and camels that were all heavily loaded with large side bags, they were headed on a wide open road towards Meccus and guarded by many men who were heavily armed, Lucifer knew that these men would have once been soldiers of Annon. The trail of horses and camels were coming from the mouth of a mine that Lucifer knew would lead down to the diamond or gold seams within. Lucifer became invisible.

When Lucifer entered the mine he realised that it was relatively new and raw and he knew that it was a diamond mine by the bags of sparkling gems that the men were carrying out.

Lucifer looked at the pitiful workforce that now surrounded him. They were obviously men of little means, *probably from the suburbs of Shakas and Khamit* thought Lucifer. He also realised that some of these men were probably forced labourers, sentenced to work in dangerous mines for whatever crimes they had committed. Lucifer knew that this was hard physical work and long hours and that many of the older men would not survive that long doing it. He began to feel pity for these mortals but he knew that he could not dwell upon it, he had to remember the reason why he was there.

The mine was dimly lit and smaller side tunnels forked away at either side of Lucifer. Men were cutting away at the seams with large sharp pit axes, carving out what diamonds they could. The majority of the diamond clusters were large and would have to be cut and cracked by heavy metal machinery and strong men in Meccus but Lucifer noticed that every now and then smaller diamonds fell to the ground and these were placed into the smaller heavy halfa grass bags.

Just what I need thought Lucifer and then in a darkened area between two wall lamps, Lucifer saw a desperate man quickly put one of the small diamonds into his mouth.

Lucifer smiled.

But the man had been seen by one of the many taskmasters, one that had been hidden in the darkness of a side tunnel. The taskmaster's sword swiftly pierced the back of the would-be thief with the speed of a cobra, cutting right through to the man's stomach. The startled man's mouth opened gasping out blood and the diamond. Nearby workers turned in fear. The taskmaster lifted up the bloody diamond in his hand and held it over the body of the dead man as if he was displaying a trophy he had just won.

"This is what happens to diamond thieves!" he shouted with the blood splattered leather sandal of his foot now on the still body. The other workers turned away not wanting to catch the eye of the sadistic taskmaster and returned to the drudgery of their labour. Another man had failed to steal a diamond and now he was no more.

Lucifer became angry and without thinking too much about it, his cloak of invisibility disappeared and he was now in his true blackened burnt state of appearance. He truly must have looked like some damned demon from the deepest depths of Hell to those in the diamond mine.

"What the…?" the trembling taskmaster called out to the fearsome sight before him. All the miners were dumbstruck and instantly fled from the dark mine not worrying about leaving their place of work without permission but the taskmaster stood frozen with fear. Lucifer swiftly grabbed the man by the neck before he could flee away.

"You kill that poor wretched worker because he wanted wealth, some deben perhaps to feed his family?"

The taskmaster's throat was now as dry as the Annon desert but he tried to respond to the demon that he now thought to be Anubis, the god of death who had come to claim the soul of the man he had murdered.

"It… is not allowed… great Anubis" he stuttered, it was all he could manage to say.

"I am not Anubis" declared Lucifer and he suddenly remembered the circumstances of his own mortal death, "but if there is one thing that I truly hate, it a cruel heartless taskmaster."

Lucifer snapped the man's neck and his head flopped to the side in Lucifer's hand.

"Now you can speak with Anubis" Lucifer laughed and as soon as he said that the man's bulging eyes re-opened and this time they were solid black.

"What sorcery is this?" Lucifer gasped in surprise.

"Can it be?" the dead man spluttered, *"Your body is black and severely burnt and your eyes are as red as any demon I know… but I never forget a voice."*

"And… I recognise your voice from many a year ago, the voice that sounds like a hissing snake that is about to bite something."

"Yes, from a time when you were mortal and I must add that you looked much better than you do now Lucif-er."

A strange laughter echoed throughout the mine, it sounded broken and frail.

"You are the one that was Nameless."

"That is right and if I remember rightly, I did say that out paths would cross again did I not."

"Perhaps it was inevitable but I go my own way now, I behold unto nobody."

"Ah so you have been cast out and quite violently too by the look of it, I told you that the ways of the Akhet were not to be trusted."

"You did but that does not mean that I trust you now, I trust nothing and nobody so you can get on with business of recruitment and I will proceed with what I want to do."

"Stealing from a diamond mine, is this the Lucky Lucif-er that I remember?"

"I need wealth for what I intend to do in the land of the living."

"And just what is that thief of Meccus?"

"I… think you will have to find that out for yourself, I will not explain my intentions to you, why should I?"

"Then it will most joyous and pleasurable monitoring you and do remember that the eyes of the dead are everywhere, my spies are infinite in this sad mortal world so until we meet again Lucky I will bid you farewell for now. I sense the road that you are embarking on now is very similar to mine and I sense that we now have similar goals and ambitions, the Angelic will weaken and that will be the day that you will elect to join with me, of that I am quite sure my dear friend."

The dead taskmaster's head flopped down again. Lucifer dropped him as if he had been infested by something and of course he had been. Lucifer then took the four large bags of small diamonds and flew from the now deserted mine. He headed towards the northern Egyptian city of Tanis which was on the Uat-Ur coast, a place that had become affluent because it was where the river Nile started. He intended to make it a base from which he would cross the sea to travel and explore the world.

But things were not to go exactly as Lucifer planned.

Not immediately that is.

PERNEB

Lucifer learned from temple engravings that it was the year 2,500 BC and that the Pharaoh Khafre was now ruling Egypt.

Has it really been that long since I departed the mortal coil of existence? pondered Lucifer as he stood studying the hieroglyphics which he found quite easy to understand because they were so similar to those that were used in Annon.

Next to the temple was a large statue to the sun god Ra and as he gazed up at it he was joined by a large rotund man whose robes immediately suggested that he was a man of wealth and influence. Behind this man waited a large golden carriage that was pulled by two magnificent white horses and driven by two black men who were obviously guards.

"Magnificent is it not?" asked the man and his voice sounded gentle and kind. Lucifer looked up again at the statue.

"It is but I think that it lacks emotion, Ra is a joyous god that brings sunshine to this world, that is not shown here" replied Lucifer and it was an honest opinion and response.

The large rich man was completely surprised by Lucifer's words.

"Really, you criticise easily my good fellow but what gives you the right to do so?"

Lucifer turned back to face the man.

"I… am an architect of art, I specialise in sculpture and statues."

This reply was spontaneous and completely dishonest but Lucifer had said this for a reason - the man was obviously rich so Lucifer thought that by saying this it might lead to him being introduced to the higher social circles of Tanis, much quicker that he had anticipated.

The man's face lighted up, there was no reason to disbelieve Lucifer especially as Lucifer was wearing robes as fine and as rich as his own but he did have to ask, "And what commissions have you completed may I ask?"

"Oh none that you will have heard of because they were for rich families in Annon, large family busts and sculptures for their houses and private temple statues of gods which I have to say are more flamboyant and exciting than the one we gaze upon now."

"Well this is most interesting because I am Perneb, the High Commissioner of Tanis and we do have an imminent commission planned, a grand statue of the great sea god Yamm that needs to be started soon. Please tell me with whom I am conversing with."

"I am Lucifer Heylel of Meccus" Lucifer said with pride, "and I am here in your beautiful city on a journey of leisure. I plan to eventually cross the Aut-Ur and explore the new civilisations there."

"Then you surely are a man of wealth and means but would you have time to take on such a task of ours?"

Lucifer smiled, "I think so, I seem to have all the time in the world now."

"This is so exciting then, I am always looking for new designers and men of art for Tanis. Have you any immediate plans for this evening as you are most welcome to attend a social gathering at my house, we are celebrating the birth day of my son Chisisi."

"That sounds perfect to me, it will be a chance for me to get to know the good people of Tanis."

Perneb told Lucifer that he would send a carriage for him when the sun was about to set and asked Lucifer where he was staying. Perneb's house was situated by the sea, on top of high cliffs which looked out toward the Mediterranean sea, He bade farewell to Lucifer and returned to his waiting carriage, he smiled at Lucifer as he waved and Lucifer felt that this was an honest and easygoing man despite the important and complicated duties he surely had to perform in overseeing Tanis. Men that failed as city High Commissioners where usually not treated so well by ruling Pharaohs and Lucifer knew this, *If I do create a monument for this man then it will be one the greatest in all of Egypt* Lucifer pledged to himself then he looked up at the god Ra.

"Art and sculpture? No problem" he laughed then just before Lucifer walked away he added, "I think you should smile more oh Great Ra."

THE PLEASURES OF THE FLESH

Lucifer had booked himself into the most expensive rooms in Tanis' elite travellers house which was called The Moon And Stars. The first thing he had done was request four heavy metal strong boxes for his diamonds which were held in The Moon And Stars safe room, a sturdy re-enforced room that led to an underground labyrinth of hidden tunnels which was constantly guarded both night and day by fierce ex-warriors who demanded a high wage for their services. Lucifer thought that these men were obviously potential thieves but he knew that they would be hunted down and executed for any such action and the men knew this also.

When Lucifer returned from his morning walk and his meeting with Perneb he ordered a sumptuous meal which mainly consisted of the rich sea life that was readily available in Tanis - a variety of fish, lobster, crab and oysters was served to him adorned with a mouthwatering variety of luscious salads.

After Lucifer had ate his fill which was everything that was served to him (there was no need for Lucifer to eat, he simply just enjoyed it) he asked for a selection of women which was to be his chosen dessert. Five women were brought to Lucifer in his expensive suite, women of different race and colour that had been 'recruited' for the pleasures of the flesh.

Lucifer had not experienced the delights of a woman's touch since he had made love to the Angelic Desire and that was now hundreds of years ago and it felt like it to Lucifer. The woman Lucifer chose had the most beautiful shining skin that seemed to be made of pure ebony, she was as black as the most starless of nights and the perfect sensual shape of her body was unlike any he had ever seen and it seemed to Lucifer that her body had been formed purely for the art of sex.

"A good choice my lord, we only acquired her yesterday but she is aware of her duties and what is required of her. Her name is Caress and she is believed to be a northern Sahara tribal princess, she does not speak our tongue but I am sure that you do not intend to converse with her that much" the concierge said smiling.

Caress looked defiant but as she looked into the startling brown eyes of Lucifer her facial expression seemed to soften, she had immediately sensed something different about him., maybe a heart that was as sad as her heart but she did not know why she was thinking this.

"I will leave you now my lord and if you require any of the other women afterwards than please let me know."

"I will require no other, Caress will be my only choice today."

"Of course my lord and I am sure that she will serve you well."

The grovelling concierge left the room. Caress stood in silence.

"Take a seat beautiful one" Lucifer said and he nodded to the long comfortable sofa that looked out towards the coast. Lucifer poured out two goblets of Tanis wine that was reputed to be the finest in all of Egypt because it came from vineyards that bordered the Mediterranean Sea.

Caress sat on the sofa and took the goblet but she did not drink from it, Lucifer however drank greedily from his.

"There is no need to fear me Caress and I do sense that you are a princess, your pride is obvious and genuine, it is there for everyone to see."

Caress looked at Lucifer and tried her best to understand what he was actually saying. For some reason she did not fear or loathe this gentle handsome man and that intrigued her greatly.

Lucifer poured himself more wine.

"Drink Princess Caress, you are safe with me. I am now going to touch you, I am going to give you my 'tongue' with my mind, do not be afraid."

Lucifer gently reached out and touched Caress' silken arm, she did not pull away.

Thoughts of her home flashed to him...
Images of her people
Their grand huts and land
Caress was dancing barefoot with a line of topless women
It was a ceremony celebrating her age of consent
Then…
The riders came
On horses and camels
With curved swords and vicious dogs
The guards of Caress fought bravely

But were ultimately defeated
They gave their lives for her without question
Unlike the others of the tribe
Caress was not raped
The man in charge indicated that she would not be touched
That she would bring more golden deben by being pure
Lucifer felt her sadness
And a tear fell from his eye
Caress noticed this and was puzzled.

"You cry" she said and was astounded by the Arabic language she was now speaking.

"Yes, I felt your pain" answered Lucifer.

"How could you and how do I now speak in your tongue, are you some sort of magician?"

Lucifer laughed.

"No sweet Caress, I am no magician but we shall not speak of that… I… have plans for you."

"What plans do you have, the pleasures of the flesh no doubt!"

Caress stood up defiant again.

"Please sit down princess and sup your wine, it will calm you down."

Reluctantly Caress sat down again beside Lucifer, *What kind of man is this?* she thought and then she drank from her goblet.

"I must confess that your beautiful body does indeed tempt me, it has been so long since I have been with a woman but then your story changed what I desired…"

"And what is that now?"

"We will not talk of this right now, not until tonight when I return from the house of the High Commissioner, there is something I want from him."

"So I am to stay here?"

"Yes while I am here, there is another room with another bed which can be yours."

"And that vile man will not bother me?"

"The concierge? I guarantee it."

"So I am yours then, have you bought me?"

"No, I have not bought you but you will be free after tonight and I will give you a choice."

"A choice?"

"All will be revealed later my little princess."

"I am not little, look..."

I remember Lilith saying something like that…

Caress stood up and Lucifer once again looked at her tall desirable shapely body and the short red garment that looked like it had been painted on her. Lucifer laughed which did make Caress smile, suddenly things did not seem so bad for her.

"I will order a new wardrobe for you soon, the very latest designs, you will look like a princess again and not some painted lady of the night."

"I have no paint on me?"

Once again Lucifer laughed then he went to a wide wooden table where there were sheets of large papyrus and ink. He began to draw the sea god Yamm, how he imagined Yamm to be and Lucifer was surprised by how good his drawings actually were, a latent talent no doubt that had never really been given the chance to surface during his mortal life.

Caress watched with wonder over Lucifer's shoulder as the sea god came to life, had the man who she thought was going to rape her turned out to be some sort of an angel she wondered?

Is this strange man an Amadlozi?

Caress did not realise how close she was to the truth.

CHISISI

Early evening and Lucifer was notified by that weaselly concierge that a horse-drawn carriage had arrived to take him the house of Perneb. The carriage was not like the chariots that would come to be associated with Egypt, it was a much more modest vehicle, more like a common rickshaw and Lucifer considered it a novelty to be riding in it. Of course, Lucifer could have took to the air to get to his destination but he wanted to act out his mortal guise in full.

Lucifer clothed himself in expensive looking garments which were concocted by his power of Angelic light. His upper tunic was blue and wrapped over his right shoulder and was held on the other shoulder by three thin leather straps. Around his waist and above his golden kilt was a thick brown belt which was covered in solid gold studs. On his wrists were long leather bands that were decorated with intricate overlapping patterns. His leather sandals had thin straps that curled up around his lower legs like two brown snakes. Just like his father, his Annon army symbol scar was visible on his upper left arm and Lucifer could have easily hid it but it was something he never did as the symbol still filled him with pride; it was sense of place, a moment in time for him, something that he knew would always keep him grounded in reality.

The cool sea breezes were quite bracing for Lucifer as he stepped out of the carriage at the main door to the house of Perneb, with him was the various designs for the statue of Yamm that he had drawn and he knew that Perneb would not be expecting these graphic ideas so soon.

A tall muscular black male servant greeted Lucifer and took him into the house, Lucifer noticed that a large dagger was sheathed on his belt.

Does Perneb have enemies? thought Lucifer immediately, *I suppose he must have, everyone in high authority in Egypt and indeed Annon are always in danger of being assassinated by those that want their position of power.*

Lucifer was taken through a series of rooms that displayed just how rich and important Perneb was until they came to the largest which was full of people enjoying tables full of food, wine and heqet which was a thick dark Egyptian beer. In the corner of this vast room, three musicians were supplying the background music, one of them who was a woman was playing a large curved benet which was the equivalent of a harp and it did sound very beautiful to Lucifer's acute hearing.

Very Angelic he thought and this made Lucifer smile.

"Ah Lucifer Heylel, welcome to our celebration." a voice boomed in Lucifer's ear. It was Perneb, with a broad smile that was as wide as his stomach.

"Please, take some wine or heqet if you prefer then I will take you to meet my son."

A black female waitress who looked very similar to Caress and who Lucifer immediately thought was of the same tribe, offered Lucifer a selection of drinks and he chose the heqet.

"I have not had the chance to taste Tanis heqet yet" and he supped his drink heartily.

"You will surely like it my friend, the barley and fruit are superb here in Tanis and we do have an exceptional heqet-master that brews it, I am quite sure that the sea air adds to the production of our heqet, you cannot beat the freshness of it can you?"

"You do have a point there Perneb" replied Lucifer and he began to think about his early army days on the coast.

Perneb then took Lucifer out of the crowded room and onto a wide balcony that looked out to the sea. The house was very near to the cliff edge and Lucifer noticed that the sea was calm and still, still red from the giant orange sun that was slowly going down behind it.

"Great Ra will sleep soon and the red glow of the evening will bless us now" Perneb said almost reverently then he said to Lucifer, "This is my son Chisisi."

A young man of now twenty years was seated on a wide basket chair but he stood up when his father and Lucifer approached him. Lucifer was somewhat surprised that Chisisi was alone.

"This is Lucifer Heylel, the man I met this morning" Perneb said and as Chisisi neared them he held out a hand and placed it on Lucifer's left shoulder.

This is a soldier's greeting thought Lucifer, *But surely this son of Perneb is not a military man?*

Suddenly fragments of Chisisi's mind surged through Lucifer, images that Lucifer was somehow not expecting…

Chisisi moving on the back of a man

With a man moving on top of him

Chisisi was smiling as a naked man came towards him

His large black penis erect and wanting

Then there was a jumble of images that Lucifer did not want to access

Until a grisly one appeared…

Chisisi with a knife at his father's back

Bloody

Stabbing repeatedly into Perneb

And Chisisi grinned

Content with his actions…

Lucifer knew in an instant that Chisisi intended to murder his father and inherit all of his money and possibly even his power.

Lucifer knew that he had to break these thoughts.

"Your hair Chisisi, is very fashionable, has it been colourised in any way?"

Chisisi smiled and it was very similar to the smile in Lucifer's mental images; he had completely misunderstood Lucifer's comment on his looks, he immediately thought that Lucifer was sexually interested in him.

"Oh no, it is my true colour, like my mother's hair."

"She must have be a very beautiful woman."

"She was."

And it was true that Chisisi was handsome but in a very feminine sort of way, Lucifer even noticed that Chisisi had powdered his lips to make them a brighter red.

"I see that you prefer solitude rather than the celebrations Chisisi?" Lucifer noted.

It was another perceptive comment by Lucifer.

"Oh yes, the majority of people in there are my father's friends and associates, I am just here because I have to be, soon I will join my friends in the city for my night of celebrations."

Perneb was slightly embarrassed by this, as if he knew what his son had planned for his evening entertainment.

"Ah, the pleasures of the young Perneb, those were the days." Lucifer laughed.

Perneb laughed too then had to say, "But surely you are not that old Lucifer, I would guess that you are a man in his early thirties?"

Lucifer took out his Yamm designs that he had rolled and carefully concealed in his tunic then looked at his open hand that was not holding the papyrus drawings.

"I may be a little older than you think Perneb… but enough of me, here are my preliminary drawings of Yamm."

"What, you have completed them already?"

"Time is short Perneb, I thought that if you like what you see it will take about two years to complete."

Lucifer handed the papyrus designs to Perneb who rolled them out on a nearby table.

"Dear Ra, these are magnificent, everyone of them. And you did all this in one afternoon?"

"Time is also money Perneb, I always work fast. I thought that if you did not like them then I would continue with my immediate plans."

"No, no, these are wonderful, you must stay in Tanis and complete this commission, money will be no object and the Pharoah Khafre will love these."

"Good, as soon as you choose one then the real work will begin."

"I have to choose now?"

Lucifer laughed.

"No, of course not Perneb, think about them, discuss them, it is your choice."

Chisisi pointed out the one he liked immediately.

"This one, it has to be."

The drawing was of Yamm standing defiantly, one arm was held out with an open hand and the other stretched arm had a clenched fist. The head of Yamm was that of a fearsome sea serpent and on his back were fish scales and large fins which almost resembled wings.

"He is controlling the sea here" added Chisisi, "You can see it, feel it."

His father Perneb smiled and agreed, "My son has an artist's eye Lucifer, I am quite sure that this design will be the one chosen."

"As I have said, there is no immediate rush but I do think that you have chosen my favourite."

The three men laughed and in that instant Lucifer could not understand why Chisisi hated his father so much.

"Come then Lucifer, join the party and meet the elite of Tanis."

"I will enjoy that but first I have to ask you something."

"And what is that?"

"That I may buy The Moon And Stars."

Perneb was surprised by this just as he had been surprised by the drawings, he immediately thought, *This man from Annon does not mess around.*

"I… think that can be arranged, I will say that it is part payment for Yamm, a sign of our gratitude and as of now you own The Moon And Stars."

"The owner will not be annoyed then?"

"I own it Lucifer" Perneb laughed, "It was to become the house of Chisisi after I had died."

Lucifer looked at Chisisi and saw that he was obviously angry, an inner jealously was beginning to build up within him.

"I… must take my leave now" said Chisisi and the tone of his voice reflected his bitter emotions, "My friends await me. Nice to have met you Lucifer Heylel and I look forward to meeting with you in a more informal setting, you can tell me about that intriguing scar on your arm."

Chisisi smiled but it was a predatory smile which Lucifer did not respond in kind to.

"Yes, I will look forward to that" and Lucifer's eyes burnt with an intent that Chisisi misunderstood.

After Chisisi had departed the balcony Lucifer had to say to Perneb, "I think that your son is not happy with you giving me The Moon And Stars?"

"Oh he understands really and he stands to inherit much more than a traveller's house, let me tell you."

Perneb laughed.

"But enough of business for now, let us join the party and celebrate the statue of Yamm and your new acquisition the Moon And Stars."

TENDER IS THE NIGHT

Lucifer did not stay late at the celebrations which he knew would last until daybreak, he stayed just long enough to get to know the people he wanted to, *Knowledge is power* he had always thought, *even in this new modern age, some things will never change.*

Lucifer did not want to take a carriage back to The Moon And Stars, instead and when he was completely alone, he reverted to his original burnt state and opened out the black crackling Angelic energy from his back. Lucifer took to the air unseen and glided in the soft hazy moonlight. He flew out to sea and back again and looked down on the house of Perneb and to where his statue of Yamm was to be erected, on the beach and close to the cliffs and directly in front of Perneb's house. He imagined that the back of Yamm's head would be directly in line with the balcony that he had been standing on and then suddenly a thought hit him, something that he would have to make Perneb aware of but not this night, now he had other things on his mind in the sensual shape of Caress.

THE EXPLODING STARS

When Lucifer walked into his rooms at The Moon And Stars, everything was deathly quiet, he had been hoping that Caress would still be awake so that he could converse with her but she had obviously retired to her bed or so he hoped because *Maybe she has fled, to try and make it back to her homeland?* Lucifer knew that this would be virtually impossible for her, a black woman without money attempting to cross vast barren deserts without a camel would be suicidal but then he thought, *Maybe she found my money-box in my bedroom?* Lucifer walked quickly to his room and when he entered he was pleasantly surprised, Caress was lying totally naked on his bed as if she was waiting for him. She seemed to be asleep and Lucifer found this quite heart-warming, *The poor girl has been through a lot recently, the rape of her village, her abduction into the slave trade, all of this must have been horrific for her. But now she is safe with me this night and that is all that matters.*

As Lucifer slowly and quietly approached the bed, Caress' eyes opened slowly…

"My Lord Lucifer… you have returned" she purred almost dreamily.

"I am not your lord Caress, we are equals now and your future is now as bright as the moon that shines down upon your wonderful ebony skin."

"You are my saviour then Lucifer, come to me."

Lucifer slowly joined Caress on his bed, he discarded his clothing with his mind but Caress did not notice this, already she was beginning to writhe with the want of Lucifer's body.

"So long… so, so long" Lucifer whispered softly in Caress' ears and their lips met like hungry night wolves, their tongues like fiery slippery serpents, licking and searching for the delights within and when Lucifer finally entered Caress she was almost at the point of climax, Lucifer did indeed wonder if she was a virgin princess and that this was the first time that she had ever made love.

Lucifer moved gently within her and then faster as the intensity of their lovemaking increased; he increased the size of his penis with his Angelic power to a size that he felt was just right for Caress and when she did come it was as if all the stars of the night had exploded within her as if the African goddess of love Oshun had entered her; and Lucifer was satisfied too even though he had not ejaculated any Angelic sperm. This was something Lucifer would come to realise was difficult for him to do, a side-effect of his time around the sun but Caress had been satisfied and that was all that mattered to him at the moment. He knew that the virgin princess was a mortal woman he could love but he did have plans for her, something he would discuss with her in the morning and not while they were in bed together…

And Caress wanted more

More and more

Time and time again

Until the Great Ra awakened and sent his light to them

And they slept
Until Ra was high in the sky directly over them.

THE PLAN

When Lucifer finally awoke, Caress was not beside him on the bed. He covered himself in a large white robe then went into the main room and again Caress was not there. Once again he began to think that Caress had left The Moon And Stars but then he heard movement in the adjoining dining room and he could smell the exotic scent of Caress as well as the enticing smell of cooked mortal food.

"Ah my lord, you have risen from your slumber. I have prepared lunch for you, fried oxen and peas with my village gravy that is full of eastern spices."

Lucifer sat down, a large plate of food was waiting for him and he licked his lips with the delicious odour.

"I have told you Caress" he started after biting into the tasty hot meat, "I am not your lord."

Caress had sat down opposite Lucifer and had begun to start her meal, "Tell me again Lucifer."

"I now own this place and all within it, you included and therefore from this moment you are a free woman again. But I want you to run this place, make it a sanctuary for other captured slaves, offer them the choice to return home or stay here with you."

"But what about Kabal, how will he react to that? He will not like it."

"Who is Kabal?"

"The man who owns the cruel vicious slave traders. I believe that he is not Egyptian, I think that he is a Shiwei from the northern countries."

"Good, you have told me me who I need to see but that will be later tonight after I have seen Chisisi."

"Who is Chisisi?"

"The son of the High Commissioner, I have something in mind for him too."

BUSINESS

When the sun began to set, Lucifer went to see Chisisi. He had learned at the celebration party that Chisisi spent most of his time at the other great traveller's house which was called The Mouth Of The Nile. Lucifer assumed that he would still be there after his indulgences of the celebration night and he was right. Lucifer announced who he was to the concierge and he was taken to Chisisi's suite. He was allowed to enter but Chisisi was not in the main room.

"Stay here a moment my lord please" the concierge said and then he went into the bedroom. Moments later he returned to Lucifer.

"You my enter my lord. I will leave you now."

"I may enter his bedchamber's?"

"Yes my lord, he will see you in there."

Lucifer slowly entered the room to find Chisisi on a large king-sized bed with two men, a white man and a black man.

"Lucifer, you have come to see me as you promised you would."

"Did I?"

"Yes, I could tell by the look in your eye at my father's house that you would."

Lucifer smiled, *This is a vain young man, I am going to enjoy this.*

"Yes of course but in private please."

"You want my friends to leave? It would make for a nice foursome."

"Yes, I want them to leave."

And Lucifer's eyes began to burn red which made the two men quickly scuttle away and out of the room.

"Sit then beside me on this bed and you can tell me why you are here" Chisisi said and there was that same lecherous look and smile from the previous night.

"No Chisisi, I am going to be quite blunt with you and you may not like it."

Chisisi sat up, his expression had changed to one of intrigue mixed with mild fear.

"What do you want Lucifer Heylel?" Chisisi then asked, his voice suddenly stern and bold, too bold for Lucifer.

"The answer is simple, I want your soul Chisisi and you are going to work for me."

"What, how dare you come here, to my rooms and demand such a thing!"

"I dare do anything, you will come to realise that."

Chisisi laughed but there was a hint of panic in his laughter.

"I will have you apprehended and slain for thinking such a thing, Do you remember who I am?"

"You are nothing to me. You are the son of Perneb, a man I like and you will work for me if I say so."

"My father will not allow this, he will not like you coming here saying such… stupid things."

"And he would not like you stabbing him in his back."

Chisisi seemed to freeze when he heard this.

"How dare you say such a thing, where the Duat do you think you are?"

Lucifer thought about Duat, the Egyptian term for the underworld then replied, "Duat is the right word my young friend."

And then he changed into his true appearance.

Chisisi recoiled back in horror and a sickly fear instantly consumed him.

"Who… or what are you? Are… you Anubis to take my soul or are you Osiris, here to take me to your dark kingdom?"

"Maybe I am both… but you will know me as Lucifer as before."

"Yes of course, oh Great One."

Chisisi was trembling like a fragile leaf in a storm now, his stomach felt like it had turned to liquid jelly and he was on the verge of losing consciousness.

"What… do you want of me?" he eventually managed to say, "Do you want my physical body, to have sex with me? I am open to you now, take me my lord."

Chisisi opened his legs which immediately revolted Lucifer but he did smile, a dark sinister smile.

"No, I do not want your scrawny body pitiful one, as I have said, you are going to work for me. I am going to buy this Mouth Of The Nile and you are going to manage it for me. You are going to start my financial empire in this realm, you will look after it, nurture it and make it grow."

Chisisi was astound by what Lucifer was proposing as he thought that he was surely going to die at the hands of this black demon.

"You will not kill your father because if you do, I will kill you, it is as simple as that."

"But… why me? If you know my plans and my ambitions, why would you trust me?"

"Exactly because of that, you are ambitious and ruthless so therefore you will be successful for me. But you will never interfere with Caress and The Moon And Stars, do you understand?"

"Yes, of course my lord… but who is Caress?"

Lucifer told Chisisi about Caress and Chisisi replied, "But Kabal the slave trader, he will be displeased by this."

"Where is this Kabal?"

"He is here this night in The Mouth Of The Nile, he brought the Africans here a few days ago."

"Then I will go to see him now."

KABAL

Lucifer reverted back to his mortal state then found out where Kabal's rooms were. He entered the rooms unannounced.

Kabal was naked in bed with three black slaves, all of whom did not want to be there and Lucifer knew this.

"Get clothed" he said to them, "and go to Princess Caress at The Moon And Stars, a new life awaits you there."

Kabal jumped out of bed and reached for his sword then held it at the throat of Lucifer. Kabal was a large muscular man who had a short black beard and a thick scar just above his left eye. He looked fierce but his appearance meant nothing to Lucifer only that he reminded him of the evil Abrax of Meccus from all those years ago.

"Who are you, how dare you enter the rooms of Kabal, you are not even armed?"

"I would enjoy killing you but I suppose slavery is just a business to you and my business with you is this…"

Lucifer turned black and burnt and grabbed Kabal by the throat. He then flew with him out of the room and high up into the night sky. Kabal struggled but he was weak from confusion and sheer terror. Lucifer flew miles and miles out into the desert and Kabal still tried to wrestle with the black demon that held him but his resistance was pathetic to Lucifer. Lucifer then dropped Kabal into the sea of sand that was vast and endless, there was no sign of life for miles, no oasis, no water to save Kabal.

"I have not killed you Kabal remember that. The desert will kill you for for your evil deeds, for the people you made as slaves. You are now a slave to the mighty desert god Seth, your fate now lies with him."

Lucifer then flew back to Tanis, to the princess that waited for him and the beginning of their new lives.

YAMM

It did take two years to carve and erect the statue of Yamm, just as Lucifer had predicted. Within that time Caress had turned The Moon And Stars into the House of Heylel which was also to become known as The Old Sanctuary because of all the people Caress was to save from slavery.

Chisisi and The Mouth Of The Nile prospered and he branched out into many other businesses which made both him and Lucifer very wealthy men. Chisisi had no idea though as to how rich Lucifer truly was because over those two years Lucifer made more visits to the Annon gold and diamond mines. Chisisi never interfered with the work of Caress and he never killed his father.

Lucifer entertained himself by killing the most evil people he could find in Tanis and the surrounding areas; murderers, rapists and sadists whom he did not consider had the right to exist and infest mortal life. He thought that his actions would attract the attention of Nameless but it was only on the eve of the official opening of the Yamm statue that he appeared before Lucifer.

Lucifer was excited, he was looking down from one of the balconies of his new residence towards the sea to where the large statue of Yamm stood when suddenly he was aware that one of the servants was standing behind him…

"Lucifer the artist then, Lucifer the sculptor, the designer of gods?"

Lucifer turned and noticed that the servant had solid black eyes but this did not register with him immediately as it had been some time since he had witnessed such eyes.

"How dare you speak like that to me?" Lucifer said instinctively but he was beginning to remember…

"I speak to you how I want, we are equals are we not?"

Lucifer recognised the voice that sounded like it was coming from the depths of some cold deathly tomb.

"Nameless, I was wondering when you would come to me again."

"Well you have sent me some fine recruits these past two years so I thought it was only good manners that I should thank you in person for that."

"I did not do it for you, I did it for the people of Tanis, the mortals that I like and care for here."

"Yes, you have carved out a nice empire for yourself here, I would imagine that you are a very wealthy man of power now."

"Gold and deben will pay for what I want to do here in this realm."

"And that is good is it not, that craving for power over mortals, that feeling that you can do what you want with them, the taking of life, the pleasures of the flesh, it is all here for you to relish..."

"Look Nameless, what exactly do you want? I have no need for you."

"Maybe not but as I have said, I will have need for you in the future, of that I am quite certain. I will leave you now and I do hope that you enjoy tomorrow's festivities and all the artistic acclaim, I think that there may be someone there that will interest you greatly and I do sincerely hope that you enjoy your time with this mortal woman."

The servant's eyes returned to normal and immediately he looked confused and frightened.

"I… do not know why I am here my lord?"

Lucifer smiled.

"Do not worry, just bring me a cool glass of heqet."

"The servant hastily scurried away leaving Lucifer to ponder Nameless' last words.

What woman?

Nameless was referring to the Annon Princess Lanar who was attending the opening ceremony. Word had reached the city of Meccus that an Annon artist had designed the sculpture of Yamm, so she had decided to see the statue in person because she had a commission of her own that she wanted to complete. This of course was a big coup for Perneb, a big feather in his cap, Annon royalty visiting his city would mean that Pharaoh Khafre would be most impressed.

But what of Caress and Lucifer's love for her, had it blossomed during the last two years? For Lucifer it had become more of a caring love, each day over the months he became more like a father figure and Caress was aware of this. Eventually she fell in love with a tall handsome African captive slave who she bought and made free and Lucifer was pleased for her. When she came to confess to Lucifer about her new love he was already aware of it and he thought that it was the right time to reveal his true self to her so that she would understand why he would give her his full and total blessing for her mortal future.

"I... am here dear Lucifer" she started to say in Lucifer's bedroom, "to tell you..."

"There is no need Caress, I know who you love and I am greatly and truly pleased for you... and I now think that this is the right time for me to reveal my true self to you so please do not be afraid."

Lucifer transformed into his true state and Caress was stunned and shocked but not afraid, this was a man whom she loved too much but was he an actual living man she wondered now.

"Are... you a Shetani or are you an Amadlozi like I always suspected?"

Lucifer gently held Caress' hand with his own black hand and they sat down on his large bed.

"I... used to be Angelic, but now I am simply me."

Caress carefully touched Lucifer's burnt face and looked into his burning red eyes. He knew that she would find his true appearance repulsive.

"You are not ugly to me Lucifer, if this is your true appearance then I will love it."

Caress nudged Lucifer back onto the bed, she was so pleased that he had revealed his true self to her.

"One last night then my love then you can start your new life afresh."

Caress was hungry for Lucifer's body, she actually seemed to be more aroused by his true appearance and as ever their lovemaking lasted all night, all the sweeter it seemed for Lucifer because he knew that it would probably be for the last time.

Probably.

And in the morning, Caress arranged for Lucifer's breakfast to be brought to him, the start of a very important day for him, in more ways than one.

THE PRINCESS

The excitement in Tanis was almost tangible, people from all over Egypt had travelled to the city to see the statue of Yamm. Perneb had wide steps carved in the cliffs on either side of his house so that people could walk down to the beach to see Lucifer's splendid statue. It was rumoured that the great Pharoah Khafre would actually be there but a last minute ailment had stopped his journey north.

Perneb's house was now full of the most important of people, all of whom were in Perneb's vast garden which looked out to the sea and the statue of Yamm. Perneb stood on a specially built altar to make his official announcement to his most special guests which included the Crown Princess of Annon. The altar was covered in all kinds of exotic seafood which was dedicated to and in honour of Yamm.

"Dear friends and associates and those of you who have travelled far to be here at my humble abode."

Laughter.

"We gather here today to pay homage the the Great God Yamm, to witness his first solid realisation by the hand of man and it was the hand and mind of Lucifer Heylel who designed this magnificent statue."

Perneb's hand opened toward Lucifer who was seated at a table next to the altar drinking vast amounts of irep, the rich Egyptian wine he was very fond of. Loud cheers and applause filled the garden and Perneb motioned to Lucifer to get him to stand up which he reluctantly agreed to. Perneb continued…

"Lucifer has made a dream of mine come true, a dream which came to me when I first came to live in this house by the sea and I am eternally grateful to him. So let us celebrate the Great Yamm today and as you can see, the ocean is calm and still, Great Yamm is truly pleased with our homage to him. Now drink, eat and make merry, those of you who have not yet seen Yamm close up then the steps I have constructed await you."

Some of the guests left to join the vast crowd on the beach. Lucifer stayed to enjoy his meal and his drink. He did feel very proud, he had overseen the creation of the statue, from it's beginnings in the nearby mountains to the enormous carving work that was done by many craftsmen and the end product had justified their and his handiwork. He was pleased and therefore he would rejoice, the day would be one to savour he had decided. And as he sat there he noticed that someone was observing him, someone who had two large bodyguards behind her. Lucifer immediately recognised the scarred symbol on their shoulders.

Annon army, which means…

"Ah, you have noticed the princess."

Perneb interrupted Lucifer's thoughts.

"Let me bring her to you so that she can join you at your table."

Perneb approached the princess and she obviously agreed to do what Perneb had suggested. As Lanar sat down opposite Lucifer, he stood and reached out and took her hand. Lanar was quite surprised by this and both of her guards began to withdraw their swords but with her other hand the princess indicated that the two men were to stand down. Lucifer gently kissed her hand.

"My princess, your presence here is as great as the Great Ra above who shines down upon us this day with pleasure."

"Your princess?"

Lucifer sat down again.

"I am from Annon your majesty, did Perneb not tell you that?"

Lanar told her bodyguards that they were not needed and told them to go and feast. Perneb also sensed that Lanar wanted to be alone with Lucifer so he left to attend to the other guests.

"Perneb did tell me that" Lanar eventually replied, "And I did get someone to check our extensive records of family names but there is no mention of you… there was a Lucif Heylel and he had a son called Lucifer but apparently that was hundreds of years ago?"

"That would be my ancestor then" Lucifer quickly replied but Lanar was sharp-eyed.

"And that scar on your shoulder, that is the mark of an Annon soldier, like that of my guards."

"Yes, I did my time in the army… maybe they lost my records somehow, I have travelled extensively since leaving Meccus?"

Lanar's suspicious mood changed suddenly.

"And you ended up here, creating this wonderful homage to Yamm."

"Yes I did, by accident I suppose, I had intended to to travel more but Perneb was so persuasive that I had to stay for what he wanted me to create."

"But you really wanted to travel?"

"Yes, I think I did. The world is a wondrous place and I want to explore it, to see what mysteries await me there, to travel is to feel alive."

"Then how about you travel back to Meccus with me because just like Perneb, I have a wondrous commission for you?"

Lucifer's eyes opened to take in the sheer beauty of this princess that was sitting before him. She had black hair that was cut short in the style that one day Cleopatra would imitate. And her brown eyes were as deep and as mysterious as Lucifer's with delicate and intricate patterns that seemed to dance in the light of the sun and beneath her exquisite royal gown Lucifer could make out the shape of body that immediately filled him with desire. Lucifer's decision was spontaneous.

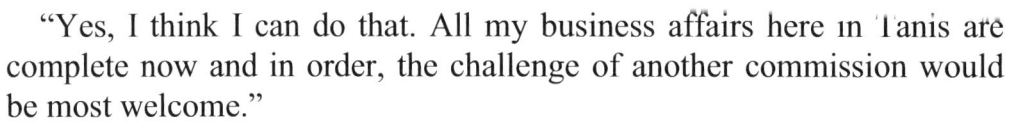

"Yes, I think I can do that. All my business affairs here in Tanis are complete now and in order, the challenge of another commission would be most welcome."

But it was not the work that Lucifer really wanted, what he truly desired was the goddess princess that was sitting before him.

LANAR

GODDESS OF LOVE

So it was back to Annon and Meccus then, Lucifer's homeland and his place of birth.

Am I going round in circles? Lucifer thought to himself, *I intended to to explore this new world and here I am back where I started and a guest of the royal household to boot!"*

Lucifer had intended to stay in the wealthiest of areas in Meccus and indeed his plan was to immediately buy property but Lanar had insisted that he would stay in rooms in the new royal palace as a distinguished guest and how could he ever refuse that?

The palace was enormous and not in the centre of the city like it had been in Lucifer's times, it was now situated on the edge of lake Mer Ek and it was almost completely surrounded by military buildings. Lucifer surmised that possibly there had been an attempted coup to overthrow the royal family at some point in the recent past. He was pleased that it had obviously failed but he was aware that there was now a government as such for the countries internal affairs leaving the royal family as a celebrated status symbol that could influence the power of Egypt and other neighbouring countries. The culture of Annon and Egypt were so alike that Lucifer often wondered how Annon had not succumbed to the great Egyptian expanse, something that would eventually happen during his immortal lifetime.

Lanar gave Lucifer a week to re-familiarise himself with his home city after which she suggested that they would meet to discuss what she wanted Lucifer to do for her. Lucifer did explore the ever-growing city, he even went back to the suburb of Shakas and to the house of his birth to find out that it had been replaced by a large tavern. He drank heqet at one of the outdoor tables that was situated where his father's back garden once was and a multitude of memories flowed back to him - the building of the extra rooms that he had constructed with his bare mortal hands, his father and then his mother who had died when he was a young boy, *Together in the Afterlife now* he immediately thought and this brought a warm smile to his face. And then he thought about Lilith and his smile faded, *But she had to keep living after I had been murdered, I cannot blame her for doing that?* This sudden acknowledgement after hundreds of years was a way of offloading his sorrow and eternal love for Lilith, *She must be happy now in her eternal life… and I have to say that I am almost happy too now.*

Lucifer then thought about Lanar. He knew that he was deeply attracted to her, *Maybe it is because of the fact that she has royal blood within her and I am nothing but a commoner, a building site worker who was once a young thief?* he thought and then, *But I am Lucifer, known as the Devil in some parts and I will have what I desire while I am trapped in this mortal world!*

Was Lucifer trapped? Yes, in some ways he was, there was no way he would be allowed to re-enter the realm of the Afterlife, he had once tried to open up an Angelic portal but the burnt black energy of his 'wings' could not do it, it seemed that his banishment by the Akhet was total and everlasting and this made made him sad that he would never see his mother and father again but for Lucifer Heylel, life went on and that meant a meeting with the Princess of Annon.

Two days before the meeting though, Lucifer paid a visit to one of the many record keepers of the Annon government. Lucifer paid the man handsomely to include him in the records from the time of his death, to basically make him a descendant of Lucif Heylel. This pleased him greatly, it meant that the legacy of his family would endure; anything he now did in Annon and Meccus would be remembered. So on the morning of his meeting with Princess Lanar, he was in good spirits.

"Your Highness, I have been looking forward to this meeting all week. I am greatly intrigued by what it is that you want me to do."

Once again they were alone, Lanar had requested that all the royal servants were to leave so that she and Lucifer had the utmost privacy.

"What do you think I want you to do?"

This was said by Lanar in a very sultry, sexy way and Lucifer realised this.

"Erm, the commission you mentioned in Tanis."

Lanar laughed, "Oh of course, that as well…"

Lucifer smiled, he knew that she was sexually attracted to him by this frivolous intimate banter.

Lanar was wearing a see-through tight white dress with a thick royal belt around her slender waist. Lucifer noticed that her large nipples were hard and erect and this excited him. Lanar continued…

"So it will be business before pleasure then" Lanar continued.

Pleasure?

"I want you to design and construct me a statue for this great lake of ours, a statue of the goddess of love. The lake is wondrous is it not, the long fingers of the Nile bless our country creating a shining blue jewel in the desert, a jewel that is surrounded by mountains that are filled with gold and diamonds that challenge the wealth of even Egypt herself."

"I know those mountains well" Lucifer exclaimed suddenly.

"You do, have you climbed them then?"

"I have visited the mines there many times now, business trips you could say."

"So you are indeed a wealthy man then?"

"Yes, my family is. I did check with the city records clerks and I found that my family status is up to date."

Lanar looked slightly puzzled, "My researcher was obviously wrong then and I am pleased about that so let there be an end to that matter."

Yes indeed thought Lucifer, he did not want the spectre of suspicion spoil this blossoming friendship.

Lanar then poured out two large goblets of rich red wine.

"Is it too early for irep Lucifer?"

"No, of course not, life is short and I intend to live it to the full."

Lanar's sensuous eyes seemed to clasp on Lucifer, as if they were somehow trying to hypnotise and control him and he enjoyed this.

"I like your philosophy, that is exactly what I intend to do also. What I want I usually get. Maybe I am spoilt but I am quite grounded too, I trust my instinct when it comes to things that I like and I like you Lucifer Heylel, there is something different about you which makes me want to know you more intimately. You will make an excellent suitor for me, a fine prince, not like the trite irritating bumpkins that are always sent to me for my hand in marriage."

Lucifer was flabbergasted, as flabbergasted as any immortal 'Devil' could be, he was actually lost for words to say.

"Cat got your tongue Lucifer… I am like a cat sometimes, mysterious, playful and also ruthless, do you think that you are worthy to be my prince?"

Lucifer slowly put his goblet down and then gently grabbed Lanar's shoulders.

"I am worthy and you will be astounded by what I can do for you."

He then kissed Lanar, gently at first then more passionate and she responded immediately as if it was the first time that someone had actually kissed her.

And in that moment, Lucifer knew that he was in love again.

HATHOR

The engagement of Lanar and Lucifer was received much better than Lucifer expected as he was obviously not of royal blood, in fact, the common people of Annon were greatly pleased that one of them could achieve such a thing. The king of Annon had died the previous year and his last wish was that his daughter would be happy so his wife gave the engagement announcement her full blessing and like Lanar she was intrigued by his otherworldly charm.

The statue of Hathor, the goddess of love that Lucifer designed was splendid, as tall as the statue of Yamm in Tanis and just as wondrous. Once again Lucifer knew that the imposing sculpture would take at least two years to complete and once again his time was devoted to this work. Of course he honoured his oath to seek out evil in the city whenever he could and whenever possible he eliminated it. Lucifer knew that this was now an addiction, one that would become more and more obsessive and he did enjoy killing his prey, sometimes in the most imaginative and devilish of ways and sometimes this worried him slightly because he thought that maybe he was becoming too sadistic, *But the Devil's work is never done* he would always muse and this filled him with humour, *They are evil people and the world is a better place without them* he would conclude.

When the carving of Hathor's head had been reached, Lucifer knew that this was an important moment and needed his constant supervision. There had been a royal visit to the coastal city of Khnumar planned and Lanar requested that Lucifer accompanied her but he had to refuse because it was a crucial moment in the construction of the statue. Lanar understood and decided to still fulfil her royal requirement without Lucifer.

This would prove to be a fatal mistake.

This was the moment that the Vaagen would enter their lives.

And when Lucifer truly became the Devil he was always thought to be.

VAAGEN

The Vaagen were roaming seafaring cannibals, centuries old and feared greatly throughout the known world. The one island that was considered to be their only homeland was known as Vaaga, which was situated near to what would come to be known as the Canary Islands in the Atlantic Ocean off the coast of the Western Sahara or Al-Sahra as it was once known. Lucifer had heard gruesome tales of these vicious cannabals over the years and he knew that the Vaagen island was to be found somewhere near to the African coast but he did not know exactly where. Lucifer had often considered trying to find the Vaagen but his private life always took priority.

This was something that he would come to truly regret.

Something that would haunt and taunt him for the rest of his life.

FEAR

There was not a fleet of Vaagen ships that night, just one that had landed stealthily on the Khnumar shore, it was always easier for one boat to go ashore undetected and the Vaagen knew this. The sails of the Vaagen ship which were gruesomely made out of human flesh, were taken down, lowered to help hide the vessel's presence as it anchored offshore. A small rowing boat with six Vaagen warriors came ashore on the Khnumar beach and they had only one objective, food for the journey home.

The sun was just beginning to rise as the Vaagen made their way to the part of the beach that they knew was used only by early morning fishermen. But the fishermen had already set sail and all was quiet and still except for lone female and two men who were walking along the beach, unaware of the Vaagen behind them. Unfortunately for Princess

Lanar, she liked to take early morning strolls along the beach to watch the awakening Ra slowly ascend into the blue heavens.

For the Vaagen, this seemed to be fairly easy prey for them but Lanar's two loyal bodyguards fought with all their might to protect her. They fought bravely as they had been trained to do but they were outnumbered, both men were killed at the expense of three Vaagen and taken for food but Lanar was untouched and spared even though she had fought as bravely as her dead bodyguards. The Vaagen suspected that the woman that had resisted them so fiercely was a woman of great importance, a catch to impress their king and when they had secured her on-board their ship and had inspected her jewellery, they realised that Lanar was an Annon princess. Lanar had boldly resisted her capture but now she was tied and gagged, a prisoner that was to be taken to to the cannibal island of Vaaga.

It was only when the returning Annon fishermen found the bodies of the dead Vaagen and a gold royal bracelet which Lanar had cunningly dropped that they realised what had happened. The Vaagen had made a mistake, they did not particularly like eating their own and they had two Annon guards to feast upon so they left their dead assuming that the incoming tide would claim them therefore leaving no evidence that they had been there. But the tide did not reach inshore that far so the fishermen were to conclude that their visiting princess who they knew loved to walk early along the beach had been captured.

"Vaagen!" one of them gasped, "I can tell by the chalk white zigzag markings on their faces. We must notify the palace official immediately, they will activate the fleet at Ramiton."

Two things happened immediately, a rider was indeed sent to Ramiton while a group of riders were sent to the capital city of Meccus to notify the queen of the dreadful news. It was over a week then when Queen Aissar told Lucifer about her daughter's horrendous abduction.

"What... the Vaagen you say, I have heard of these evil creatures!"

Lucifer's heart was beating like a large alarm bell, he felt an immortal rage build immediately within him.

"But how can you be sure that they have captured Lanar?"

"She has disappeared Lucifer and the fisherman of Khnumar... found this."

The queen held out her hand and in it was the engagement bracelet that Lucifer had given Lanar, both their names were engraved on it. Tears formed immediately in Lucifer's eyes.

"I... gave that to her."

"It lay beside three dead Vaagen."

"Then I will go and find her... maybe... maybe they will realise that she is a princess and not..."

Lucifer could not finish his sentence, the thought was far too gruesome and horrific for him. The queen gently held his hand.

"I think that we should pray that our fleet finds them."

"You can pray for Lanar Queen Aissar but I will leave immediately, I vow that I will find these vile devils and they will pay dearly for what they have done."

"But Lucifer, how can you find her, how can you do what only our fleet can attempt?"

"I will find her, I promise you that and the Vaagen will suffer greatly for this, of that you can be assured."

The queen felt a great pity for Lucifer, she knew that like herself he was suffering greatly with a heavy worried heart *but how can he possibly find his beloved Lanar?* she thought, *what can one heartbroken man do?*.

Lucifer stormed out of the palace to a secluded spot where he immediately took to the air, a grim faced black demon with only two determined thoughts on his mind, the safe return of Lanar and the destruction of the evil Vaagen, even if it meant revealing his true self to Lanar.

SEARCH AND DESTROY

For days, Lucifer searched the Mediterranean Sea, then the Tyrrhenian Sea then onto the North Atlantic Sea. He had lost all track of time but he reckoned that it had now been three or four weeks since he had begun his constant search and he was now heading down towards the Canary Islands off the coast of the Al-Sahra, he was now only a few days behind the Vaagen ship that had captured Lanar.

After the Vaagen ship had berthed on one of the many jetties of Vaaga, the excited Vaagen dragged their prize possession to their king who resided in the only village on the island which was large and not overcrowded because many of its residents roamed the seas in search of new human flesh.

Their king who was revered as a god lived in a large palace which was adjacent to an even larger temple which had been built so that his people could worship him. The king was an immortal that had a shape-shifting ability to become the person he had just consumed. His name was Vaag and he had arrived as a form of alien bacteria on a meteorite which had landed on the island millions of years ago.

Slowly over the eons, by consuming the emerging primitive lifeforms from insect to rodent and then eventually monkey with his internal green acid, he had evolved over the years until the first human beings had arrived on his island in their crude rowing boats. He consumed and became one of them almost immediately and as he fed upon these primitive people he became a god to them and this created a vile cannibalistic culture that began to thrive and grow.

The Vaagen then became feared seafaring cannibals who struck terror into everyone that they came into contact with, they were the nightmares of young children and were spoken of only in hushed whispers by all that knew of them. They did inhabit other isolated islands but only temporarily, they were just places were they would enjoy eating their captives. The island of Vaaga was their one and only homeland, the place where their god ruled and when Lucifer approached the island from high above he noticed the many jetties below with his hawk-like Angelic vision.

Lucifer flew down and hovered over the large village which he knew would have been much larger if the Vaagen had not been sea people. The palace and the temple immediately attracted Lucifer's attention.

This must be it; Lanar must be alive!

Below Lucifer were many temple guards who were allowing people to enter the temple. Lucifer swooped down on them like a great giant black eagle and destroyed the guards and anyone else who was near them. Villagers scattered as quick as they could at the sight of this fearsome winged demon but Lucifer stood in front of the temple and studied the structure he was about to enter. The temple was surrounded by many large poles which had bloodied skulls on top of them, the walls were covered in small stones which had the faces of many different people carved upon them.

This is a house of death thought Lucifer and suddenly his belief that Lanar was still alive began to wane, he actually felt sick as he entered the temple. Many Vaagen were praying inside, side lamps on the walls showed them to be kneeling towards a long altar that glowed with strange green veins that looked like they were full of emerald blood… and as Lucifer focussed his eyes he did not believe what he saw, it was Lanar, standing behind the altar, looking as beautiful as the first day he had saw her.

"Lanar, Lanar my love… I thought I would be too late but I am here now, to take you away from this evil and damned place."

Tears had now formed in his eyes and he immediately reverted back into his human form as he did not want to scare her with his demonic appearance but there was no reaction to his bodily change by Lanar and this did make Lucifer curious. But his mind put this to one side, here was Lanar, here was his princess, his bride-to-be, safe and alive. But then another question flashed through his mind, *But why do the Vaagen kneel before her?*

At first, it was as if Lanar had not recognised Lucifer, she became thoughtful as if she was trying to remember who he was and then she said,

"Take me to my bed-chambers first… Lu… cifer, I need your body now, then we can leave here."

These seemed strange words to Lucifer, an unnatural reaction to his sudden presence but he raced to Lanar and kissed her as if he had not seen her for years…

But reflected in Lanar's eyes was the empty withered flat skin of the real Lanar which had been left carelessly on the top of the glowing green altar…

"What… how can this be!" Lucifer shouted in shock as he pulled away from Lanar, revolted by what he was now looking down at… the thin face of Lanar with all the life sucked out of it.

The Lanar in Lucifer's arms extended her mouth towards his lips, it was grotesque, unnatural and alien and Lucifer pulled away from it, a green substance was glowing in her mouth'

"You are not my Lanar, you are something from the pits of Hell, what sort of twisted creature are you?" Lucifer cried out in disgust.

Lanar's deadly mouth returned to her beautiful face…

"We can be one, we can be together forever Lucifer" she said seductively but the look on Lucifer's was one of sudden anger.

"No!" screamed Lucifer looking at what was left of his beloved Lanar on the altar. He then turned back into his true demonic form and the other Lanar tried to flee, this creature was powerful but not as strong as the immortal Angelic Lucifer.

Lucifer grabbed the false Lanar with the speed of a cheetah…

And threw her onto the glowing green altar

Beside the skin of his Lanar

Which seemed to enrage him even more…

The other Lanar tried to fight but it was hopeless

She was in the grip of the Devil

Her mouth and sharp teeth

Tried to piece Lucifer's skin

As she growled with an unearthly venom

Trying to inject a green acid that would consume him

But his skin was as hard as stone…

Lucifer then grabbed one of the altar's oil lamps and set fire to the demonic creature that he was holding, the flames licked at him too but there was no pain for him. The Vaagen people fled from the temple as the false Lanar slowly burned, Lucifer's black arms keeping her pinned to the altar as the hungry flames began to consume her. In his red eyes there were tears again as he watched the remains of his beloved Lanar ignite beside the other Lanar.

In his moment of pure rage Lucifer had forgot to move Lanar's skin away from the deadly flames of revenge…

"Lanar… Lanar, my love, my love, forgive me please, I did not think… I was consumed by hate my… darling" Lucifer said sadly as he watched the ravenous flames instantly turn the withered remains of his real love to ash and it was as if his heart was burning and being eaten too.

Lucifer then went on a bloody rampage of hatred and revenge; destroying the Vaagen village and anyone he came across within it; old men, old women and children were included too…

Then when Lucifer was satisfied that all were dead, he flew away from the island of death; the beating and crackling of his strange wings as they took to the air echoed around the village and his anguished cries and screams of pain filled the air.

What Lucifer did not realise at the time though was that the dying flames of the oil lamp did not completely destroyed the creature on the altar, it's heart was still beating but only just, it was breathing but only just. It would take hundreds of years for the burnt and withered shape-shifting body of the creature known as Vaag to slowly regenerate… and one day it would find another host, an unsuspecting visitor to the island of Vaaga who had no idea who and what the Vaagen were.

RAGE

For days Lucifer raged in the skies, not setting foot on land. He flew as a lost soul, heartbroken and angry until slowly his rage subsided, a rage that had taken the lives of many Vaagen. He had no idea though that Vaag had managed to survive, an unmovable burnt carcass that would eventually slowly start to heal. The Vaagen who were not on the island that day continued their gruesome bloodthirsty lifestyle and when they returned to Vaaga they saw that their king was dead, on the same altar that he had fed upon. They assumed that a greater god had destroyed Vaag so they left the island and never returned. Vaaga Island became a place to avoid like it always had been and over the years it became known as an island to definitely steer clear of, a place were shape-shifting monsters lived, a place were you would be eaten alive.

And when the heart and mind of Lucifer had finally calmed down to a state where he could almost function normally, he realised that he should go to Queen Aissar so that she could have closure on the death of her daughter. He knew that it was the right thing to do even though he knew that he would have to relive the events of Vaaga all over again. He knew that he would be consumed by a great sadness that would be too unbearable but Lucifer was a man of principle and once his mind was set, he would do what he intended.

Lucifer's royal account was that he had hired a ship full of the fiercest mercenaries he could find and that eventually they had found the island of

Vaaga but they had been too late to save Lanar. Lucifer said that he had killed the Vaagen king, that he had burnt him and his people but unfortunately the remains of Lanar had been in Vaag's temple too and had it had accidentally suffered the same fate but Lucifer finished by saying to the queen…

"She is with the Angelic now, the Akhet will grant her eternal peace."

Lucifer left Meccus and became even more determined to destroy as much mortal evil as he could.

LIFE GOES ON

Lucifer's worldly wealth increased and Chisisi continued to expand the Heylel financial empire which would become respected and also feared throughout the known world. The mark of the Annon army became synonymous with the Sigil of Lucifer and rumours that Lucifer was indeed the 'Devil' began to quickly circulate and grow.

Caress did as Lucifer had expected and The Moon And Stars eventually became known as an underground cult called The Old Sanctuary which also honoured the Sigil of Lucifer.

Lucifer was now to be found in many countries, his fame and fortune increasing year by year and the most trusted of his private network ensured that his immortal status was always concealed so that Lucifer could continue his mortal life doing the things that he wanted to do. Sex with mortal women eventually became important to him again but he vowed that he would never fall in love as before not knowing that in the future it would happen again but this time it would be more of a fatherly love like that of the love he held for Caress. But the continual destruction of those that were evil was always his main concern, this had now become Lucifer's real passion.

It was only around the time of 30 AD when something happened that made Lucifer re-assess his constant destructive and deadly obsession.

A man preaching the peace and love of the one god had begun to walk the Earth and make a name for himself; this man was known as Yeshua Nazarite.

YESHUA

DESIRE

One night, Lucifer was wandering through the dusty streets of Nazareth, he had gone there because he had heard about a young new prophet whose teachings were causing quite a stir throughout the Roman Empire.

This so-called Son of God intrigued Lucifer greatly as he sensed that there was something different about this prophet, someone who was not prophesying the destruction of mankind and the end of the world, here was a man talking about love and the forgiveness of sins and how the world can change because of that. Lucifer though, had no time for the 'forgiveness of sins' because he only believed in the swift hand of vengeance so he was eager to meet this unusual man called Yeshua of Nazareth, he thought that it would lead to interesting conversation.

It was late at night and no house lamps were burning nearby, only the bright light of the full moon lit up Lucifer's steps. And then in the shadows of a nearby narrow alleyway Lucifer heard a voice call to him…

"Money for a poor man please."

The man stood in the darkness between the walls, a thick grey cloak covered his body. Lucifer walked into the alleyway.

"I am looking for Yeshua Nazarite, do you know of him?"

"I have heard of him, a false prophet. I was one of them who tried to throw him from one of the nearby hills after his pathetic so-called teachings."

"You… tried to kill him?"

Suddenly there was a knife at Lucifer's throat.

"As I will kill you traveller if you do not give me your purse. You are a wealthy man are you not, I can tell by your fine clothes."

"And I can tell that you are no beggar."

Lucifer hardened his skin and it began to sparkle like a rough diamond.

The man's eyes opened wide in disbelief.

"What… is happening, your skin… has changed!"

"It has changed… look into my eyes, the eyes that will claim your soul this night."

The man dropped his knife and began to tremble, his strength sapped by what he was seeing, "You must be Satan, the Devil Incarnate!"

The man slowly backed away from Lucifer, his knees were beginning to buckle from his sudden fear… then he turned and tried to run.

Lucifer just laughed, he could have easily killed the would be thief but he had decided not to as his mind was on other matters. Lucifer continued his walk through the streets until he came to a large house, the home of someone wealthy and here he saw something that he had not seen for a very long time, the brightness of Angelic light. And out of this light stepped a familiar figure, the unmistakable figure of Desire.

"I thought that our paths would cross again some day Lucifer."

"Desire… what are you doing here?"

"I await the mortal death of someone within this house, a young child who has an incurable disease."

"So the love of the Akhet is still pitiless is it not?"

"Life and death goes on as before Lucifer, it is the way of mortal life, the path that we the Angelic have to follow."

"And do you know about my path back here, my years held captive by the sun, my physical form burnt and disfigured forever?"

There was pain in Lucifer's voice and Desire was aware of it.

"I… did not know of that but eventually I became aware that you had returned here."

"And you did not try to find me?"

"I wanted to but I was warned not to, I was told that I might suffer the same fate if I was to contact you, I think the Akhet was worried that you would somehow influence me, make me forget my Angelic duties."

"And still you work for the Akhet?"

"I know no other life Lucifer, no other existence."

"Then I feel pity for you, sad that you have not seen the real light yet."

Lucifer was then suddenly overcome with emotion, memories that he had tried to avoid for thousands of years…

"And what of my mother and my father, what do you know of them?"

"They live happily as before, their love is eternal as I am sure you know. They miss you every day but nobody knew what happened to you. I told them that you were probably continuing the work of the Angelic in the realm of the living, that you had most likely taken up full-time residence here as some Angelic do."

Tears were now streaming down Lucifer's cheeks.

"I do not do the work of the Akhet!"

"I… only told them that to ease their sadness, to comfort them and it is true now is it not."

"I was banished, cast out into the black void of space then made a captive of the sun but then even the sun had his fill of me and then he threw me back to this world with one of his mighty fire bursts… and… my burnt appearance terrorised those that saw me, they thought me a demon, the Devil Himself even… and now I do my own work, the work that the Akhet should do."

"You interfere with the fate of mankind?"

"No, I swore that I would never do that, I do not want to be blamed for anything else, if the mortal world falls apart and ceases to exist then it will not be my fault… but I do my bit, I eradicate the evil that infests mankind and that can only help increase the quality of mortal life here."

"And yet you let that thief in the night go?"

Lucifer smiled.

"You know of that? Maybe he was not truly evil, maybe he was just hungry?"

"That is the Lucifer that I remember."

"Oh, that Lucifer is long gone, like Moses in the corn."

Lucifer laughed which made Desire laugh too.

"So what are you doing here Lucifer in the dusty streets of Nazareth I may ask but I think I know the answer."

"I came to find the Nazarene, the one who is making such a name for himself."

"Yes, this is the town of his childhood but it was nothing but a village then."

"So he is who he claims to be then?"

"I… think that only he can answer that. You should go and speak with him, I sense that he might be in danger."

"In danger?"

"He has gone into the Judean wilderness, he has been there for nearly forty days. He went there to pray, meditate and fast. You will find him at the foot of the Jebel Quruntol mountain which will be known as the 'Nursery of Souls' one day"

"But how is he in danger, he must be weak from lack of food certainly, is that what you mean?"

"He is weak which makes him easier prey for those that are Nameless."

"You know of Nameless then?"

"I am one of the few that do know but I am not to talk of him."

"And yet you just have."

"Because you are no longer one with the Akhet… and because I think that you can help Yeshua in his hour of need."

"And you cannot?"

"I am here for the young child whose soul is close to passing now… but I send the place of the mountain to you."

Desire held Lucifer's hand and gently kissed him on the lips and instantly he desired more, he saw her naked, he remembered how she had made love to him and his heart ached suddenly… but he now had something important to do and Desire had the soul of a departed child to comfort and protect.

"Until we meet again then Desire."

"I fear that we may never meet again my dear Lucifer but my love will always be with you."

Desire's Angelic light faded, Lucifer knew that she was now with the child and he now had to go and be with the man called Yeshua.

THE WILDERNESS

Lucifer turned black and took to the night sky, it was not long before the peaks of Jebel Quruntol came into view.

"Hear me oh Nameless One, you will not have the soul of Yeshua this night!" Lucifer shouted to the dark winds that surrounded him.

And then Lucifer spotted something, a shadow of a figure in the moonlight, lying beneath a palm tree at a small oasis. The man was not moving so Lucifer assumed that he might be sleeping and dearly hoped that he was not dead. Lucifer immediately swooped down, he was aware that he must have looked like a dark angel descending so he hoped that the man's eyes were closed. Just before Lucifer's blackened feet touched the sandy ground, he changed into his mortal form then approached the figure with caution. He knew that the entity known as Nameless could be near and he knew that this mortal could well be important to him, someone that he would dearly love to consume, a frail mortal prey that he might even fight for.

They were at the bottom of the mountain that would come to be known as the Mount of Temptation and the ground was abundant in green vegetation. The man had obviously been trying to crawl to the water of the oasis.

The man's robes were stained and dirty, Lucifer could smell that he had not bathed for some time and he knew that he was still alive because he could hear a faint heartbeat, hear his feeble breaths. Lucifer knew that the man was close to dying…

And yet there are no Angelic nearby, no Angelic to take the man's soul to safety? If this man is truly the Son of God then where are the Akhet?

This thought puzzled Lucifer then he heard and saw a snake, dark and threatening in the moonlight, it's tongue darting in and out, sensing the heat of the man nearby… and it was near to his outstretched hand that was reaching toward the oasis.

With preternatural speed, Lucifer grabbed the snake's neck and squeezed it hard so that it's eyes and tongue squirted from it's dead body. Lucifer then threw it into the nearby bushes where he heard the rustle of hidden rodents that were waiting to devour it.

Then Lucifer held the man's hand and a sudden unexpected warmth consumed him, a sense of love and forgiving that he had long forgotten… and Lucifer realised that he could not access the man's mind but it was not his main concern at that moment. Lucifer dragged the man gently to the oasis and bathed his face softly, spilling water from the cup of his hand into the man's mouth.

The man's breathing became stronger, his heartbeat more solid and eventually he opened his eyes and gazed weakly upon Lucifer. The man's eyes were the most glorious deep blue which was quite unusual for a man with light brown skin.

And the blue eyes stared at Lucifer in horror.

"Begone Satan…" he stuttered fearfully, "Are you still here to plague me with your vile temptations? I… will never yield to you."

Lucifer knew that he was referring to some dark demon that was most likely Nameless and that maybe Nameless had now departed, *beaten by a stronger soul?* Lucifer checked his hands to make sure that they were not black and burnt.

The man had now recoiled away from Lucifer and was visibly shaking.

"What do you see?" Lucifer had to ask.

"I see… your darkness, your grotesque skin, your evil red eyes and black smoky wings."

Lucifer was astounded by this but then he thought that maybe the man was hallucinating from being so close to death.

"Look again my friend, I am not evil, surely you can sense this? The one called Nameless has departed, most likely he left you for dead but I think that you have defeated him this night. And I have saved you from the bite of a snake, I have given you water so that you live now."

Suddenly the man's face softened as if the dark form he had been looking at had vanished.

"You have… saved me?"

"I think so, you were so close to the water when you collapsed."

The man tried to stand up and Lucifer helped him. His brown hair was shoulder length and he now had a beard that was in much need of a trim. He was a handsome man, as handsome as Lucifer who immediately felt the power and presence within him.

"Do you remember who you are?" asked Lucifer.

"I am… Yeshua Nazerite" he replied, "I came into the wilderness to meditate and contemplate my existence… but I was followed here by a dark entity who tempted me, tried to consume me, take my very soul…"

"Nameless" Lucifer uttered but he did not think that Yeshua had heard him."

"This vile creature tempted me three times but I did not succumb… I am sorry that I thought it was you and I am most thankful that you have helped me."

Lucifer was aware that Yeshua was very weak and that he still needed his help to survive the night.

"Where can I take you Yeshua? You are urgently in need of food and sustenance."

"My mother lives in Nazareth, she is called Maryam, Yoseph my father was a carpenter, she…"

Then Yeshua suddenly lost consciousness and Lucifer knew that he had to act fast, He immediately changed into his burnt form and took to the night air with Yeshua. He headed north away from the Mount of Temptation as fast as he could fly with a mortal and soon he was over Nazareth.

Yeshua had said that his father had been a carpenter so Lucifer circled the town looking for any sort of workshop and on the outskirts he saw a house with wood and tools outside of it.

That must be it thought Lucifer and he descended quietly as the light of dawn broke. Lucifer banged hard on the door of the house.

"Maryam, I have your son Yeshua" Lucifer shouted and the door opened and Maryam appeared looking very worried but also pleased that her son was now home.

"Yeshua, Yeshua, what has happened to you my dearest?" Maryam called out and she went immediately to her son who had been laid on the carpenter's table by Lucifer.

"Help me please" Maryam asked Lucifer and he took Yeshua to his room where Maryam immediately attended to him. Lucifer sat quietly in the main living room and waited patiently.

He needs… food, hot soup.. and milk Lucifer thought then, *I am sure that he will recover, the love of his mother will make it so.*

Returning to the room, Maryam informed Lucifer that Yeshua was resting peacefully now, she had managed to feed him bread and milk but then she had to ask, "He has been gone for forty days, I was so worried about him. How did you come across him though, how did you find him… and how did you get him here, you have no camel, no horse that I see?"

"Do not worry about that Maryam, all that matters is that your son is home and safe now."

"Are you… Angelic?" she had to ask bluntly.

Lucifer smiled at this question, a smile that was tinged with sarcasm.

"I… am no angel now" he quickly replied, "Just someone who was in the right place at the right time."

"Praise the Lord then" Maryam proclaimed.

"Yes… maybe we should."

Maryam kneeled in front of Lucifer then softly kissed his hand.

"I think that you are an angel" she whispered, "What is your name kind one?"

"I am… Lucif-er Heylel of Meccus."

"Not Lucifer of Hades then?"

Maryam smiled but it was a nervous smile.

"No, I am not the one called Nameless."

"Nameless, who is the one called Nameless?" asked Maryam and Lucifer sensed that maybe he was saying too much to a mortal woman.

"Nameless… is an eternity to beware."

"Ah, I see, it is good that you have not given this being a name then, I shall remember this. Will you now share bread and wine with me?"

Lucifer looked around Maryam's humble household, it was spacious, clean and well decorated, a house worthy of a messiah.

"Yes, I would like that very much and maybe you can tell me more about your son,"

"That will surely take some time" laughed Maryam.

"I have all the time in the world" replied Lucifer and once again there was a curious look on Maryam's face.

THE CRUCIFIXION

Lucifer became a follower of Yeshua and listened to and contemplated his teachings. At one point he thought that he might become the thirteenth disciple but he did have too other matters to attend to. At the start of 33AD, Lucifer went to Alexandria to check on the affairs of the House of Heylel. Annon had long ceased to exist, a country that had eventually been consumed by the Great Egyptian Expanse. This had come as no surprise to Lucifer at the time and he held no animosity towards Egypt whatsoever as it was a country that he dearly loved, the country where the House of Heylel and The Old Sanctuary had originated. Lucifer was now a man of unlimited wealth and he was a man who covered his tracks well to conceal his true identity.

After his business affairs had been completed, Lucifer returned to Judea on the third of April where he decided to visit Maryam in Nazareth. Her husband Yoseph had died in 20 AD but Lucifer knew that she still grieved for him so he made regular visits to see her. He had brought her a selection of the finest new fashionable linen and cloth from Alexandria and he knew that Maryam would make beautiful dresses and shawls for herself with his gifts. But when he knocked on the door to Maryam's house he was told by a neighbour that a woman named Desire had told her that her son may be in grave danger and that Maryam was now in Jerusalem. He was also told that Yeshua had been arrested by the Romans.

Lucifer flew at once to Jerusalem where he joined the many who had gathered to watch the crucifixion of Yeshua. The sun beat down without mercy upon the overcrowded streets and Lucifer pushed his way to the front of the crowd to get a better view.

How can they do this? What could he have done to deserve such a thing? This is madness!

The road was steep and Lucifer saw Yeshua in the distance with the large wooden cross on his back. Lucifer could see that Yeshua was struggling to carry such a heavy load by himself.

"What is happening my friend?" a man next to Lucifer asked. The man was old and frail and blind.

"The messiah is carrying his cross on his back, he slowly approaches us old man."

"And do you now see what the Akhet truly is Lucifer?"

The man's voice had changed.

It was the dull voice of Nameless.

Lucifer looked at the man and saw that his eyes had turned a deep swirling black, eyes the seemed to have tiny dark snakes swimming in them.

"It does not surprise me that you are here Nameless… this is something you would surely enjoy."

"The death of a messiah, a man who is teaching about love and forgiveness, how can the Akhet let this happen son of Lucif? I am here to witness their folly, their inability to act, to save one of their own. They are a joke, a liability to the life of man, can you not see that now?"

Lucifer did not know how to respond to Nameless, there was a lot of truth in what he was saying and this worried Lucifer.

"You had nothing to do with this then?"

"Me? I had no need to, the crowd chose a known murderer and terrorist over their 'Messiah,' how crazy is that fallen angel?"

The laughter of Nameless was deep and cruel sounding and taunted Lucifer's thoughts as he mused over what Nameless had just said. Lucifer did not know how it had all happened but he was there to help Yeshua in any way that he could and he would make sure that Nameless would not stop him.

"This is The Big Mistake Lucifer, mark my words. This is the Great Day when my kingdom truly begins to dawn in this realm, from now on with the death of this pitiful messiah, my seed will grow in man and woman, it will take root and prosper, the rise of my kind has truly begun."

Before Lucifer could respond, he noticed that the old man's eyes had reverted to their white blank look, he had no idea that he had been possessed. It was then that Lucifer noticed that Yeshua was right beside him on the road. He was beaten and weak, blood poured down his face from the cruel crown of prickly thorns that had been placed upon his head. Yeshua collapsed, the heavy wooden cross fallen by his side. A man rushed out of the crowd to get water for Yeshua and Lucifer joined him, he went straight to Yeshua.

"It is me Yeshua, your friend Lucifer. What have they done to you dear one?"

Lucifer could feel tears forming in his eyes, tears that came straight from his heart.

"They do what they have to do to me my friend… it is good to see you again" Yeshua gasped.

"I have followed you, listened to your words, you surely do not deserve this!"

One of the Roman soldiers glared at Lucifer but he allowed the other man to give Yeshua the water. Yeshua thanked the kind man who he seemed to recognise. The man looked at Lucifer and shook his head, the man was crying.

"I… can save you now Yeshua, fly you away from all this, my wrath upon the Romans will be great this most darkest of days."

"I… know that you were once Angelic, I can sense it but this is my destiny Lucifer, it is The Great Plan that will save mankind."

"How can your death possibly achieve that?"

Yeshua smiled, his teeth were bloody and broken from the persistent Roman violence he had recently suffered.

"You will see… my friend. Help me now please because I have not the strength to carry my burden and my courage is fast beginning to falter."

More tears formed in Lucifer's eyes and then crashed to the ground, he was confused, his heart confused but he did as Yeshua asked.

And when the nails penetrated Yeshua's flesh, it was as if Lucifer felt his pain too…

Why, why is this happening? Lucifer thought repeatedly but of course there was no answer to his inner frustration, no sign that the Akhet were near or that they even cared, *Can it be that Nameless is right, that the Akhet is utterly powerless this day and that they do not even want to try and save Yeshua? Are they truly fearful of Nameless now?*

Worrying thoughts for Lucifer indeed and when the cross of Yeshua was lifted and erected, Lucifer joined Maryam and her family to keep vigil with them. The last words Lucifer heard Yeshua say was "Forgive them father for they know not what they do."

Then the sky darkened and thunderclouds raged in the dark sky overhead, a great rain washed the blood from Yeshua as he passed from mortal existence…

And Lucifer was angry, as angry as he had ever been, a great rage of confusion burst from him. He went to the Roman guard and grabbed his spear. Curiously though the guard did not resist, it was as if he were mourning too. Lucifer then carved out a large deep cross in the wet ground.

"Remember Yeshua this way, this will be the symbol of life for all mankind!" Lucifer shouted out to all that could hear. Then he dropped the spear and walked away, his head numb from the death of Yeshua.

And when was alone he flew up into the swirling dark sky and the clouds that seemed to be crying and shouted out to the heavens above, "Are you happy now Akhet, that this brave man is now dead? Why did you not protect him or even try to save him? You let this be the Day of Nameless, the evil in this realm will increase and multiply now because of this… but I am here, I will do what needs to be done in this world of the living!"

Of course they was no answer.

Lucifer flew back Alexandria.
He needed to find evil.
He needed to destroy it.

CANDIDA LUX / LU'NA

ROME

In 82 AD Lucifer went to Rome to see a business associate of the House of Heylel. Lucifer had not been to Rome for quite some time, a fire in 64 AD had destroyed much of The Eternal City and Emperor Nero had killed a vast multitude of Christians in response to the fire using them as scapegoats for the cause of the catastrophe. Lucifer knew that the word of Yeshua had now reached Rome and the followers of his teachings were growing in numbers but their new religion and lifestyle was constantly under threat by the emperor and the Senate. Lucifer was intrigued to see how Rome was being rebuilt after the fires and he was also interested to see how this growing underground religion known as Christianity was perceived by those in power.

Lucifer's host was a man called Marcus Marius, a man of sixty two years who was one of the richest and most influential business men in Rome, his magnificent house had not been affected by the fires.

Lucifer arrived on horse, riding was something he really enjoyed, it reminded him of his army days in Annon which were now thousands of years ago in his memory. Anything that made him recall those days he now cherished.

A black male servant of Marius who had been waiting for Lucifer greeted him at the gates of Marius' estate which was on the outskirts of of Rome and not in the city. Lucifer was immediately aware that there were many security guards present but he thought that this was quite natural for a man of Marius' wealth and standing.

"This way my lord, you are expected" the tall strong servant said and he grabbed Lucifer's horse by the bridle and he began to walk slowly along the wide long road that lead to the main house.

"What is your name?" asked Lucifer.

"I am known as Protego my lord."

"Ah 'Protector' then and where are you from originally Protego? I know that you are of African origin."

"I am from the north of Africa, a village whose name I have long forgotten now, I was bought by Lord Marius when a was a young boy."

"And you have served him well since?"

"He has treated me almost like a son, I know no other life."

"That is good then, I knew Lord Marius would be a fair and good man."

Lucifer immediately thought about Caress and the work of The Old Sanctuary in saving and freeing slaves but here was a servant who seemed more than content with his life.

"You have never met my lord then, I do not recall you ever visiting him in my time here?"

"No Protego, we have never met, just conducted our business affairs by papers over the years."

"You look much younger than my lord if I may say."

Lucifer realised that Protego was a very intelligent and observant man, someone who had been well educated under the supervision of Marius. In an instant Lucifer aged his skin slightly.

"Maybe the early evening light is deceiving you Protego, look again."

Protego looked up at Lucifer on the horse again and was surprised by the different appearance.

"Yes… it must have been a trick of the light, please forgive me my lord."

"There is nothing to forgive Protego, thinking that I was younger is a compliment to me."

Lucifer laughed.

It was not long before they arrived at the main house. Another servant came and took Lucifer's horse and Protego took Lucifer to see Marcus Marius who was in his large study attending to business papers, he immediately looked up from his table of work…

"Ah Lucifer Heylel, at last we meet in person!"

Marcus Marius rushed to Lucifer and generously shook his hand, "We have made a lot of money for each other over the years have we not?"

Lucifer smiled, "My accountant assures me so dear Marcus… and yes, it is a pleasure to finally meet you after all these years."

"Come Lucifer, sit and share wine with me on the porch, the setting sun in Rome is always glorious."

Is the sun setting on Rome? thought Lucifer, *Were the fires a sign that the Great Empire is beginning to crumble?*

Marius was right, the view from the porch was magnificent, showing Rome in all its rebuilt glory in the distance. A servant quickly brought two large goblets and a decanter of wine and once again Lucifer noticed the presence of guards surrounding them. Marius was aware that Lucifer had seen his security arrangements.

"I am afraid that they are a necessity these days… these are dangerous times."

"Dangerous? Is not the Empire thriving?"

"I saw the great fires as a warning Lucifer… and of course the threat of the new religion is rippling through the Senate now."

"You refer to Christianity?"

"Yes, their numbers seem to be increasing day by day."

"So you see them as a threat?"

Marcus Marius looked suddenly thoughtful and placid, not angry as Lucifer expected.

"Well they are threat to our old gods, beliefs that have existed for hundreds of years… but maybe we need a change, the gods did not put out the fires, the people of Rome did."

Lucifer nodded, this attitude surprised Lucifer though, it was almost as if Marius was sympathetic to the plight of the Christians. Then Marius suddenly said, "This is not a business trip is it Lucifer?"

"No Marcus, all our affairs are well in order… I came to see how the Eternal City was changing."

"Then that is good, there will be no talk of making money then. Come, my wife has prepared a lovely evening meal for us, she has been waiting to meet you for a very long time."

Marius took Lucifer and his goblet of wine to the spacious dining room that truly displayed the wealth of Marius. There were two tables, a long wide one and a smaller more intimate one and this was where Marius bade Lucifer to sit. On the long table was a selection of exotic foods, some hot, some cold, two servants were waiting to serve the two seated men then Marius' wife Messalina entered the room. She went to Lucifer and bowed her head graciously.

"Lord Lucifer, this is truly a great honour for us."

Lucifer stood up, The honour is mine Messalina, I cannot believe that we have never met before."

"The years pass so quickly, do they not?"

"Quicker than we realise" Lucifer replied and he became thoughtful but he had to snap out of it quickly because he knew how the memories of the past could affect him.

Lucifer noticed that the attractive Messalina was much younger than Marius, *Probably by at least ten years* he thought. In contrast to the mature beauty of his wife, Marcus Marius was not a handsome man but the years had been kind to him, his amicable face and slightly rotund body reminded Lucifer of his old friend Perneb, here was a man who had enjoyed the obvious success of his life. Lucifer liked this couple very much.

A hot spicy tomato and vegetable soup was first which Lucifer thought was delicious and it was Messalina who broke the comfortable silence.

"I hope that all the business talk was completed on the porch, I know how obsessive Marcus can get when it comes to making money."

Lucifer laughed, "I have told Marcus that this is no business trip, it is one of leisure."

Messalina smiled, "Then that is good, what have you planned to do Lucifer?"

"Oh, a bit of sightseeing, that sort of thing. I cannot stop here long as I do have business commitments elsewhere."

"Of course Lucifer" interrupted Marius, "But you are welcome to stay here as long as you want. Rome has become a beautiful city again but the winds of change are in the air as we have just discussed. Maybe we should go to the Colosseum tomorrow to see the darker side of our new city?"

Messalina stopped eating, "You want to take Lucifer there Marcus… you know what a cruel bloodbath it can be?"

"Lucifer has said that he wants to see what Rome has become, what better spectacle is there to show him then?"

"Spectacle? I call it a damned atrocity."

Messalina was obviously agitated and it was at this point that a female servant entered the room and approached Messalina; the hesitant servant whispered something in Messalina's ear.

Lucifer's acute Angelic hearing heard what the servant was saying…

"Madam, I have an urgent message from Candida Lux, she needs to see you urgently at the Sanctuary."

Messalina immediately stood up and offered her apologies.

"I am sorry Lord Lucifer but something quite urgent requires my attention. I will leave you two gentlemen to discuss the 'wonders and magnificence' of Rome."

Lucifer stood up and Messalina left the dining room, he knew that her words about the wonders and magnificence of Rome had been sarcastic.

The proposed visit to the Colosseum now intrigued him greatly.

BLOOD IN THE COLOSSEUM

It was midday when Lucifer and Marius arrived at the Colosseum in Marius' large horse drawn carriage. Marius had a private viewing area which he jokingly called his 'box' but Lucifer knew that this was a safe place for Marius to watch the proceedings, A servant brought wine and food for them while a guard stood in the shadows behind them. Protego was allowed to sit with them which was no surprise to Lucifer; he also drank the wine with them. Lucifer knew that Protego's relationship with Marius was more than just as a protector, he seemed to be looked upon as an adopted son.

Lucifer looked around the imposing Colosseum, he had been to visit it before when it was first built in 72 AD when the Emperor Vespasian ruled but Lucifer did not tell Marius this. Lucifer saw that the current Emperor Domitian had added a fourth level to the gigantic structure.

"Very impressive Marcus" noted Lucifer, "And what delights does this magnificent place hold for us today?"

"I'm not sure that 'delights' is the right word Lucifer" replied Marius, "Messalina would never think that about this place."

"Has she ever been here before?"

"Only the once… but she left as soon as the Christians entered the arena."

"And what happened to them?"

Lucifer knew what was happening to Christians in the Colosseum but he wanted to hear it from Marius.

"The same as what will happen to them today sadly. We do not have to stay to witness it if you do not want to… but it will show you the flaws of our modern community."

Marcus Marius looked around nervously, as if he had suddenly realised what he had just said. It was at that point that he looked to another nearby private 'box' where two ladies were sitting. One of them looked up and waved to Marius and he waved back in acknowledgement.

"Who is that?" Lucifer asked, "She is a very beautiful woman."

"That is Candida Lux… a woman of great mystery but she never misses the games, especially when she knows that Christians will be involved."

"And who is the woman next to her and why does she wear a hood to cover her face?"

Lucifer noticed that the woman's hands seemed to be almost as white as marble and this intrigued him greatly.

"She is called Lu'na Aurora and the hood is a mystery to me too, she is a very private woman, I have no idea where her wealth comes from and she is rarely seen in public during the day; I think she does not want to be seen here?"

"And yet you know that she is here."

"My wife does know Candida Lux but maybe I am saying too much…"

Marius's words stopped for a moment and once again he looked around nervously, "The Lady Lu'na is very wealthy, she lives on the outskirts of Rome like me. Candida Lux seems to be a permanent house guest of the Lady Lu'na but I have no idea where Candida is from originally, as I have said, they are two ladies of mystery."

"Candida's long blonde hair is stunning" noted Lucifer.

"And Lu'na's hair is a pure white, they could almost be sisters."

"Maybe they are?"

"It would not surprise me as they are involved in a very secret project."

Once again, Marius looked furtive and Lucifer had to ask, "You must tell me more dear friend."

"Maybe I…"

But then Marius' words were interrupted by the echoing sound of loud horns, horns that heralded the start of the Colosseum games. Lucifer noticed that this was when the Emporer Domitian appeared in his large gloriously decorated box.

And still the horns sounded as the first event began which was a re-enactment of a famous Roman victory in the north lands. This was a vicious realistic tribute to the victorious Roman army and blood was spilled by many of the participants. The crowd cheered and loved it, it was obvious that blood and violence was what they wanted. After a short interlude, various animals were released into the arena from the newly built hypogeum below; tigers and bears on long chains, half starved animals that viciously began to fight and kill each other. Then gladiators entered the arena to combat these animals, some of these men were mortally wounded and once again the crowd gasped and cheered at what they were watching. After the dead animals were dragged away it was time for the gladiatorial event which once again the crowd loved. Another bloodthirsty spectacle that resulted in the death of many gladiators. Lucifer could actually smell the mortal bloodlust in the air and he noticed how concerned Marcus Marius looked…

"You do not approve of this Marcus?"

Marius turned to Lucifer, "No… I do not and I do not approve of what we are about to witness next."

Lucifer was now quite certain that Marius was or about to become a Christian.

After the dead gladiators were unceremoniously cleared from the arena Lucifer saw that the ground sand of the Colosseum was now covered in blood and there was no attempt to clean it up for the final event.

Twenty Christians were marched by armed soldiers into the centre of the arena, men, women and even children. Tears instantly formed in Marius' eyes and he began to tremble.

"I… have never seen this before… children, dear Lord what have we become! I… do not think that I can watch this."

Lucifer held Marius's arm, he was about to say something when the emperor began to speak, shouting as loud as he could to the silent still crowd.

"Let this day be a lesson to this new so-called religion. The gods of Rome will not tolerate it, the gods of Rome are angry, anybody who opposes them will be crushed without mercy. This is what will happen to you if you turn your back on our gods! Their wrath will be immense, witness and beware. I have spoken!"

"He… speaks as it he is a god!" growled Marius and he banged his fist hard against the wall causing the skin on his knuckles to tear and bleed .

The crowd roared as if they were now animals themselves and the noise was deafening, there seemed to be no sympathy for the trembling Christians who had gathered together in fear.

Then starving lions were let loose into the arena of death.

Lucifer wanted to fly down and protect the Christians but that would have meant revealing himself to all in the Colosseum and he knew that would mean that he was interfering with the fate of mankind by disclosing a mythical being to them. He could not and like Marius, Lucifer found it very difficult to watch what happened next. Marius looked away but Lucifer watched in horror as the hungry lions slowly approached the Christians, almost puzzled by the living fearful meals before them.

The children were crying and screaming hysterically but the women and men began to pray and look up to the sky as if expecting a host of angels to descend and save them.

The Akhet is not here this day thought Lucifer and his anger and extreme disgust increased.

As the lions viciously tore into the group of Christians, Marius began to cry while the frenzy in the Colosseum increased tenfold.

"I… feel sick Lucifer, I need to leave now. Protego, go and ready our carriage."

Lucifer and Marius did not speak until they arrived back at Marius' house. A strong wine was served to both of them immediately.

"I am sorry that you had to witness that Lucifer… it is the first time… women and children… my God."

"Your God, was God there in that bloody arena?"

Marius looked at Lucifer and the truth was now in his eyes.

Then Messalina rushed into the room, she was wearing a long hooded night cloak and seemed very distressed, it was obvious that she was aware of the terrible and horrendous events that had occurred at the Colosseum. She made no attempt to make any excuse for her immediate departure.

"I have heard what they have done this day, I go now to join with them."

"I… am coming with you my love" replied her husband.

"Where are you both going?" asked Lucifer.

Marius did not seem bothered about Lucifer knowing what they were about to do.

"We are to be accepted as Christians."

"Then I will come too."

THE NEW SANCTUARY

Lucifer went with Marius, Messalina and Protego to a secret place in the nearby hills of Rome. They went through a hidden entrance that led to a series of tunnels and caves that were large, spacious and well lit by many oil lamps on the walls.

Shortly they were standing in a large area in which men woman and children had gathered, some still crying about the dreadful news of the day. Lucifer knew that these people were the persecuted Christians who had fled from their homes for the safety of their lives.

There were tables full of fresh food and fireplaces in the walls that seemed to be somehow well ventilated for the smoke from the fires. Some of the people were praying in front of a long altar that was against the main wall on which a large wooden cross was nailed. Lucifer smiled contently because he remembered what he had said at the crucifixion of Yeshua, that the cross should be how Yeshua was to be remembered, and here was the living proof that it had.

Maybe I have interfered with the fate of mankind? he suddenly thought but he did not dwell on it. It was ironic though, the 'Devil' creating the Cross of Christ, the symbol of everlasting life. Lucifer did not know how important this was to become at the time, his action of carving the cross in the ground and demanding that this was how Yeshua was to be remembered was instinctive and purely motivated by love and grief.

Candida Lux and Lu'na came to greet Messalina and her husband but they were obviously concerned as to who Lucifer was.

"This is Lucifer Heylel, a trusted friend and business associate of mine" Marius said immediately, "He sympathises with the plight of the Christians."

"Is that true?" asked Lu'na quite bluntly, her eyes glowing white in the lamplight.

"Yes, I do. I am well acquainted with the teachings of Yeshua" Lucifer replied but he did not elaborate on it, he just looked up lovingly at the cross on the wall.

"I trust Marcus and Messalina, therefore I trust you" said Lu'na almost expectantly, "Welcome then to The New Sanctuary."

Lu'na held Lucifer's hand to formally greet him and immediately Lucifer's mind was bombarded by images that were strange and unusual; white people, white buildings, a large white sun… then black demon-like creatures that were drinking the blood of people they had cruelly attacked and killed. Lucifer knew that Lu'na was not human.

"Come, break bread and drink wine with us" said Candida Lux and they all went to a table that was near to the large cross.

Lu'na seemed fascinated by Lucifer, he knew that somehow she suspected that he too was not mortal.

"Where are you from Lucifer?" Lu'na asked.

"I… am originally from Meccus in Anno… Egypt."

Lucifer winced at this because Meccus was part of Egypt now and he hoped that none of them realised the implication of his slight mistake.

"A very beautiful city I hear."

"Yes it is Lu'na and it does have a rich history which stretches back to when it was the capital of Annon."

There was a sparkle in Lucifer's eyes, he knew that he was going to enjoy talking with this enigmatic Lu'na.

"Perhaps we can talk in private Lu'na, I suspect that we both may have something to tell each other."

Lun'na smiled then she said to Candida Lux who was deep in conversation with Marius, Messalina and Protego, "Lucifer has remarked how well ventilated the Sanctuary is, I will show him what our engineers have constructed and achieved here."

It was a feeble excuse but nobody questioned it.

"Come Lucifer, this way" said Lu'na and Lucifer followed.

She led him through a series of short tunnels and very soon they were outside of the New Sanctuary and looking at the large red sun that was beginning to set in the distance.

"Beautiful isn't it" Lu'na remarked.

As beautiful as you thought Lucifer *but obviously a setting sun is not so dangerous to you.*

"The sun affects your skin doesn't it?"

Lu'na looked surprised by Lucifer's words, not many people knew the reason why she avoided the light of the sun.

"I am Luxar. I am from another dimension. I am here to protect humans from The Malos."

"The Malos are dark creatures that drink human blood."

Lu'na was quite shocked by Lucifer's knowledge, "How do you know that Lucifer?"

"My mind received images from you when you held my hand.

"Then as I suspected, you are not human too, I can sense such things."

"I… was once but that was thousands of years ago now."

"You sound as old as me Lucifer, how can that be?"

"I… was once Angelic but I disagreed with the Akhet. I was viciously expelled and trapped in orbit around the sun for years then a miracle returned me back here."

Lu'na was astounded by Lucifer's words, "So I am actually standing in the presence of an angel?"

Lucifer laughed, "I am no angel now, an angel of death maybe, my purpose now is to destroy the evil that the Akhet allows to live, an evil that the Akhet thinks will magically disappear one day."

Lu'na smiled, "Then maybe we are not so dissimilar are we ?"

Lucifer smiled too, he was very attracted to this beautiful exotic woman from another dimension.

"And now you protect Christians too" Lucifer noted.

"How could I not help, the cruelty that is inflicted upon them is terrible and should be condemned. Candida Lux and I created this New Sanctuary, it was the least I could do."

"I also created a sanctuary years ago, it is known as The Old Sanctuary."

Suddenly Lu'na looked a little concerned, she had heard rumours about The Old Sanctuary.

"So… you are Lucifer the Devil then?"

Once again Lucifer laughed.

"I think that my image has become somewhat distorted by people over the years, bad publicity I think."

More laughter.

"I saved Yeshua in the wilderness, I offered to save him from crucifixion but he declined. I carved a cross in the ground at the time of his death and demanded that this was how he was to be remembered and it has come to be."

"So you are not the real Devil then?"

"Of course not, I was mortal once, I have family who are now long dead and at peace. The real entity that is a threat to mankind is known by me as Nameless."

"A very apt name, both in this reality and my reality. There is so much I want to discuss with you Lucifer but I do feel that we should return now. Maybe we can talk further in my house some day?"

"I would enjoy that."

Lucifer and Lu'na returned to their mortal friends whose conversation was still about the new atrocities that had been committed in the Colosseum.

"There is much work to be done here now" Lu'na remarked to Lucifer and he had to agree.

"Yes there is and there will be more dark days of blood here unfortunately."

SAD TIDINGS

A year later, Lucifer was informed by Marcus Marius that Candida Lux had been taken and convicted of being a Christian by the Roman authorities. She had sadly met her end in the Colosseum beside many other Christians but she never disclosed the existence or whereabouts of The New Sanctuary.

Tears suddenly filled Lucifer's eyes and his heart burned with the need for revenge.

Marius had taken over as head of the Sanctuary as Lu'na had moved to northern Britannia, she had told Marius that there was important work to do there. Lucifer suspected that she had been ordered to go there by her elders from the other dimension.

When Marius died, Protego became head of The New Sanctuary and in his later years Candida Lux returned. Only Protego knew that she was now Angelic.

JACK

LONDON

Over the many following years, Lucifer continued his crusade against evil and what he really enjoyed was handing out his kind of justice to known serial killers that had long evaded capture by the relevant law enforcement authorities. In 1891, Lucifer went to London, he was intrigued by a series of vicious murders that had been committed in Whitechapel since 1888.

Lucifer owned the largest property in the richest area of Mayfair and this was where he stayed whenever he visited London. His mansion was within walking distance of the secret London headquarters of The Old Sanctuary. Lucifer claimed to be a direct descendant of the original House of Heylel and only the Sanctuary leader knew who he really was.

The Old Sanctuary leader was not in attendance the night Lucifer went to the Sanctuary. On the surface, The Old Sanctuary appeared like an upper-class social club like so many other rich clubs in London at the time, the local authorities had no idea of the real reason for the club's existence and it was simply known as The London Branch.

Lucifer took a seat in the main recreational room, he sat in a large leather chair beside an enormous black Victorian fireplace where he was served large Napoleon brandy's while he smoked a large expensive cigar and pretended to read the evening newspaper. What he really was doing was listening in to nearby conversations.

And all the talk was about the fiend known as Jack The Ripper.

He repeatedly heard the names of various suspects, names that even included Prince Albert and the famous painter Walter Sickert.

Conversations about the fact that Jack The Ripper had an accomplice abounded but others argued that the Ripper was a loner, someone who probably lived close to Whitechapel, Lucifer noted that Sion Square and its surrounding roads was mentioned several times for some reason. Lucifer decided that this was where he would start his search then and just before midnight he went to Sion Square.

It was a typical Victorian night, the air was covered in the infamous London fog and the street was dimly lit by the gas lamps that would be soon turned off. Sion Square was deathly quiet and inactive, the majority people who had common sense were now safe inside their houses and Lucifer totally understood why. But he began to think that maybe Sion Square was a 'red heron' so he walked on into Whitechapel and soon he found himself at the start of Brick Lane from Hanbury Street. Once again the street was deserted but suddenly at the end of the road he saw a woman enter from Old Montague Street. Lucifer focussed his vision to that of a hawk and he saw that she well and truly inebriated, the only reason why she would be walking this late alone in the notorious area.

This fool of a woman is ideal prey thought Lucifer so he instantly turned invisible and watched the woman walk up the street towards him.

Then out of the shadows of Osbourne Place, a man emerged like a phantom carrying what looked like a doctor's bag. The man was smartly dressed with a top hat and a large black cloak that seemed to move unnaturally in the still night air.

Lucifer could hear the man's heart beating…

Fast and uneven

His breath heavy in anticipation

Almost like he was sexually aroused

Lucifer knew that this man was no late night doctor

This man was the murderer known as Jack The Ripper.

The man walked slowly toward the drunk woman who was now singing an unintelligible song like she was a imagining that she was a music hall singer .

"Now then, what have we here?" the man in the top hat said, his voice cold and emotionless, his mouth drooling from the thought of the imminent kill.

"Ooh... hello my lovely... have you come to escort me home? ...I will make it worth your while... bet you never had a real woman like me."

The woman cackled loudly and then continued to sing her dreadful song and Lucifer was astounded by her ignorance.

How could she get herself in such a pathetic state at a time when a vicious deadly killer stalked these streets?

The man looked carefully around the street then he slowly reached into his bag like he had all the time in the world and pulled out a long sharp knife that glistened in the moonlight that had managed to pierce the patchy dense smog...

"I have come to escort you to Hell drunken one, I am going to kill you."

Suddenly the woman's eyes opened wide as if she had sobered up in an instant.

But before the blade of the knife cut the woman's throat, Lucifer spoke...

"And I am going to kill you."

The man froze.

And then turned in anger.

The knife pointing at Lucifer.

"Where... did you come from?" the man growled but there was fear in his voice.

"Hell" was Lucifer's simple reply and he turned into his dark form, the black energy from his back crackling like the wings of a demon.

"My... God!" the woman stuttered and uncontrollable lines of urine dribbled down her legs.

The woman fainted as Lucifer grabbed the man and took him high into the air...

"Are... you Satan? ...I do your work, I have heard your voice that commanded me to kill worthless women, those dirty prostitutes that infest our streets and our minds."

Lucifer flew to the river Thames then followed it out of London. The man kept babbling on about why he had murdered the women, why "they had deserved my knife" but Lucifer paid no interest to Jack The Ripper's crazy excuses.

Soon they were hovering above a deserted part of the river.

"I have no interest in who you are and neither does the cold water below…"

Then Jack's voice changed, he suddenly became calmer.

"But you know who I am Lucifer."

It was Nameless.

But Lucifer was in no mood to converse with him, he snapped the Ripper's neck and dropped dead body into the silent river below.

He then flew back to 'The London Branch' for a much needed late brandy.

Was he celebrating? It did not feel like it, this time it felt as if Nameless had touched his very soul.

WAR

Soon a Great World War began and Lucifer witnessed the invention of even greater mortal killing machines; great clumsy metal tanks that fired ammunition from within, lethal gas bombs that scarred and killed without discrimination and new aeroplanes that could kill from the sky, a new deadly technology was emerging.

Lucifer now sensed that maybe Nameless was winning, that what he had said over the years was now coming true. Lucifer also felt that the numbers of the Angelic were decreasing even though he did not know for certain. But he did know that attendance numbers were decreasing in Christian churches in the cities, that young people were shunning the words and teachings of Yeshua, followers of The Old Sanctuary were definitely on the increase and he knew that this would be a dilemma for him if he let it be.

In the 21st Century almost empty churches were to be found everywhere, people were finding their 'gods' in the shape of worthless and mostly untalented social media celebrities that seemed to be wherever there was a movie screen or a television, personal computer, tablet or mobile phone which Lucifer found quite amusing but it did make him wonder about the future of the mortal world going forward. Sometimes he did think that the world of the living was culturally and morally doomed and that good old fashioned mortal values and ethics were now very much a thing of the past

So the world seemed to be growing more and more evil to Lucifer and with World War Two, a new evil emerged like never before with the name of Hitler.

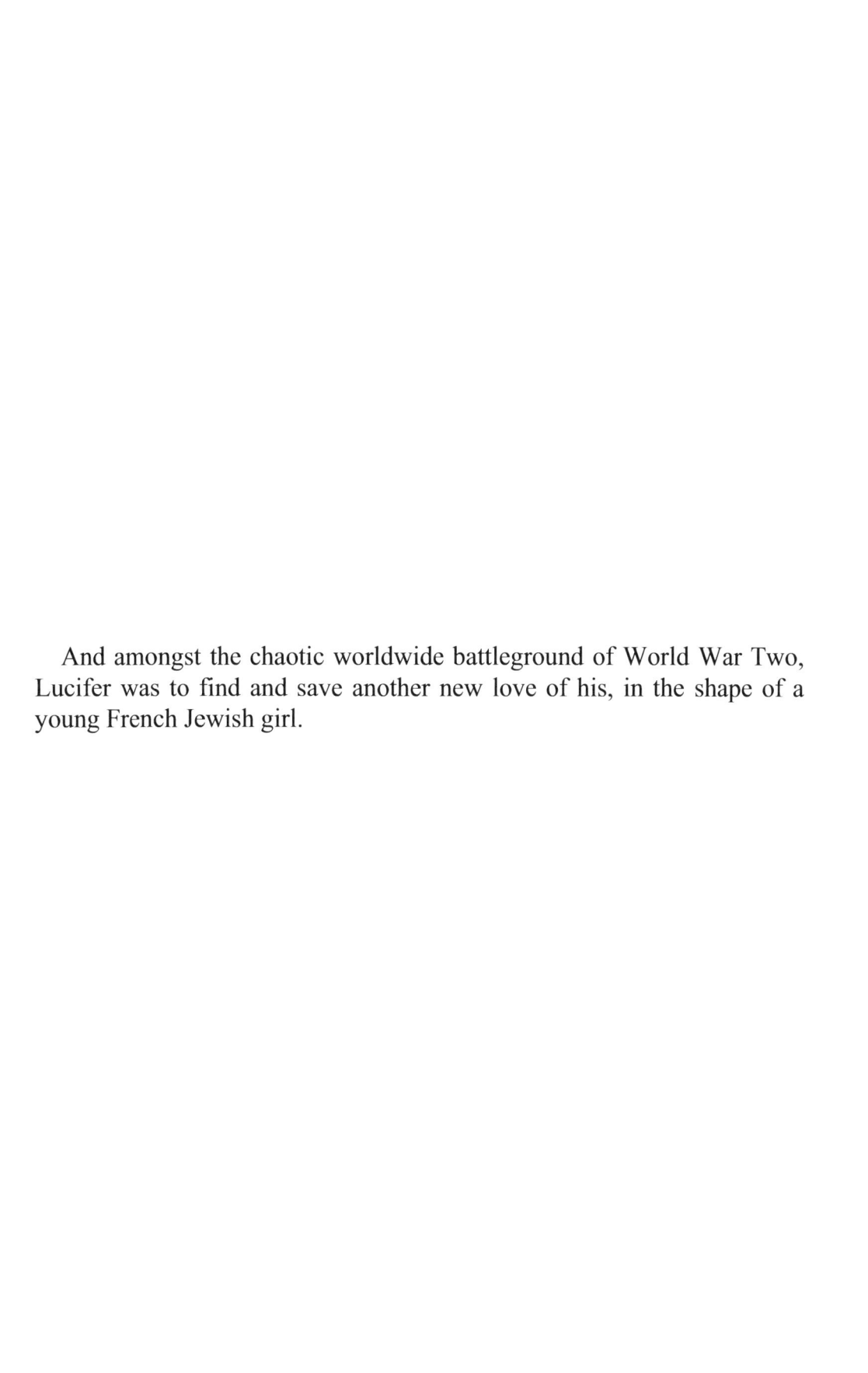

And amongst the chaotic worldwide battleground of World War Two, Lucifer was to find and save another new love of his, in the shape of a young French Jewish girl.

NOW

THE FALLEN ANGEL

THE THIN MAN

Lucifer Heylel looked out across the New York skyline at the sparkling multicoloured blinking lights that heralded the start of night. Lucifer liked his modern Manhattan penthouse but like all the other dwelling places he owned throughout the world he could not call it home, home was still buried in the dim and distant past, a past that still haunted him when it wanted to.

Lately the past had been trying to resurface in his mind and this puzzled, intrigued and irritated Lucifer; he had been experiencing strange dreams and dreaming was something that he did not usually do or indeed did not remember and he thought that these dreams were triggering this new latent nostalgia.

Lucifer was standing completely naked as he looked through the large wide window admiring the magnificent view before him. The sun was setting on a cloudless clear day and its vibrant red orange rays seemed to caress the tall buildings as it descended down amongst them. The pulsating night life would soon come alive and this night Lucifer wanted to join it, to merge with it, to forget the unwanted memories that were being forced to emerge within him.

His desire to kill had to be satisfied.

Lucifer had spent the afternoon having sex with a lady from one of the expensive escort agencies that he trusted. The lady was beautiful as was expected, tall with dark brown hair and the most perfect sensual body. She was a New Yorker and although she tried to sound like a high-class business woman sometimes her accent would betray her working class roots.

"Hey Lucky, are you going to stand there like God's gift to women or are you coming back to bed, we have unfinished business or should I say that you have unfinished business" said the naked lady from the bedroom door.

Whenever women asked what his name was, Lucifer would always say that it was Lucky, of course he had a reason for this but he never told them, there was no point because they would never believe him unless he revealed his true self to them. Lucifer turned toward the sultry woman, indeed they did have unfinished business because Lucifer had not climaxed during their hours of lovemaking, it was something he found difficult to do now, something that had almost been taken from him by the searing heat of the sun. It did mean however, hours of satisfaction for the women he chose to have sex with; he could make love for hours, for days, weeks even and no Angelic sperm would leave his penis, a penis that had an almost unlimited growth capability. When Lucifer made love to women, it was something they would never forget and for Lucifer it was still a highly enjoyable erotic experience as he brought the women to unimaginable heights of ecstasy. Sex for Lucifer was a way to forget.

This night though, it was more than just sex he craved, he knew that he needed a victim. Lucifer casually thought about the woman in his bedroom and what he could do to her but the woman was basically a good woman trapped in an unfortunate profession due to personal circumstances; she was not at all evil, he knew this because he had touched her head and had accessed her memories and thoughts, this was an Angelic trait that had survived his banishment. Lucifer only killed those that followed, worshipped or were consumed by Nameless and this night would be no different.

Lucifer pondered what he would do as he watched the first sparkling stars appear in the darkening electric blue sky… *I will have rampant sex for the next two hours, then I will have dinner delivered and then I will walk the nearby streets until the opportunity for death presents itself to me.* Evil is never far away in the city when the sun goes down and that is why Lucifer preferred to reside in the city rather than the countryside sometimes; of course there was evil to be found in small, isolated places but the city was the large breeding ground, that was a simple fact and had been for thousands of years. The city was the place of money, power, sex and debauchery, the place where every type of ungodly sin could be found, the place where the morals of the Akhet no longer existed. The city therefore was the ideal place for the work and wants of Lucifer Heylel.

After the satisfied lady left with a much fuller purse, Lucifer decided to have lobster for dinner. Seafood was always a delicacy for Lucifer probably because he had been born in a desert city and he could have eaten more even though he did not even have to eat. The lady had been delicious too and Lucifer had been tempted to ask her to stay the night but his urge for the mortal death of someone evil was too overpowering, he knew that the New Yorker had left a richer, happier person and this pleased him greatly.

After Lucifer had showered, he looked at himself in the large mirror covered bathroom and he admired his ever youthful body – he was tall, lithe and muscular, like a modern day sportsman he always thought. Lucifer's straight brown hair had been shoulder length for years but now he preferred it short cut at the back and sides and long on top which would always be combed back over his head, he knew that this was a thirties era style and indeed he had worn it this way since those days and he found it amusing to know that this style was now very much back in fashion.

Like his hair, Lucifer's eyes were a deep brown with a complex pattern that glowed with an inner intricate beauty, another Angelic trait he replicated with effective precision. Every now and then he would add tattoo designs to his body but would discard them when he became bored with them, only his Annon army symbol which was now known as the Sigil of Lucifer was ever present. Lucifer knew that his bodily appearance was desirable to both men and women but he also knew that if they knew what he really looked like this would not be the case, like all Angelic he had the ability to change his appearance and he was eternally grateful that this gift of light had not been taken by the greedy cruel sun. Again this was a memory that he did not want to think about at the moment.

After drying himself, Lucifer went to his computer desk and browsed through his list of wanted murderers, criminals, known drug-dealers, seedy pimps and other such undesirables. Lucifer's database of these reprobates was immense and he had a list for just about every city in the world; over the years, compiling these lists had become something of a hobby for him, an enjoyable activity that appealed to him as a natural predator.

After staring at the screen for some time, Lucifer decided that he could not be bothered to choose this night, he decided that he would just walk the streets and let fate decide his lethal hand.

Lucifer dressed in a black suit and plain white shirt, the only luxury he allowed himself apart from his antique silver wristwatch were a pair of large diamond cuff-links which he knew would definitely attract people of a nefarious nature.

As Lucifer left the ground floor entrance to the building, he tipped the doorman Max as usual. Lucifer liked Max, he trusted Max and he knew that his salary was not what it should be so every year, no matter where Lucifer was in the world, he would make sure that Max received a huge monetary bonus with many gifts for his large family for which Max was eternally grateful.

As Lucifer walked the streets of Manhattan, he breathed in the city air, it was a scent that always rejuvenated him, a smell that was vibrant with the energy of life and tonight he knew that the scent of death would be an added ingredient.

As Lucifer passed a Catholic church, he was tempted to go inside but he knew that he would linger there too long, he had always found churches lovely calming places to sit and contemplate his current lifestyle, a place that always made him think of his dear friend Yeshua. Lucifer never confessed his sins when in church though as he never wanted the Akhet to forgive him. The church he was now passing reminded him of the small white church of his recent recurring dreams, he suddenly realised that this small church probably existed somewhere in the world and that meant that it was calling to him, it meant that he would surely have to seek it out and find out why.

Deep in thought now, Lucifer wandered deep into the city and soon he was standing at the entrance to Retroz nightclub. *Perfect* he thought as it was a nightclub he really liked, a nightclub that played music from different eras on varying nights and tonight it was the nineteen seventies.

Once inside the club, Lucifer took a seat at one of the bars on the upper level and surveyed the active scene. Multicoloured strobe lights scoured the dance floor and Lucifer noted that many people had indeed bothered to dress in clothes from the era that was being remembered – tonight it was flared trousers and jeans, flowery paisley shirts, tie-dye t-shirts and bright colours, girls with flowers in their hair but it was also the era of punk rock and the so-called 'new wave' so leather studded jackets, safety pin decoration and spiky hair were in abundance. It really was a vibrant scene, a 'happening' as Lucifer seemed to remember and he smiled broadly as he drank his large vodka.

Lucifer then noticed that his smile had seemed to attract the attention of a man standing at the side of the bar. This thin gaunt looking man was dressed in a large shabby green coat and was wearing a yellow t-shirt that displayed the Beatles Sgt. Peppers album and the slogan 'All You Need Is Love' but it was the man's eyes that drew Lucifer to him, deep sunken dark eyes with an aura of malcontent and distrust about them.

Lucifer stood up from his stool and walked past the man and went to the Gents room that was two doors down from where the man was standing.

Lucifer pretended to relieve himself then as he washed his hands he listened to the song Sympathy For The Devil by The Rolling Stones that was being piped into the room. Lucifer liked the music of The Rolling Stones and had met them on various occasions in the clubs of London during their early days and he was convinced that the song now playing had been inspired by him. Again he smiled at this thought and as he dried his hands he noticed that the thin man from the bar was now standing beside him.

"I was just admiring your cuff-links man; I think they're pretty cool."

Lucifer kept smiling.

"But I thought that you might prefer a different kind of 'ice'?"

The man was a petty drug-dealer and drug-dealers were among Lucifer's favourite victims, they were abhorrent people that made a living from other people's misery, they were people that preyed on the vulnerable and the weak without any feeling of remorse.

"Yes, I could be interested" said Lucifer looking around the men's room to check that they were quite alone.

"Don't worry, we can conduct our business in here" said the man as he pointed to one of the wide invalid cubicles.

"Please step into my office sir" he said with a grin that displayed gold and silver capped teeth. After the man had shut the door, he sat down onto the toilet seat and reached inside one of his jacket pockets but Lucifer abruptly stopped him, "Before I check your merchandise, I thought you might want to check mine?" he said looking down between his legs.

"Oh, you're the business with pleasure sort, cool, but it will cost you more."

"Money is of no consequence to me but you are" growled Lucifer as he loosened his trouser zip to reveal his penis.

"Wow man, now that is impressive, you might get reduced rates for that" the evil man slobbered as he took Lucifer's penis into his mouth. Lucifer held the man's head as he probed the man's mind. Lucifer had been right about the man, he was evil through and through and had even killed two people, two murders that he had managed to get away with but tonight, justice would be finally served to him.

Lucifer was not particularly aroused by the man's mouth; it had been a ruse that had enabled him to access the man's thoughts. Lucifer's penis grew larger inside the man's mouth causing the man both pain and twisted pleasure, "I do hope that you are enjoying yourself" said Lucifer looking down at the man who was now red in the face and sweating, "because the taste of me will be the last thing you will taste in this world."

Lucifer increased his grip on the man's head and thrust his throbbing penis further down the man's throat then he increased the size even more and suddenly there was cold fear in the man's eyes as he struggled to break free but Lucifer was too strong… garbled pleas for help and to stop were ignored by Lucifer as he pushed deeper and deeper down the man's throat.

The man could no longer breathe, his eyes became bloated and began to bulge out of their deep sockets and it was then that Lucifer revealed his true appearance to the dying man…

The thin man stopped struggling.

Fear became disbelief then disbelief became instant insanity as the man looked at the black and charred creature that was choking him to death.

Burnt red eyes stared mercilessly down at their prey, red eyes that were now burning deep into the man's soul.

The man stopped struggling suddenly and slumped down to the toilet floor, "May your soul burn in Hell for all eternity" said Lucifer who had reverted his image back to normal. He zipped up his trousers and went to wash his hands. Another man entered the men's room and noticed with alarm that there was an unconscious man lying on the cubicle floor.

"He looks a little blue and cold doesn't he, I think that he may have had a bit too much ice" said Lucifer casually, "I will inform the management" he added but of course he never did, instead he left Retroz and headed for another club. What Lucifer needed now was sex.

FIELD OF THE FALLEN

Lucifer found what he wanted in a back alley, another unfortunate lady of the night but it was what he needed, perhaps now he would be able to have a restful night's sleep without having to go semi-catatonic. Unfortunately it was not the case though as the dream of the little white church with the old blood stained wooden cross returned and this time it was more vivid than the nights before…

This time there were Angelic in the dream
Dead angels
White marble statues
Statues frozen in the throes of death
Angels crucified
Angels hung by the neck with black rope
Angels gripped by sad and deadly despair…

Lucifer rolled uncomfortably on his king-sized bed but he did not wake up. The carpenter that had built the church was now making coffins in which to bury the fallen Angelic.

"We need to talk" he said to Lucifer as he began to dig another grave.
"Why do we need to talk old man, who are you?"
"I am a carpenter and I have much work to do but he needs your help."
"Who… who needs my help?"
"Come to me and I will tell you."
And then the voice faded...
The gruesome images of the Angelic faded
The church faded…
And the last thing Lucifer saw in his sleep was a field full of white crosses and a place name…
The Field of the Fallen.

THE WHITE CHURCH

As soon as Lucifer was awake he went straight to his computer and searched for The Field of the Fallen. Many pictures and places came up but he persevered until he found what he wanted, the small white church from his dreams, a church that was situated on the west coast of America in California, in a town called White Palms.

Lucifer felt the need for coffee, he made himself a pot of his favourite brand and took it to the veranda of his penthouse to sit and ponder what to do next.

Lucifer had always been an impulsive person, a man who usually reacted to things by instinct but this time he decided that he would take a little time and think it all through before flying to California. For some strange reason he thought that it might be some sort of a trap but he was not quite sure why he thought this. The only real enemy he was aware of was an entity known as Nameless but he had thought that they had reached some sort of amicable agreement throughout the years, that each would go their separate ways uninterrupted by the other.

Lucifer did not readily admit it but he did know that it was his soul that Nameless desired and that somehow his soul would increase the power and influence of Nameless.

And he also knew that the numbers of Nameless were increasing daily which was a serious worry for Lucifer if he let it be.

Lucifer always thought it humorous that he was the one that was thought of as the Devil, he did understand why though and that was rooted in the past with the House of Heylel and then The Old Sanctuary but he suspected Nameless as the reason for the seemingly continuing decline of the Angelic which was resulting in Lucifer being one of the 'last angels' even though he did not truly realise this. Nameless had foolishly said that Lucifer was doing *his work* but Lucifer had disagreed venomously, claiming that he was ridding the world of the living evil that infested it. Nameless had just laughed at this saying that Lucifer was *misguided, twisted and delusional*, stating that Lucifer was as *evil* as those he killed and that he *enjoyed taking lives* and like any murderer he would be *damned forever*. The last thing Lucifer could remember about Nameless was the echo of his sick laughter that rippled throughout his mind with a multitude of different voices.

Lucifer sipped his coffee; again those past thoughts began to bubble up inside him and for the first time in years he said, "Come, come to me, I need to remember…"

And as the warm rays of the morning sun caressed his naked body, a small boy in the desert city of Meccus ran through the market, a boy who people called Lucky…

Faces of all the people he had loved
Floated through Lucifer's mind like ghostly phantoms
He felt warm inside as their love flooded throughout him
It had been some time since these memories had filled him so
But he knew that he needed them now
And that they needed him
He felt that there was a reason for this
But he did not know why
Once again he believed that the small white church of his dreams
Was the answer.

WHITE PALMS

This memory of his life and all those that he had loved had flashed through Lucifer's mind in an instant, there was so much more but he now wanted the vivid images to stop, he could only endure the ecstasy and pain of this in staggered doses.

Lucifer sipped his coffee then decided that it was time to seek out this mysterious white church that was now attracting his curiosity like a magnet; *I will go to White Palms now* he declared to himself. The dreams, the resurgence of memories were more than just coincidence he felt and the answer had be found in California, he was convinced of this.

Lucifer went to his bedroom and dressed in something casual, white t-shirt, blue jeans with a thin brown leather jacket and classic Ray-Ban sunglasses for the west coast sun, of course all these clothes could be conjured up by his control of Angelic light but he did always prefer the feel of real man-made garments on his skin. Lucifer then went back to the balcony and opened out the dark light of his black wings and took to the sky.

Lucifer flew as fast as he could which was like that of a speeding bullet. The land of America below became a blur and soon dawn beckoned over the Pacific coast.

As Lucifer approached White Palms he began to scan the area for The Field of the Fallen and on a deserted hill that ascended up from the beach he spotted the white church, *That is the church, the one from my dreams, I am sure of it* he thought and he was pleased with himself for having found the small building so quickly.

It was early morning in White Palms and the large yellow sun was shimmering over the ocean like a giant beacon that was welcoming the day as it had done since the beginning of time. Lucifer could not see any mortals walking about but he still deployed his cloak of invisibility as a caution as he alighted to the ground in front of the church. He checked again that he was alone before he became visible, for Lucifer this process had become natural over the years.

The church was exactly the same as the church from his dreams except the brown cross above the door was much smaller and for Lucifer this was a surreal feeling. Lucifer walked to the back of the church to where the graveyard was situated, The Field of the Fallen - gravestones and burial grounds with simple wooden crosses dedicated to military personnel who had fallen in battle from as early as the American Civil War up to the first and second World Wars. There were none of the endless white crosses from his dreams here though he immediately noted, here was a graveyard that was overgrown and neglected, burial places that had not been cared for or visited for years.

Lucifer went back to the front of the church and called out, "Hello; is anybody there?" but there was no reply. Lucifer then entered the church and felt an instant peacefulness surround and comfort him; it had been sometime since he had been in a church he realised again but it was always the same feeling once inside. The morning light was cutting beautifully through the painted windows as he walked towards the altar which displayed a solitary large silver cross. This was a church that few came to he concluded, it was the Field of the Forgotten not just the Fallen he mused.

"Why have you brought me here, who needs my help?" he said towards the cross. Lucifer looked around the church and there was no answer to his question *but did I really expect one?*

"The dreams, the memories… why do you taunt me with them then!"

I think that you taunt yourself

Lucifer turned to see an elderly woman sitting at the back of the church and he was surprised that his Angelic hearing had not alerted her presence to him. The woman was dressed in the style of the fifties and was wearing wide angular sunglasses from that period.

"And who are you old woman, what do you know of me?" Lucifer asked and he almost spat out his words with contempt and frustration.

I know everything of you

The woman smiled but it was not a natural smile.

"Nameless… you take the guise of this old woman, why?"

She was near
She saw you flying in the sky
Like a pathetic bird

"She is one of you then?"

She always has been

"So it was you who brought me here… why Nameless one?"

Not me
I want to know

"This is not your concern."

You are always my concern
We work together

"I work for myself, not for you… not for anybody."

Not even for the god known as Yahweh?

"Not even Yahweh or the Akhet or whatever they are known as, why should I? We do not exactly see eye to eye do we."

But we do

"No we do not, do not tempt me again Nameless."

Me tempting the Devil
That is quite strange
Is it not?

"It is strange that I am here, talking to an old woman that seemed to appear from nowhere… and I note that your voice has changed, it is colder, darker, distant, bolder even; you are trying to trick me no more I think, I can hear the true you speaking."

You are at a crossroads
I think
"I am at a church; that is all."
Churches are crossroads
"You do know why I am here then?"
Suddenly the old woman stood up as if in trance…
Be careful which path you choose
Lord Lucifer

And then the woman turned and ambled awkwardly out of the church leaving Lucifer with his troubled thoughts, he turned again to the silver cross.

"The Akhet have deserted this world and I curse them for that, there is only one pathway for me, the one that I have walked for an eternity."

THE OLD MAN

Outside of the church, Lucifer breathed in the fresh salty air and a cool sea breeze caressed him, he had confronted his dream and nothing had come from it, *a wasted journey?* he then thought with disappointment but before he left White Palms he decided that he would take a relaxing stroll along the soft sands of the beach, he knew that it might help clear his perplexing thoughts.

And just as he was about to descend the steep stone steps towards the beach below, a voice behind him asked…

"I hope that you enjoyed your visit here my friend, there is not much to see inside but the church still stands and that is the main thing I guess."

Lucifer turned to look at an old man in battered weather worn denim overalls.

"And who are you, another Nameless voice?"

"I… am just the man who looks after the church, nobody comes here much these days. I just look after it with limited funds, repairs, cleaning; it gives me something to do."

"Then you have done a good job old man, the church and graveyard are well kept considering your circumstances."

"Thank you… I'm sorry, I don't know your name" and the old man reached out his hand.

"My name is Lu…Lucky" and Lucifer took the old man's hand but was puzzled that he could not easily access his thoughts, nothing much was in his mind, just the church, the graveyard and the silver cross.

"That is a good name, I like that; maybe you will bring good luck to this church?"

"The church is lucky having you" replied Lucifer, "and you have not told me your name."

"Oh my name is of no concern to a gentleman like you… some days my memory plays tricks on me, some days I don't even remember my name" said the old man and this was followed by a deep chesty laugh that suggested a lifetime of too many cigarettes, "Enjoy the day sir, it is all we have."

"Yes quite so, it is all we have."

Lucifer turned to walk down the steps then he heard these words behind him…

"You are not the last!"

Lucifer froze and contemplated what he had just heard and when he turned to look back, the old man was no longer there.

THE FIRST ANGEL

THE OUTLOOK HOTEL

You are not the last!

These words echoed throughout Lucifer's mind with an ominous refrain. Lucifer looked at the small white church that was glowing brightly in the Californian sun and considered where the old man had gone. Lucifer thought that the man was some sort of a caretaker, a handyman working to upkeep the church in his retirement and that he had most likely wandered off to tender to the graves at the rear of the church, a task that was clearly getting the better of him but at least the old man tried and cared.

Lucifer then thought about his walk along the soft sandy beaches of White Palms that had been interrupted by the intriguing words of the old caretaker, *Maybe I should just ignore them, the man probably meant that I would not be the last visitor to the seemingly redundant church… but his voice had sounded different,* Lucifer was sure of this, it seemed to be a voice from the past, from over two thousand years ago.

Surely not, I am imagining things, my memory playing tricks on me again, probably instigated by the sight of the cross?

Lucifer decided that his walk could wait, why not; he indeed had all the time in the world after all. He went to find the old man.

The caretaker was at the rear of the church in the Field of the Fallen, tending to some flowers at the grave of a soldier. Lucifer went to him but the man did not turn to look at him, he just continued to prune the flowerbed, cutting away the strangling weeds.

"I see you have returned Mr. Lucky; I thought that you were going to enjoy a stroll along our lovely coast"

"I want to know what you meant by *You are not the last?*"

"Did I say that, I don't recall it?"

The old caretaker stood up gingerly and breathed out, "I think maybe I am getting too old for this job, I don't think that my knees will take much more of this hard ground."

"Yes, you did say that I was not the last."

The caretaker looked puzzled, "I'm sorry, maybe I meant… that you would not be the last visitor, but we get so few these days, the fallen here belong to a forgotten generation, a time gone by, that is why the church is so neglected."

"Why is it neglected?"

"I don't know, there hasn't been a priest here for years, guess it's the way things are going in this world today."

"Indeed."

"Do you have family here?" the old caretaker then asked.

"No, I was just curious; I saw the church from… the coast road."

"You are out for a stroll then, I see no car down there?"

"Yes, I like to walk and think, it is a quiet time for solitary reflection."

"Good for you, walking is the best form of exercise, especially at my age… funny, there was another guy here yesterday with no car and no family here."

Lucifer became instantly thoughtful and curious, was it just a coincidence?

"Did this man want anything?"

"Want anything?"

"I was just wondering why he was here?"

"Just curious like you I guess, this church is very old. Y'know, he had a similar way about him."

"Similar, in what way?"

"Similar in the way that he spoke, the look in his eyes."

"You seem very observant my old friend, do you happen to remember what his name was?"

"He didn't say, just asked questions about the church here like you."

"Did he say where he was from?"

"Now you are worrying me sonny, you're not the cops are you?"

Lucifer laughed, "No, no, I am not the cops, but I do believe in justice."

"Justice… does that even exist these days?" and the old man looked around at the multitude of graves surrounding the white church.

"Could this man be staying in White Palms then?" Lucifer asked, trying to get the caretaker to focus again.

"Well if he was, a hotel within walking distance would be the Outlook Hotel which is just down the road apiece… nice place, art décor period."

"Thank you my friend, I do need a place to stay tonight" said Lucifer and these words lit a curiosity in the old man's eyes, "Oh and one last thing maybe, what did this man look like?"

"Well I said that he had a similar look to his eyes as yours, that sparkling brightness but he was a rough looking man."

"In what way?"

"Black hair, close shaven beard, big head with a large brow above deep set blue eyes. His body was solid and muscular… funny, he almost looked like sort of Neanderthal to me, cave-manish, a bit like Mr. Hyde from those old horror movies y'know? But the funny thing was, he spoke ever so gently and politely which was completely at odds with his appearance, he sounded and seemed like a real old fashioned gentleman which is very rare these days."

"Judge not a man by his appearance" said Lucifer thoughtfully and his own true appearance flashed quickly through his mind.

"Quite so, quiet so Mr. Lucky, my father always said that to me. Well, time for a break I think, gonna brew up a pot of coffee, care for a cuppa with me young fella?"

"Thank you my friend but no, I think I will continue with my walk."

Lucifer pulled out his large wallet and took out a wad of one hundred dollar notes, "Here, this is for your kindness and information" he said to the old caretaker. The old man looked astonished at the amount of money being flashed in front of him, "Hey, no need for that much, we get by, but there is a donation box inside the church."

Lucifer stuffed the money inside the man's top pocket, "Then you put it in."

Lucifer then turned to leave but once again the caretaker had to say something.

"If you do stay in the Outlook, watch out for the 'Widow' mind."

Lucifer turned and the caretaker was smiling.

"Widow?"

"The hotel ghost… a young couple were killed on their wedding night at the hotel in the early thirties, they say she waits there for the return of her husband, they reckon his body was dumped in the sea."

"Sounds sad and gruesome" reflected Lucifer.

"Sure was, poor kids on their wedding day, somebody there will tell you the full story I'm sure of it."

"Yes, I suppose every hotel like every castle has a ghost maybe" and Lucifer became immediately thoughtful for a moment, "that sort of thing is good for business."

The caretaker began to laugh, "Sure is, but if I were you I would keep away from the honeymoon suite."

"Ghosts are of no concern to me, we will all become ghosts one day" said Lucifer as he began to walk down the steps to the coastal road. The old man watched him go and as he did he whispered to himself, "I think you're right sonny, I think you're right."

THE HOTEL

As Lucifer walked along the wide coastal road, he admired the Californian sea view. *Maybe I have been in New York too long?* he thought; he had flown to White Palms from Manhattan because of the recurring dreams of the white church but there was no reason why he could not enjoy his visit? The mystery of the dreams had not been resolved so it made sense to stay in White Palms until there was some sort of conclusion. Lucifer liked mysteries; it made his eternal life more interesting.

The old caretaker had said 'walking distance' and soon The Outlook Hotel came into view. Facing the sea and the blue horizon, Lucifer realised that the caretaker's description of a thirties style art décor hotel had indeed been correct. The main building which seemed to be four levels in height was flanked by two circular smaller towers which were only three levels high. The rooms in the main building all seemed to have their own private verandas and these verandas stretched around the building. The building was primarily white with blue linage and on top of the building in blue capital letters was the name THE OUTLOOK. Palm trees at the front of the hotel added an exotic touch to what seemed a very enticing hotel. *Much better than those many plain modern structures I have stayed in* Lucifer immediately thought as he approached the main doors.

After Lucifer had completed the signing in formalities at the reception desk, the young lady seemed a little surprised by Lucifer's lack of baggage "No luggage sir?" she had to enquire.

"No, I am travelling light today it seems, I was not expecting to stay in White Palms but my personal circumstances have recently changed."

"Of course, and I am quite sure that you will not be disappointed by what White Palms has to offer" replied the receptionist, blushing slightly because she had suddenly realised that her question may have been a little too personal.

"I hope so" grinned Lucifer because he liked the beautiful look of this young lady, "now could you show me to my room please?"

Lucifer had asked for the most expensive suite and was given the rooms on the top floor that were next to the Honeymoon Suite; both apartments looked out toward the sea. Lucifer was generous with his tip for the young man who had taken him to the suite and the man was surprised and delighted considering that there had been no bags for him to carry. Lucifer gave him an order for the best cigars and Champagne that the hotel had. The suite was known as the Mariner's Suite which was named after a famous sea captain who had stayed there after retiring.

The suite was spacious which delighted Lucifer and the interior design was in keeping with the art décor style of the building; thirties, forties, fifties design elements were all prevalent, Lucifer saw that there was even a real ship's anchor on the veranda which he assumed was a small homage to the sea captain. Inside the suite there were basically four large rooms, a bedroom with a large adjoining bathroom, a reception and private room with kitchenette and all the rooms except the bathroom opened out onto the veranda. Lucifer walked through the main reception room and stepped out onto the wide balcony. Again Lucifer looked out towards the sea and took in the view. To the left of him he saw the beginnings of White Palms; to the right was the road back to the church and here the buildings along the coastal road became sparse, these buildings were probably holiday dwellings or retirement homes thought Lucifer.

On the veranda next to the large anchor was a table with two chairs and in the corner an unopened sun umbrella. Before sitting at the table the doorbell rang and it was the young porter with Lucifer's order; Davidoff Winston Churchill cigars and three bottles of Moete Chandon Champagne. Two of the bottles he placed in the fridge in the kitchenette and the other bottle he placed in a silver ice bucket and then he asked, "Where would you like your Champagne sir?"

"On that balcony, I feel the need to watch the waves of the sea" replied Lucifer.

"Indeed sir, it is a most wonderful sight from here."

"From anywhere" Lucifer instantly replied.

"Can I get you some sun lotion?" asked the porter which was a sensible question because he knew that Lucifer had no luggage with him.

"No, I will purchase what I need tomorrow; the sun and my skin are well acquainted."

Lucifer laughed but the young porter was puzzled by his words.

"Of course sir; will that be all?"

"For now yes" said Lucifer and again he gave the young man a generous tip.

Back on the veranda, Lucifer cut the end of one of the cigars with the silver clipper provided in the box and poured himself a glass of Champagne; he did not bother opening the sun umbrella. As he lit the cigar he relaxed back into the comfortable table chair and gazed out at the tranquil sea. Lucifer lazily rolled the cigar around his fingers and enjoyed the thick plumes of smoke that flowed smoothly from his mouth and as he sat there his thoughts began to drift…

Back to another time, another place…

Suddenly German Stukas and English Spitfires were flying through the skies in the distance, engaged in deadly dogfights. Lucifer laughed, the name of Churchill on the cigar had evoked memories of World War Two, the bloody conflict that had claimed so many souls, both young and old.

AUSCHWITZ

As the smoke trails and the planes faded from Lucifer's mind, other images and memories took their place. Consummate evil had festered and thrived throughout that period, culminating in one the worst atrocities known to mankind, the Nazi's abominable Final Solution that was implemented in their evil death camps. It was as if the time of Nameless was now clearly at hand, a time for Nameless to revel in the depths of humanity's despair, a time for Nameless to feed dark temptation to the multitude that were susceptible to it. One such man was Adolf Hitler and Lucifer was convinced that at some point Nameless had possessed him, driving him to do the unthinkable. Many times Lucifer had thought about killing Hitler during that period but he always concluded that he should not because of his vow to himself that he would not interfere and alter the fate of mankind, *I am not a god* he would always think. And he knew that such an act would weigh heavily on his shoulders if the assignation created some sort of venomous backlash from the Nazi hierarchy, an even greater evil if that was possible might take Hitler's place, Nameless might make sure of that. *No, mankind has to solve it's own problems*, Lucifer would deal with evil at it's grass roots as he had done for hundreds of years, It was this decision that had prompted him to visit one of the death camps he had heard about during his war travels… the chilling place known as Auschwitz.

Lucifer followed the trail of the Jewish people to the railroads of death and travelled with them on the top of the train to their deadly destination. When he arrived at Auschwitz, he could not believe what he witnessed, Lucifer thought that he had seen it all throughout his second life on Earth; mass sacrifices, torture, war, horror of every kind and description but the way in which the Nazis were controlling their sickening genocide was truly reaching new depths of evil… cold, calculated mass murder in concentration camps that were nothing more than human abattoirs; people thinking that they were being taken for a shower were then being gassed to death instead. At the same time these poor unfortunate people were being starved and worked to death and when selected, executed in the name of Aryan supremacy, sometimes at the whim and by the camp commander.

Walking slowly around Auschwitz, invisible to all, Lucifer noted that in some warped way it resembled a small village; there was a grocery, a hairdresser, a bar for the German soldiers, recreational sports facilities, a small cinema and theatre and even a brothel in which Jewish women were forced to perform immoral and degrading acts of sexual gratification and perversion. It was late at night, street lamps lit the narrow roadways in this most evil of places as Lucifer approached the red brick house which was the camp brothel. Two soldiers were standing in front of six new female arrivals to the camp and the higher ranking officer spoke first.

"This one I think, I will take this one to my private quarters."

This man was small and overweight, a man not particularly suitable for combat but suitable for what was required at Auschwitz. Lucifer could hear his heart beating faster after he had made his choice, a young girl with fair hair who was far too young and innocent for what lay ahead of her this night.

Lucifer followed the man and the pitiful girl and as they entered the officer's room, he entered with them.

Slowly the man took off his uniform jacket, he then went to the young girl who was now white faced and shaking uncontrollably with fear.

"Good… good, this is your first time I think, I will fuck you in your shabby clothes where you stand first" the vile officer said and the side of his mouth began to dribble with saliva as his rate of breathing increased. The girl tried to scream but the man held her mouth tight.

"No, no noise, we do not want to wake up the rest of the camp do we? You can scream later with pleasure" and he laughed at his own words as he pushed the girl up against the wall of his room.

"I feel your fear young Jewish and it excites me greatly, tonight you will know how good a German fucks and tomorrow night, if there is a tomorrow night for you, you will want me to do the same to you again."

The officer now had his hand around the girl's throat as he took out his small erect penis but just as he was about to put it through the girl's under garments, Lucifer grabbed it tightly.

"How does it feel Nazi scum?" a voice from seemingly nowhere said.

The man stumbled back in pain and instant terror. Lucifer then grabbed the man by the neck and increased his grip on the man's penis. The girl standing behind them was confused and scared and could not move; fear had frozen her limbs at the strange unbelievable sight before her.

Lucifer wanted to tear the man apart but he was aware of what that would do to the girl's state of mind, also there would be reprisals, the Nazis would maybe think that somehow the girl was responsible for the officer's gruesome death and was sure to be killed at once. Lucifer listened to the man's heart again and could hear that it was about to burst open with fear…

Lucifer dropped his cloak of invisibility and revealed his true sunburnt black appearance to him.

"My God… you are the Devil!" was all the astounded man could mutter just before his heart stopped beating. The officer slumped to the floor and Lucifer turned to towards the girl, his red eyes burning in his black molten face… the girl fainted, it had been all too much for her, she had expected evil in the camp but not to meet the Devil face to face!

Lucifer grabbed a sheet from the bed and wrapped it gently around the girl, he had decided to intervene this night; he had spontaneously decided that he would save the young girl. Lucifer needed a new housekeeper for his lonely mansion in Scotland and this girl would be given the opportunity to be that housekeeper for him.

Lucifer flew with the girl who was still unconscious, away from Auschwitz until he reached the outskirts of Berlin; it was now nearly dawn and he found what he wanted, a deserted woodcutter's cabin in the forest. Lucifer laid the girl gently on a small bed, reverted to his human image and waited for the light of the sun to awaken the girl.

Lucifer was seated beside the bed on a makeshift wooden stool when the girl woke up… at first she screamed when all the terrors of the night came to mind but Lucifer gently held her.

"Ssh my pretty, you have had a bad dream; that is all."

The girl's deep blue eyes were now wide open as she peered frantically around her new surroundings for any sign of the beast that had walked toward her in the officer's room.

"Where... am I? Who are you?" she asked then her heartbeat increased, "You... you are the Devil, aren't you? Keep away from me!"

Lucifer laughed quietly, "Do I look like the Devil?"

The girl seemed confused suddenly, "No... no but..."

"I know that you have questions, and so do I, what is your name girl?"

"I... am Elize Montel."

"Good, I am Lu... Mr. Heylel, people call me Lucky and I think that you have had a lucky escape, don't you?"

"But, how?"

"That can wait Elize Montel, I will explain everything to you later. There is coffee here, tins of beans and spam for breakfast, the name on this woodcutter's cabin suggests that he has most likely been taken by the Nazis. I want to take you to Scotland with me, would you like that Elize?"

Scotland seemed a million miles away to the girl but she knew that she would be safe from the Nazis there and this was a question she would never have expected to be asked but she tried to compose herself, "Why... yes, of course, both my parents are... dead now."

The girl burst into tears, instigated by her sudden strange new circumstances and the painful memory of what had happened to her parents and Lucifer hugged her immediately.

"Now, now my pretty, I understand your sadness Elize and your safety and well-being is my main concern now, life has to go on and you will be safe in Scotland, no matter what happens in this mad world."

Lucifer lit the fire in the small stove and filled the kettle from the water pump outside then placed the kettle on one of the hotplates, "Right, I want you to stay here, wait for me, I should not be long, there is somebody I want to see in Berlin."

BERLIN

The war between England and Germany was at its peak now; Lucifer guessed that Hitler was most likely at his headquarters in Berlin, overseeing military operations.

Lucifer knew where the army headquarters building was as he had been there before but Hitler and his henchmen were parading through Paris at the time, he also knew where Hitler's private room was and he went straight to it and entered unseen. Lucifer's hunch had proven to be correct; Hitler was in deep conversation with two of his generals over a large folded out map which was on his wide executive table. An anger began to build within Lucifer as he watched the little corporal descend into an enormous tantrum.

"No… no… no!" Hitler repeated with fury, "Get out, get out, you incompetent donkeys, you know nothing of war, nothing of strategy and conquest!" he shouted and both of his clenched fists thrashed through the air as if he were hitting out at irritable phantoms. The two generals picked up their brown leather folders and left the room hastily like two frustrated sheep. Hitler was still shaking as he went to the drinks cabinet and poured himself a large Schnapps, mumbling wildly to himself as he did.

"You seem a little flustered" said Lucifer behind Hitler but he remained invisible. Hitler turned in surprise, his hand tight on the glass he was holding, he looked around the room but nobody was there.

"That is right, you cannot see me, I am the voice of your conscience" whispered Lucifer. Again Hitler said nothing, his eyes rolled around his head and up to the ceiling as he took a large drink from his glass of Schnapps and Lucifer noticed that his hand was still shaking. Hitler's face contorted into a manic grin.

"My conscience? I have no conscience; you are just a random thought that wastes my precious time."

Lucifer had decided not to kill Hitler; again that oath about interfering with mortal affairs was just too strong to break, however there was another tact that he knew he could employ and that was what a cat would do to a mouse that it had just caught.

"I am more than just a thought; I am the one who will take you to the edge of insanity, you will pay for your acts of pure evil, one way or another."

Hitler was so seriously agitated that he went to a drawer in his desk and took out a box full of various pills and shoved a handful of them into his mouth then hastily swallowed them with the Schnapps. Hitler was sweating profusely now; his eyes were swollen and bloodshot as he manically looked around the room.

"Still here conscience?" he said sounding like a pitiful patient in some mental health asylum.

"Oh yes, very much so, I have been here for hundreds of years."

Hitler's eyes now took on a look of fear, Lucifer knew that it was time to reveal himself, *surely it will send the madman over the edge* he thought, *taunting this evil man is such immense fun!*

Lucifer slowly shed his cloak of invisibility and Hitler began to shake uncontrollably in revulsion at the dark vision he was now looking at. Lucifer stood before him, black and burnt as if all the fires of Hell had consumed him. Black light was crackling from his back and his red eyes stared intensely at the man known as Adolf Hitler. Hitler screamed like a young boy who had just awoken because of a nightmare and then ran out of the room as if the hounds of Hell were after him shouting wildly, "Guards, guards, save me... the Devil himself has come for me!"

Lucifer laughed at this sight and his laughter echoed around the spacious room as he listened to the nearby chaos but now it was time to leave the German High Command and their raving lunatic leader, it was time to get back to Elize and as he flew high in the sky away from the city of Berlin to the woodcutter's cabin, he looked forward to seeing Herr Hitler again one day.

ELIZE

As Lucifer alighted in front of the wood cabin door he changed his appearance, the only way he could access the black light for flight was when he appeared as he truly looked and that sight was definitely not for Elize.

Lucifer opened the door to find Elize sweeping the floor, she had washed the dishes and had tidied the cabin but Lucifer suspected that this work had been done to relieve nervous tension, to help her forget the events of her traumatic night.

"There is no need to that dear Elize, we go away from this miserable shack now."

Elize still looked scared and Lucifer saw it in her eyes, not surprising he thought as she had seen him for a moment in his true state, he knew that what he was about to reveal to her would be a lot for her to comprehend but her mind was young and open to what the world had to offer.

Lucifer had revealed himself to mortals down the centuries both male and female, he had even nearly taken a mortal wife once which was truly a painful memory so he only confided in people he felt he could trust, people that worked for him and he had decided that there was something Elize could do for him.

Elize was shaking, "Where do we go now, do you intend to take me to Hell?" she blurted out but Lucifer was sympathetic to her words and he was aware that she had not run away from the cabin which meant that there was a big part of her that trusted Lucifer.

"My dear young one, I know that you are scared, that you think that you may have flown through the night with a demon... but you flew away from Hell remember and you do know that I have saved you from certain death. There are things I will tell you but not here, I said I would take you somewhere where you will be safe from the cruel hand of Nazi persecution."

"To... Scotland then?"

"Yes, to a mansion I own, a place called View Ness."

This was simply an offer Elize could not refuse; she fought to put the memory of Lucifer's true appearance and what he really might be to the back of her mind… and the fact that she had flown through the night sky was indeed a wondrous thought, hard to believe of course but it had truly happened and this being called Lucky had saved her life. Elize had to trust him, what other option did she have?

"Is that a smile I see little one? Do you want to come with me to the beautiful romantic hills that surround Loch Ness?"

"Yes… yes I think I do" Elize stuttered as if destiny had suddenly taken her gently by the hand.

"Good, good, a better life awaits you now but only if you want it. You are not my prisoner, you are my special guest and you will be able to leave any time that you want to, to come and go as you please" said Lucifer and suddenly he realised that he might have fallen in love with the young French girl called Elize but not as a lover, more as a fatherly figure.

"Now to access my light for flight, I have to be in my true state but my Angelic light has the power to make me invisible to mortal eyes so when I disappear do not be alarmed little one, I will then hold you as I did last night and we will take to the sky like two birds."

"I… will not be scared" said a brave Elize but Lucifer could see that she was trembling again.

"You must close your eyes now Elize so that my dark appearance does not disturb you and if the journey becomes too much for you, you must remember that I will not let you fall. Flying is a wonderful feeling, try to enjoy it, I am sure that you will want to do it again and again and remember, you will always be safe with me, I give you my word my dear one."

Soon, they were high above Berlin heading to the coast and the North Sea of the United Kingdom and Elize kept her eyes open, she was flying like a bird or maybe she was in some fairy tale, maybe she was Wendy with Peter Pan heading towards Neverland. Elize wanted to fly with Lucifer forever.

VIEW NESS

The moon was full and welcoming and the man in the moon seemed to be smiling like never before as they finally reached Loch Ness. Lucifer glided down gently towards a huge grey stone mansion that was partly obscured by thick bushy trees. Lucifer placed Elize in front of a large wooden double door then reappeared before her in his normal mortal guise.

"This is View Ness young Elize, a place where all your worries can be forgotten and all your dreams can come true."

Lucifer was standing before a large marble statue of an angel that was next to the main doors, the angel was looking up to the sky with both arms outstretched as if pleading for heavenly guidance. Lucifer grabbed the statue and moved it carefully to the side revealing a small metal box that contained a key to the doors. Elize marvelled at the strength of Lucifer and asked, "Is that a statue of you, you did mention Angelic light?"

Lucifer smiled as he mused, "Yes, I suppose it could be."

Once inside the vast View Ness, Lucifer took Elize to the main reception room where a fire was prepared and ready in the large ornate black marble fireplace.

"I have a groundsman and housekeeper that live in a self-contained cottage not far from here, they always keep View Ness ready for me as it is one of my favourite habitats, the couple are called Jim and Joan McTaggart and I have known them for years."

"And they do not question your ever youthful appearance?"

"My, you are sharp my little one… I have touched both their minds, my appearance has changed over the years so what they see is not what you see."

"So they do not suspect your true identity?"

"They do not, at least I think they do not" replied Lucifer and this made him laugh, "Maybe I will reveal the truth to them one day? I think they deserve that."

Lucifer then turned and lit the fire and said to Elize, "Have a seat before the fireplace and I will get us something to drink, a brandy for me and a glass of wine for you, I think that you are old enough."

"I am sixteen… and a half, nearly seventeen" Elize said trying to sound older.

Lucifer laughed again.

As the thick logs on the fire began to burn brightly, Lucifer returned with the drinks and noticed that Elize was staring intensely at the thick framed painting above the fireplace.

"It's beautiful."

"Yes it is, Raphael's Portrait Of A Young Man, stolen by the Nazis and I have stolen it from them. Do you like paintings Elize?"

"Yes… yes, of course" Elize said quite excitedly, "my ambition has always been to be an artist."

"Then that is what you shall be, if you like it here."

"Oh, I think I will like it here!"

"Good, then we shall drink to that."

Lucifer raised his glass to her and smiled, he felt so glad that he had saved the life of this girl.

"I love art" Lucifer suddenly said, "Here at View Ness in the underground vault is my main collection, some of which I have bought but some I must confess that I have stolen, mainly from the Nazis after I had found out about what they were doing."

"So you will return them after the war?" asked Elize and Lucifer smiled that mischievous smile of his, "Maybe… maybe. From now on, you are in charge of my collection, my library is full of books about art and I will ask Jim to ready an art studio for you, a room at the top of View Ness for the light and the scenery, there are great views of the loch from the top floors."

Elize's broad smile filled Lucifer's heart with joy, "You will meet Jim and Joan tomorrow and I will tell them to make all the arrangements."

"But who will you say I am?"

"The daughter of my friend in France whom I am shielding from the Nazis and the horrors of the war there, they will like that, they will take you into their hearts and treat you like the daughter they lost" then before Elize could ask any questions about what he just said, he asked, "And now you shall tell me more about yourself."

Elize suddenly looked sad but she wanted to tell Lucifer, it was almost as if he was suddenly a sympathetic psychiatrist that could help heal her pain and loss.

"We lived in an apartment in Paris, my father was a bank clerk…"

Tears formed in the eyes of Elize as her head drooped down in sadness, "My father was helping fellow Jews to escape then one night they came for him but he resisted and was immediately shot… my mother went to him and she was shot also… both in front of me… I was taken, they said that I could be used in the camps."

Now the tears flowed freely from Elize's eyes and she began to shake again.

"There there little one, they will be in Heaven now, let that thought comfort you. Now we must concentrate on the living and your new life here at View Ness…"

Lucifer's daydreaming had stretched into the evening and Lucifer's memory of View Ness and Elize abruptly faded, disturbed by a presence he suddenly felt, a figure to the right of him.

THE WIDOW

Standing on the veranda of the next suite was a woman with flame red hair, she was dressed in a floral patterned brown dress that seemed perfect for the art décor surroundings.

The bright moon and stars that were now above the Pacific made the woman's jewellery sparkle as she stood in silence, staring out towards the sea. Lucifer felt compelled to speak to her, pleased that he now had company that he could talk to.

"Good evening, it is a lovely night isn't it?"

The woman turned as if in a dream, it was as if she had not noticed Lucifer sitting at the table. The woman smiled but there seemed to be a sadness to the smile.

"Yes, it is lovely" the woman replied dreamily then turned to look again at the gentle waves that were rolling in silence towards the shore.

"The sea is so quiet tonight, so peaceful" Lucifer noted.

"Like the lull before the storm" replied the woman and this time there was an urgency to her voice as if she had suddenly remembered something…

"Forgive me; my name is Heylel, Lu… Lucky Heylel."

"Lucky? That is an unusual name, and do you feel lucky tonight Mr. Heylel?"

"Oh yes, I feel lucky all of the time" said Lucifer smiling.

"Then you have been surely blessed… my name is Mary Myers" replied the woman and she seemed to stutter as she said this.

"And is Mary Myers alone tonight or does she have a partner or husband that will soon join us underneath these beautiful stars?"

"I… have a husband but he is not here at the moment, I am waiting for him."

"May I join you on your balcony?" asked Lucifer who felt suddenly drawn to this woman of mystery, "I will order more Champagne when your husband arrives."

"Yes… yes you may, it seems to have been some time since I have talked with someone."

Lucifer noticed that the verandas were joined by small almost unnoticeable gates, obviously something that helped the cleaning staff of the hotel he assumed. Lucifer went to the kitchenette for another of the large Champagne bottles and with the one from the ice bucket he joined the woman on her veranda. There was a table similar to Lucifer's apartment and as he put the bottles and his glass on it he said, "I'm sorry but it seems I have forgot to bring another glass."

"It seems a long time since I have drank Champagne, do not worry I will get a glass" replied Mary Myers.

Lucifer opened the new bottle and when Mary Myers returned he poured out two large glassfuls.

"To this night I think" toasted Lucifer and Mary replied, "Yes this night… but not the sea."

It was an odd remark but this only intrigued Lucifer more, "The sea can be a cruel monster but tonight it is like a gentle giant that seems to be at peace with the world."

Mary Myers did not say anything, she just looked out again across the still ocean.

"You say that you are waiting for your husband?"

Mary Myers began to tremble; it was as if she was finding it hard to breathe suddenly. Lucifer held her hand to comfort her…

And then they were in the bedroom

A large four-poster bed

Flowers, cards, Champagne

A dance record playing the latest jazz

This was the bridal suite

And Mary Myers had just been married…

Her husband Jack opened the Champagne, "Well, we did it honey, we tied the knot and that money is safe and untraceable, it's going to be easy street from now on babe."

Mary Myers lounged back on the sumptuous bed against the lush large pillows and sipped her drink and as her hand rubbed sensually against the soft silk sheets there was a knock on the Bridal Suite door.

"Did you order anything Mary, any supper?"

"No?"

"Must be more Champagne then" said Jack grinning widely.

At the door Jack asked who it was before he opened it.

"Room service for Mr. and Mrs. Myers sir."

Myers opened the door and a gun nozzle greeted his face.

"Evening Jack, thought we'd just drop by to say congratulations."

Five men, smartly dressed in suits and hats entered the room, "Where's your wife Jack?" growled the man with the gun.

"Look, she had nothing to do with it Sam… the money is safe, we thought that the time was right to get married, I was going to contact the boss about the money, you know that don't you?"

"I only know what I am told Jack, you know that and I only do what I am told to do… that's your mistake I think."

"But…"

"No buts, you're coming with us Jack, you can tell it to the boss."

"What about Mary?" asked the trembling Myers and at that point his wife entered from the bedroom.

"Who is it hun?" she asked then she saw the gun…

"It's okay babe, just business, I gotta go now and speak to someone, you stay here, I won't be long."

"Oh, she'll stay here" said the man called Sam and he nodded to three of the men who then went and stood beside Mary, "These boys here will take good care of your wife, keep her entertained so to speak, so you've nothing to worry about Jack… now move, the boss don't like to be kept waiting on his yacht."

The two men and Myers left the room and as soon as they closed the door Mary Myers raced to the bedroom, but she had been too slow, one of the remaining men had his foot wedged in the doorway.

"That's really unsociable of you Mrs. Myers; the least you could do is offer us a drink."

Mary Myers went and sat on the bed and two of the men went to the drinks cabinet while the other one remained in the room and drank Champagne.

Time ticked by slowly for Mary Myers, she lost track of how long her husband had been gone from the hotel then suddenly the phone beside the bed rang but it was the man who picked it up, "That will be for me I think" he said grinning and she noticed that one of his yellow tobacco stained front teeth was missing. The man put the phone down.

"Well, it looks like it has all been sorted" he said and the two other men joined him at the bedroom door.

It was brutal.

Mary Myers was repeatedly raped, her mouth gagged so she could not scream. She tried to fight but the three men were far too strong for her. She was badly beaten throughout her hellish ordeal and when the last man was finished with her she was stabbed to death and left like a limp bloody rag doll on her wedding bed.

The men hastily left the room and exited the hotel in secret by a back entrance.

Jack Myers was never seen again, he was wanted in connection with the death of his wife but his mutilated body was now swimming with the fishes in the Pacific Ocean.

Lucifer withdrew his hand. The widow of Jack Myers was dead; Mary Myers was a 'ghost.' Lucifer had met many dead souls over the years, he knew that the touch of their reborn skin was the same as any mortal but like his skin it could control and reflect the light, Mary Myers could disappear at any time but she did not, she was aware that Lucifer had accessed her mind.

"You know who I am now Mr. Heylel… but I could not access your thoughts?"

"I was once Angelic; I would guess that you do not have that power over me."

"An angel? Then have you come to tell me that Jack is coming back to me?"

There was a new urgency to Mary's voice, an expectant look in her now sparkling eyes…

An acute sadness suddenly filled Lucifer, "I am afraid not Mary and I do wish it was so. A portal would have claimed him I think, which one I am not sure. The puzzle is why you are still here; was there no light, no portal, no Angelic for you here at the end?"

Mary's bright eyes suddenly dimmed as if something inside of her was turning down the light of optimism.

"I… do not remember, all I know is that I have waited here for Jack every night since."

"Even when living mortals have stayed here?"

"Yes… I watched them; all of them so happy, so in love and I watched them making love, I even joined in with some of them unseen but they thought that they were imagining it, like a fantasy, a sexual dream."

"I feel so sorry for you Mary Myers, but there is nothing I can do for you, the only portal I could possibly open for you would probably be a doorway to Hell and the hordes of Nameless and you most certainly would not want that."

Mary Myers leaned over the table toward Lucifer, "Then maybe you could simply kiss me, I have been so lonely for so many years now."

Lucifer's lips caressed the lips of Mary Myers and then he gently lifted her up from her chair and took her to the bridal bed.

"Tonight I will be your husband, you will enjoy the night you never had with him" and Lucifer's appearance changed to that of Jack Myers, fully naked and wanting. Mary Myers clothes disappeared as if they had never existed and Lucifer kissed her again, it had been some time since he had made love to one of the living dead.

THE ROUGH LOOKING MAN

The next morning, Mary Myers was no longer there. Lucifer went to the veranda and then to his own rooms, he was ravenous for breakfast.

The breakfast room was situated at the back of the hotel and looked out over the swimming pool where a few of the guests were enjoying a late morning swim. Lucifer was informed that the breakfast room was about to close shortly and that the luncheon room would open thereafter.

"Good, I will have breakfast then lunch then."

The hotel waiter looked slightly puzzled then smiled, "Of course sir, what can I get you?"

"I will have bacon and scrambled eggs with fried tomatoes and a large pot of coffee; then I will have steak or possibly lobster in your lunch room."

Watching the swimmers while he waited for his breakfast, Lucifer thought about Mary Myers, he wondered why she had not been there when he had awoke; *Where do lonely ghosts go?* he suddenly thought then he imagined her walking along the beach or simply window shopping in White Palms. What he did find curious though was why a portal had not opened for her, of course he did know that this had happened to many before because the Akhet was not infinite and then he concluded that maybe her love for her husband had simply been too strong so she had managed to avoid a portal somehow to stay Earthbound, continually waiting for her husband to emerge from the sea. Lucifer knew though that it was never going to happen now and given the background of her husband, he was now probably in the realm of Nameless possibly, or maybe he had misjudged him, *Not all thieves are evil* he thought and this made him smile…

"You are right Lucifer, not all thieves are evil; you are living proof of that are you not?" said a deep gentle voice behind Lucifer, who turned quickly, surprised that someone had seemingly read his thoughts.

Standing before Lucifer was a smartly dressed man in a brown striped suit. The man was not tall but he was thick set and muscular, his hair was black and shoulder length and combed back and his broad chin was dark even though he had clearly shaven. This was the 'rough looking man' that the old caretaker had mentioned at the white church, *It has to be.* Lucifer looked directly into the man's eyes which were the most beautiful shade of blue, they sparkled and shone and seemed to dance with the reflection of the swimming pool water within them, these were eyes that could easily bewitch anyone even though they were set in a fearsome face mused Lucifer. This was certainly the man that had been described as Mr. Hyde.

"I know who you are" said Lucifer blatantly, "You are the Angelic known as Alphar, the first angel and this is a great honour for me to finally meet you."

"Quite so Lucifer and I have heard so much about you over the years that I find it somewhat of an honour to meet you too."

"Do not believe all that you hear Alphar" replied Lucifer and this made him laugh out loud, "Please take a seat, I have ordered coffee."

"Coffee will be good… strange how our bodies do not need such things and yet we find comfort in both eating and drinking."

"We are just trying to remember I think; a link to our mortal body of old."

"And I think that you are right Lucifer" replied Alphar as he sat down at the table.

"I am impressed that you read my mind without touching me" stated Lucifer, "But then you are somewhat older than me."

Alphar suddenly seemed to stare beyond Lucifer, up to the sky above the outdoor pool, "I was one of the first of mankind to walk upright, one of the first to make tools for hunting, one of the first to create fire, how many years ago now I seem to have forgotten, we did not have mechanised clocks then" and this time it was Alphar who laughed, "Sometimes I still long for that life you know, it was so simple, so easy to understand… and yet it was so hard to survive."

Alphar realised that maybe he had looking back through rose coloured glasses for a moment. Lucifer broke his nostalgic thoughts…

"I heard that you turned your back on the Akhet, that you deliberately made yourself Earthbound?"

"To help the needy Lucifer, and sometimes in the poorest and most remote parts of the globe… and I heard that you were banished for arguing with the entity that you call The Akhet?"

"I did argue, about their annoying inertia in this world and I ended up in orbit around the sun for speaking up against them, breaking their rules and showing them the cruelty that exists here. I was burnt beyond recognition in my hard catatonic state."

"But you managed to survive and return though, how was that so?"

"A gigantic solar flare sent me crashing back here… unfortunately some mortals have witnessed my true appearance, they call me the Devil because of that and because of certain things I have done."

"You cannot blame them, mortal existence can be naïve."

Lucifer laughed, "An understatement if there ever was one Alphar… but I do enjoy being the 'Devil' when it suits me."

"And so you should and I have heard that you seek out evil, that you enjoy eradicating it?"

"I do, it is the one main thing I exist for now I think."

The waiter brought Lucifer's large breakfast and Lucifer barked, "Another plate, I shall share this meal with my friend."

"That is not necessary Lucifer" protested Alphar graciously.

"I think that it is, I will not eat alone when I am with company."

Alphar smiled, he was beginning to like this Angelic called Lucifer.

Another large plate was brought and the two new friends heartily tucked into the food, they were now the only people left in the breakfast room.

After they had eaten, the two Angelic looked at each other and it was Alphar who spoke first, "This is no coincidence, the two of us here in this hotel, in this place called White Palms?"

"That is what I was thinking my friend."

"You dreamt of the white church then?"

"Yes… I was compelled to come here and you?"

"There are no Angelic left that I know of now, you are the first one I have seen for a very long time and yes, I have been to the church, spoken to the caretaker… and I fear the Heaven as we know it may have fallen."

Lucifer's face became stern, "Fallen to Nameless then?"

"I assume that this Nameless you refer to is the entity known to me as the Dark Conscious? Perhaps Nameless has something to do with it, I do not know, but something has definitely happened, I can feel it."

"Can you open a portal to Heaven?" Lucifer asked but he suspected what Alphar's answer would be.

"No, that is the one thing that was taken from me when I decided to stay on Earth, when I shunned the Clear Conscious, those that you call the Akhet."

"Your punishment then, for defiance."

"And you, I guess that your celestial doorway is blocked too?"

"Yes… I have tried to open a portal in the past but nothing happens, I think that maybe I could open a doorway to the realm of Nameless but I think that would be too dangerous, something that might suck me in and try to absorb and possess me."

"I think that you are right, that is what would happen, the realm of the Dark Conscious is not high on my 'places I want to visit' list I think" joked Alphar and this made Lucifer roar with laughter.

"So what now Alphar, what happens next, do we simply let Nameless and the Dark Conscious take control of this world of the living… but what would mortal life be like then?"

"Chaotic and cruel and surely doomed… Nameless is an entity that is as old as Yahweh Himself, it feeds upon evil without discrimination, the kingdom of Nameless both living and dead would grow until it had totally consumed this world called Earth."

"And then?"

"And then other worlds, other realities maybe, this is just the start of this dark universal cancer."

"So we are just to wait and watch as evil takes over the world, what can we do, where do we go from here?"

Alphar's face suddenly looked stern and thoughtful.

"I have sensed something this morning, a new light, something unknown to me… I suggest that it is time to go to church."

NAMELESS

A GATHERING OF ANGELS

Lucifer and Alphar took a walk, back along the coastal road towards the white church on the hill. The Church Of The Fallen was quiet as it had been when both men were last there but Alphar could hear voices inside.

"There are people inside the church Lucifer."

"I heard them too, maybe they are worshippers?"

"Perhaps Lucifer… but one of them is Angelic… and there is another who seems to emanate a new light that is different."

"Let us see then, it will be most interesting to meet yet another Angelic this day."

Lucifer and Alphar entered the church quietly and saw three men and a woman who was holding a baby, one of the men was looking at them.

"Your Angelic aura is very strong gentlemen… I thought that I was the last angel."

The man who spoke was called Mastema and he was with Major Tom Savage, his security officer Ray Gunn, Susan Eden and her child Matta, all of whom turned when they heard his words.

Lucifer and Alphar walked slowly down the aisle to the surprised group and it was Alphar who replied to the stern looking Mastema.

"I fear we may be the last, it seems like fate has drawn us all here this day for a reason."

"Not fate" replied Mastema, "It is this church that has brought us all together."

"Quite so" was Alphar's simple reply to Mastema's simple conclusion.

The tall black man known as Ray Gunn was instinctively worried and wary, "Just wait a minute Mastema, who are these two guys, they could be agents of Nameless… I mean they look like Dr. Jeykll and Mr. Hyde or maybe the Beast from the X-Men!"

"I am Alphar and this is Lucifer" was Aphar's cool reply to Gunn's less than complimentary comment.

"Man, you must be shitting me!" Gunn blurted out, "Are you saying that the other guy is the real fallen angel!" and without thinking he produced a hand gun from within his coat and pointed it straight at Lucifer, his hand shaking at the surreal thought that he just might be about to shoot at the Devil.

"No Ray!" said Mastema but Lucifer was angered by the action of Gunn and Lucifer immediately turned into his hardened burnt state… Gunn, Savage and Eden instantly and instinctively recoiled away in horror, Eden trying to shield her son from the terrifying sight that was now in front of them. Lucifer had seemed to grow in size and the black light from his back was crackling behind him like two large wings that darkened the light inside of the church… Lucifer's burning red eyes stared intensely at Gunn and the anger in his voice was there for all to hear.

"You dare point a weapon at me in this sacred house mortal, do you know who I am?"

"Yes… I fucking do now… and I don't fucking believe it!"

Gunn was scared and his hand tightened up on the trigger of the gun accidentally sending a bullet towards Lucifer which immediately bounced off his black skin and ricocheted through one of the painted windows.

Lucifer reached towards Gunn but Mastema stepped between them and took the shaking weapon from Gunn's trembling hand.

"No Ray, you are jumping to some terrible conclusion here."

"But… he's the fucking Devil, the one that we thought that you were, the fallen fucking angel for Christsakes!"

Mastema still had no real concept of the Devil on Earth because of his long banishment on the surface of the moon, all he knew was an entity known as Nameless claimed that title now. He did know of Lucifer though and that like himself he had been banished from the heaven he knew as Enolan for openly arguing with the consciousness he knew as Aenor.

"Yes he was banished from Enolan like me but that does not make him evil."

Lucifer noticed the fear in Eden's eyes at what she was looking at so he reverted back to his human appearance.

"Wise words Mastema and it is understandable why the mortal reacted so" said Alphar gently in an attempt to calm the situation down.

Mastema introduced Savage, Gunn and Eden to Lucifer and Alphar and then added, "And this is my mortal son Matta" and this he said with pride.

"Ah, the new light that I sensed then… this has never happened before to my knowledge" said Alphar and he caressed the head of the baby Matta who was still being held tightly by a shaking Eden, "There is no need to worry Susan Eden, I think that we are all here for the same reason."

"Yes, I think we are" replied Mastema who then began to tell the two other Angelic about the story of his banishment and his eventual return to Earth. Mastema told them about the Angelic Theolus and how he had managed to open a portal in which they had entered in search of Enolan. He told them about the bravery of Theolus which had sadly resulted in his death and then he said that the church that they were all in now was the same church where the dead Angelic were being buried and that they had come with the hope that the light of his son could somehow open the portal once more. Mastema still had to know where all the souls of Enolan were, he was not ready to accept that Nameless had destroyed or claimed them all.

"We do need to find this out" said Alphar, "I need to know what happened to Yahweh or Aenor as you call Him and also the Clear Conscious… and I do think that the new light of your son might be able to help us."

DARKNESS AND LIGHT

Alphar, Lucifer and Mastema stepped aside for a moment to discuss their plan of action. Savage and Gunn were understandably annoyed to be left out of this Angelic discussion but it was a chance to talk to Eden.

"Are you okay with all this Sue? Whatever they are talking about could mean danger for Matta" said Savage.

"I will agree with whatever Mastema decides, Matta is his son too and he would not knowingly put him in any sort of peril."

"I think that we should get the Hell out of this church Tom, as soon as we can" said Gunn, "All of this is way beyond the likes of mere mortals like us."

"I should agree Ray but we are part of this now, we have been since the moment Mastema walked towards us on the moon… I have been in that portal Ray, I have seen things no living man, mortal or immortal should ever see… what they are about to do could mean the very survival of humanity as we know it! You are free to go if you choose Ray, you know that."

"I'm still a member of the security forces Tom, and that means I'm still responsible for looking after your sorry ass."

Savage smiled, it was what he expected of his faithful friend.

"I appreciate that Ray" and this brought a welcome smile to the three mortals as the three Angelic approached them, again it was Alphar who took the initiative and addressed Savage.

"We think that you three mortals should leave now as we do not know what might happen here, what dark and evil forces we might encounter."

"Funny, we have just been discussing that" replied Savage.

"That's right Mr. Hyde but no dice man, we are staying" interrupted Gunn, "You might be thousands of years older than us but that does not give you the right to order us around!"

"I am millions of years older than you" replied Alphar and Gunn's jaw nearly hit the floor, "and I do admire your modern resilience… so be it then, we will now try and access the portal, with your permission that is Susan Eden?"

Eden hugged Matta tighter.

"Of course, do what you must, as long as no harm comes to my son."

"All we need to do is touch the head of your son, to channel his light through us… we hope it will activate and revive the dormant portal light within us that has long been denied to us,"

The three Angelic took the baby Matta to the altar table and gently laid him beneath the large metal cross. Together they softly touched his head and then went into an instant trance-like state as if they were praying which Susan Eden did find rather unsettling.

Eventually a bright light sparkled from the baby Matta and slowly surged through the arms of the Angelic until their whole bodies were glowing like three living white torches. Savage, Gunn and Eden had to shield their eyes as the light consumed the church which seemed to shimmer and slowly change before them. It was as if the church was now somehow vast and endless and yet still small and intimate, it was as if they had all entered a new reality where time and the laws of physics were different and unknown to man.

"It has worked" said Mastema, "This is now the church of the Angelic, the remnants of Enolan I think!"

The three mortals looked around and marvelled at the dancing glowing beauty of the church which seemed to move with a life of its own.

"You mean that we are now in Heaven?" gasped Eden.

"What is left of it my darling" replied Mastema, "But do not be deceived, dark forces do now surely lurk within here somewhere."

As soon as Mastema had spoken, the swirling light inside of the church suddenly began to fade and dark figures began to move in the new ominous shadows, crawling slowly like slithery phantoms across the walls and floors…

You are so right Mastema
But 'dark forces'
Do you have to be so melodramatic?

The three Angelic stepped in front of the three mortals who were now instinctively shielding the baby Matta on the altar.

Three Angelic
And another
An infant that really intrigues me

"Keep your fucking hands off my son!" spat Eden to the moving shadows surrounding them and she quickly took hold of her son to guard him.

A mortal with spirit
I like that
Her soul will be joy to consume

"Keep your vile claws away from her Nameless" shouted a defiant Mastema and the creeping shadows pace quickened, some of it moving with a threatening unnatural speed.

You managed to escape from here last time
And those that failed me have paid the price
But this time Mastema you will not be so lucky!

"Are you referring to me somehow, I have been known as Lucky you know?"

Ah, my dear friend Lucifer
I assume that you are here
To finally join forces with me?
To become part of my Dark Conscious

You will be made very welcome there of course
And you will not be deceived like you were with the damned Akhet
You will be my prince
My son
It is what I have always wanted for you

"I am not your friend dark one and I have no desire to be your son or prince, I am here because you threaten the balance of my world."

But this world
This reality
Is destined to become mine now
And now that the pitiful pathetic Yahweh and his grovelling Akhet
Have gone
It means that there will be more prey for you
And I do know
How much you enjoying the art of killing and murder
Dear Lucifer...

"And just where has Yahweh and the Akhet gone?" interrupted Alphar.

I know you ugly one
The oldest Angelic
The first
And the weakest
Shunned by your dear Clear Conscious
Because of your weakness

"You are wrong evil one, I am most surely the strongest, the passing of time builds strength within us, you of all creatures should know that."

Yes I do
And remember that I am much older than even you
As old as time itself
As old as Yahweh and his infernal Akhet
So beware
Ape that walks

"I have never been scared of you and I never will be" Alphar said calmly.

I think Yahweh was
I think that is why he has departed this chaotic world
And with Him and his whimpering Clear Conscious gone
Defeating the Angelic has been so easy for me
And my servants
...

There was a sudden pause in the surreal discussion as an unexpected beam of intense new light from the church doorway sought out the darkness within, the light made the moving unearthly shadows squirm away to the dim corners of the building…

They were suddenly wary, almost frightened by what was about to enter the church.

Everyone and everything inside seemed to hold their breath for a moment…

And then a voice spoke that was strong and powerful and yet full of compassion and warmth.

"The Father has gone but the Son remains. My father was never afraid of you Nameless, in fact He pitied you and those that followed you… He has gone to spread His Word to new worlds throughout this magnificent universe that we all inhabit."

From this light in the doorway stepped an old man in blue denim overalls.

"Who… the fuck is that?" exclaimed a stunned Gunn who was actually shocked and surprised that he could still think and talk.

"My God, it is the carpenter, the caretaker who rebuilt this church, the one who tends to and looks after the graves" replied Savage.

"You're telling me that an old carpenter is going to save our sorry skin?" stuttered Gunn.

"I think that he is more than just a carpenter Ray, did you not hear what he has just said, he has just told us that Yahweh is his father!"

As Savage and Gunn gawped in complete disbelief at the old man, his appearance began to slowly change; standing before them now was a young man with tanned skin, shoulder length brown hair and a short beard dressed in gleaming pure white robes.

"It is Yeshua!" declared Lucifer enthusiastically, "It has been some time since we last conversed Son of Yahweh" and his broad optimistic smile indicated that it was something that he had surely not been expecting.

Eden began to tremble as she held her son, "My God… my God" was all she could numbly repeat but Nameless was unimpressed by the presence of Yeshua.

The saviour of the world?
Who hides in a small forgotten church
In the dirty rags of mortal work
Why did you not leave with Yahweh?
Did the Akhet not want you?

Yeshua was calm, seemingly unaffected by the taunting words of Nameless.

"I rebuilt this church with my bare hands and when you began to destroy the Angelic, I took the souls of Heaven into myself, they are safe within me, within these walls."

Safe?
Here?

And suddenly the walls of the church exploded and shattered revealing an endless foreboding barren landscape full of white blood stained crosses amongst dark crawling bodies that were frightened and confused and ceasing to exist as the shadowy legion of Nameless fed upon their doomed souls…

Gaze upon your kingdom false prince
See what remains of your loyal Angelic

"I know this; I have buried them, you do not show me anything new one who is Nameless" said Yeshua and his face was sad and reflective but then stern and committed to the task at hand.

You still have not answered me crucified one
Why do you remain here?
When you can run and be safe
Lost in the stars
In the celestial wilderness
Like you once were
Do you think then that you can somehow destroy me?

Yeshua smiled and there was a look of pure love in his eyes.

"I am here to save you" was Yeshua's simple and surprising reply.

Nameless began to laugh, so hard and loud and ear-splitting that the mortals had to cover their ears.

You amuse me
so-called son of Yahweh
Nothing is to be saved here
This day
This is the moment
I will consume the last of the Angelic
The last of your Christian soldiers
Those that are trembling before me now

Lucifer smiled at this and clenched his fists hard.

He saw that Alphar and Mastema had done the same…

I will consume you
And the souls
That hide within you
Can you not feel what is about to happen?
The dawn of a new existence is nigh

"Then show yourself Nameless, I think it is you that always hides" replied Yeshua as he looked around at the desolate and dire scene that was surrounding him.

Again, a deathly booming laughter reverberated around the remains of the church and in the corner to the left of the crushed altar, a large form slowly began to take shape…

A human figure

Thirty feet high or more
That appeared to be made of clear glass
A transparent skin
That seemed to have a life of its own
That revealed moving human forms within it
Swimming and squirming
Rolling and turning
In some twisted state of agony and ecstasy
It was a vile vision
That transfixed those that looked upon it
In some ways it was macabrely hypnotic
A sight that was also somehow darkly erotic
And tempting to the eyes
That were foolish enough to continue to gaze upon it…
You can see
That my souls are content
Here within me
They enjoy being part of me
They love me
And they do not question it
Like your confused Angelic here

"Those that are within you are are mislead and trapped, imprisoned souls that will never be at peace within you" declared Yeshua and his voice had taken on a much bolder tone that indicated that he was prepared for what was to come next.

They do not seek
Your boring pathetic and outdated way of life
They never did
I give them what they want
They do what they enjoy
What you and your Angelic will enjoy
Because deep within you all
That is what you really want

Nameless waved his large hands before him and writhing deadly figures began to move from him across the ruins of the floor towards the Angelic and the mortals and Yeshua who was now standing beside them. Susan Eden wanted to run but the dark figures who were now more like grotesque giant insects and spiders that moved too fast and within seconds they had hold of her legs.

Lucifer became hard and black and he increased his size, his deep red eyes burned with fury and a dark crackling energy from his back surged towards the unearthly creatures destroying them in an instant but still they came, an unending horrific deadly swarm...

Mastema and Alphar also increased the size of their bodies, Mastema suddenly became a heavily weaponed warrior complete with shining sword and shield and Alphar now looked like a giant ape, that was growling with fierce sharp teeth as he tore into the dark hordes that threatened them all…

Savage and Gunn fired their guns like madmen but their bullets simply passed into their gruesome adversaries with seemingly no effect whatsoever, soon they were fighting with their bare hands, tearing apart the black creatures that now surrounded them.

Curiously, Susan Eden and her son were left alone by the deadly hungry abominations, it was as if Nameless had ordered this and of course he had because he alone wanted to consume the new light of the baby Matta.

The Angelic and the mortals fought without any feeling of fear of defeat or death at the hands of the servants of Nameless but they were totally outnumbered and slowly they began to be consumed by the dark multitude as the hungry forces of Nameless began to finally infiltrate their skin and their bodies…

Suddenly Yeshua spread his arms wide withdrawing the Angelic light that was within Lucifer, Mastema, Alphar and the infant Matta, this living light flowed towards Him, illuminating Him like the brightest of beacons…

"**Come to me, be one with me, my kingdom forgives you!**"

And this time it was His voice that boomed throughout the fallen church as a light as bright as the largest sun in the universe shone directly at Nameless…

You waste your time puny saviour
You have waited too long to take action
Your cowardice will be your ultimate downfall
Do not think that your combined Angelic light
Will defeat me
The new light of the infant is too young
And your remaining Angelic are too jaded now
I know that they are tired and exhausted
Almost bored with the troubles of this realm
Confused angels
Like lost little lambs
That have no real direction and focus now
No solid plan for the future
They are disorientated
Demented even
They do not really believe in you
And your kingdom anymore

My…
My strength is… supreme
I give them the Hell… they want
Because they
Truly desire it…
They…
Will never want to leave me
I will give them
what they
Have…
Always…
Craved…
But slowly the despicable dark creatures of Nameless became confused.
It was as if they were now terrified and alone…
Not one Dark Conscious no more
As if a new awareness had suddenly struck them somehow
They had been blinded by the new Angelic light
Of Yeshua
And they began to shrink
Like insects being that were being grotesquely squashed
By some greater invisible force
And those still in the body of Nameless
Began to seep from it
As if Nameless was bleeding a thick black blood
That did not want to be inside his massive form
It was like newborn spiders leaving the mother spider
But they did not him
They slithered away from him
Almost scurrying away in fear
Like rats deserting a sinking ship
Then their horrific forms began to circle in the air
Until they became small orbs of floating light…
That began to drift about like wary flying insects
Towards Yeshua and his open glowing arms…
No…
They dare not!!
Nameless screamed but more and more orbs fled from his body
Which unbelievably began to shrink in size…
More and more
Smaller and smaller
And the voice of Nameless then became weak and faint
Almost pathetic sounding
A shadow of what it was moments before…

No

***This is not** possible!*

It cannot be!!

"Love is possible, forgiveness is possible" stated Yeshua and His voice was once more calm and soothing in the swirling unbelievable chaos before Him.

The light from Yeshua filled the broken church like a giant sun rising above it.

"You were right Nameless, this is the dawn of a new day!" cried out Yeshua as He watched the entity known as Nameless shrink ever smaller before Him. Nameless fought and raged, almost like a spoilt infant at one point as a multitude of orbs continued to leave his glass-like form faster than the speed of light, until Nameless appeared as nothing more than an empty transparent shell that reflected the ruins of the church, he was now as small as a young boy...

And when the last orb left his shaking body, he began to shrink and disappear like the wicked witch in the Wizard of Oz, until his tiny withered form shattered like a broken mirror.

There were no more dark crawling shapes, no threatening shadows now...

The small church was quiet and still, calm and serene like nothing had happened.

Just Yeshua, still standing with his arms outstretched with a powerful Angelic light pulsating all around him, a light that was full of life and hope.

"What... has happened?" muttered Susan Eden as if in a dream, still holding her baby Matta tight.

"I think that love and forgiveness has conquered all" answered Mastema gently.

Yeshua walked slowly towards the stunned mortals and Angelic, only Lucifer was grinning as if he had enjoyed the fight. Yeshua seemed larger to them but that was probably just a trick of the gleaming light surrounding him and their admiring imagination.

"The gates of Heaven and Enolan are open once again" said Yeshua smiling, "and I believe that I could not have achieved this without the added power of your combined light my beloved Angelic!"

"And what of the fallen angels?" asked Alphar solemnly and Yeshua's face became suddenly sullen and sad.

"I am afraid that their souls may be gone forever Alphar, only my Father and The Akhet were capable of making mortals Angelic."

"There could be another way" replied Mastema looking at his son Matta... and this made him think of his wife and family in Enolan.

Yeshua smiled again, He had read Mastema's thoughts.

"You are welcome to visit My kingdom whenever you want Mastema as both Alphar and Lucifer are, as far as I am concerned, your combined banishment is now and forever more at an end, the portals of the Clear Conscious are open to you all once again, such is my word to you."

Then Yeshua looked at Savage, Gunn, Eden and the baby Matta and said, "Your time will come to ascend but not now dear ones… I think a spell of forgetfulness will be beneficial for you all."

And they did understand what the Son of God meant.

FAREWELL

The waves of the Pacific crashed constantly in the distance. They were all back in the solid reality of White Palms, the solid reality of their existence. Mastema, Eden and Gunn were the first to leave the shattered church and as Mastema said his goodbyes to Alphar and Lucifer he concluded, "Their memory of this great day will fade slowly, by the time we get home, today will be a mystery to them… and what of you two, what plans do you have now?"

"There is still mortal evil to seek out" replied a resolute Lucifer, "And I can only pray that Yeshua has not been cruelly tricked this day!"

"And there is still disease, oppression and poverty to overcome, there will still be demonic spirits to conquer I suspect; those that hide in the skin of mortals, those that were not here this day" added Alphar and then he noticed the old caretaker who was slowly walking up the wide steep steps looking shocked and bewildered at what was before him, the ruins of what he had so lovingly cared for over the years…

"But first dear Lucifer, I think that our priority must be to rebuild this shattered place, the place where the last church saved the world."

A NEW REALITY?

GOODBYE

Lucifer was dreaming of Mary Myers. He could feel her warm hands gliding gently across his still body, her small teasing fingers arousing his taut erect nipples. In his Angelic sleep, he remembered her face as her sparkling bright eyes looked down at him. *Had it only been a day since I last made love to her?* He could not recall exactly in that moment as so much had happened since, the living world he knew had changed dramatically and as Mary Myers moved slowly and erotically above him, he knew that she had changed also.

The night sky was clear, the large moon full as it shone its bright silver light through the open doors of the hotel bedroom. A soft Pacific breeze caressed and cooled the lovers as the intensity of their passion increased. Lucifer knew that Mary Myers was close to climaxing and she was beginning to glow.

Is this a dream? he thought, he was not sure but he was not really bothered as he was enjoying the moment… and as Mary Myers came she whispered repeatedly…

Thank you, thank you…

Softly in Lucifer's mind as she slowly disappeared above him.

Lucifer smiled. Mary Myers was dead, a 'ghost' that had been killed in that hotel many years ago. He now knew that he had not been dreaming and he now knew that she had just ascended to the New Heaven after waiting for him to return so that she could say goodbye to him.

Lucifer smiled again then a large heavy sleep overcame him as he was still quite exhausted from his fierce encounter during the day with the ancient evil entity known as Nameless. And Lucifer dreamed again, of all those that he had loved in his long existence…

Lilith
Desire
Caress
Lanar
Elize
And many more whose names eluded him in his sleep
And they all surrounded him in his bed and in his mind
But not in an erotic way
It was in a loving way
A caring way
And tears of love filled his eyes
Because he now knew that he would be able to see them again one day
That he would also be able to see his father and mother again
And a tremendous feeling of peace filled Lucifer…

Even though a dark shadow of doubt lurked at the back of his mind…
Grinning with malevolence
A twisted demonic mouth
That seemed to know a secret
Of something that had happened

Or would happen in the future
Something that Lucifer was not aware of…

A NEW MORNING

It was midday when Lucifer finally awoke, he realised again that the confrontation with Nameless had actually left him feeling drained and almost weak. He had been dreaming of Lanar before his eyes opened and it was not often that he allowed himself to think about Lanar because of the hurt and pain it evoked but something bothered him about the dream which was an irritation for him, she had been pleading with him, *Come to me dear Lucifer, make me live, we can be together again.*

Lucifer sat up, *Maybe we can be together again?* he suddenly thought, Yeshua said that he, Alphar and Mastema were allowed to access an Angelic portal, which would mean that he would be able to meet Lanar again, his parents again, all those he had not seen for thousands of years… then something hit him like a cold cruel hammer, the realisation that he was not the Lucifer of old, he knew that he had changed, not just with his now demonic appearance but also his personality and mind, *And how would Lanar react to that?* And then he suddenly thought, *Also there was the chance and a good chance that Lanar had found a new love in Heaven just like Lilith had* and that had completely broke Lucifer's heart and would do so again. Lucifer knew that it would be something that might completely destroy him and this he could not allow. So he had awoken to a new dilemma but why had the Lanar of his dreams said *make me live?* Lucifer shook his head, he needed to bathe his face, to refresh his muddled thoughts.

Lucifer went to the bathroom and splashed cold water onto his face and neck then brushed his fingers through his hair and as he looked into the large gold framed mirror above the wash basin, he noticed that his hair had turned golden at the sides… then he looked into his eyes, they were sparkling white and shining brightly as if the Milky Way was circling around inside of them, as if they had been possessed by the universe. For a moment he thought that he looked like someone else, *But who?* he wondered then he suddenly remembered, *That singer called Bowie,* Lucifer had found his Heathen album very intriguing and had really liked it. *Cool* he immediately thought, *maybe I will keep this look?*

Lucifer laughed, his mood had been lifted.

ALPHAR

THE BUSINESSMEN

After a quick shower, Lucifer felt the need for food, of course he did not have to eat but he knew that it would be something that would help revitalise him as he was still feeling the affects of his recent battle with Nameless. He dressed causally in a white shirt and black trousers and then made his way swiftly to the hotel dining room. Sitting at the table overlooking the swimming pool at the rear of the room was a muscular figure he recognised immediately.

"Ah Alphar, I suspected that you might be here" said Lucifer smiling and already he was beginning to feel revitalised.

Alphar put the thick black book he had been reading down and turned to look at Lucifer.

"You did not search the hotel for my mind then Lucifer?"

"No, that would be completely rude of me, I do respect your privacy as I hope you would respect mine."

"Of course I respect your privacy dear Lucifer, please sit with me, I have eaten but you order, please do" replied Alphar who then took a sip of Champagne from his large crystal glass.

Alphar was a powerfully built man with jet black shoulder length hair, his broad chin dark yet clearly he had shaven. He was dressed once again in a brown thin striped suit but with no tie. He was the rough looking man as before but once again he displayed the natural elegance of a gentleman.

A waiter came to the table and Lucifer ordered lobster, seafood was always a delicacy he enjoyed and after the waiter had left the table Alphar poured Lucifer a glass of Champagne.

"I think we should celebrate should we not?"

"Of course, I try to celebrate every day" replied Lucifer with a devilish smile.

"Yes, but after yesterday, I think our celebration today is rather special."

Alphar was obviously referring to their 'meeting' with Nameless and his subsequent demise at the hands of Yeshua, the Son of Man.

"I notice that your hair colouring is different today, my hair was totally white as dawn broke this morning…"

"And your eyes sparkled white like million stars that had consumed them?" interrupted Lucifer.

"Yes… the result of being in the presence of the Son of Yahweh and the power He unleashed to defeat Nameless."

"I suspect so, I think that it may have even increased our Angelic power?"

"It will have I think… even the ancient Nameless could not defeat the might of the last Angelic combined."

"And that is quite something is it not Alphar, as Nameless was an entity that came into being at the dawn of life, a consciousness that was as old as Yahweh Himself. It is a pity that Nameless chose a different path, that he was drawn to the potential evil that began to exist and develop on this planet, what a different world it could have been. I see that you have been reading 'the good book,' a book that I have read many times before."

"I thought that it was a good time to revisit it, maybe the meaning within will now be revitalised?"

"Maybe" mused Lucifer but he was not totally convinced that it would, "We shall see, we shall see my friend but do you really think that Nameless is no more Alphar, 'it' has existed since the dawn of time?"

"I really do not know, Nameless sounded as a young child just before it expired, before the Son of Man took every soul within Himself, both good and bad. Evil still exists in this world Lucifer, the living evil, only now instead of passing into the kingdom of Nameless, it will go into the kingdom of Yeshua."

"And that is what is worrying me, that Nameless has tricked the Son of Man. 'Yahweh forgives all' Yeshua has said but I am not convinced that this will actually work somehow?"

"We will have to wait and see then that is all" replied Alphar sounding practical, "All I know is that our work here in the land of the living is far from finished, especially as there is so few of us left."

"And there are no Angelic to guide souls through the portals now."

"But there is no need now as there is no threat from the Dark Conscious… but I suspect that Yeshua will somehow rebuild our numbers even though he said that he did not possess the power to do so. Perhaps a New Angelic will begin to flourish with the light of the infant Matta?"

"I have existed for years, my purpose being to wipe out evil" stated Lucifer suddenly, "That is not going to stop overnight."

"And I have existed to help those for whom there seemed no help at all, people in remote places that were suffering and struggling to survive. I cared for animals even before I became Angelic and I have handed out swift justice in kind since to any mortal I came across that was cruel to animals. I have battled demons and exorcised them when the church failed, I have even saved the world from alien intervention and invasion… and I suspect that we will be needed to continue with our good work…"

"Did you say aliens Alphar? That is something I have never encountered, beings from a different dimension and ghosts of the dead yes but never aliens, maybe they kept clear of me?" Lucifer laughed, "You must tell me all about your life Alphar, you really must! Did they have pointy ears and did they tell you to live long and prosper?"

The two Angelic laughed out loud but Lucifer suspected that Alphar had not really understood his joke about Mr. Spock. They then raised their glasses and drank to each other and at that moment Lucifer's large lobster arrived, he offered to share it with Alphar but Alphar declined as he had already eaten and he did not want to appear a glutton. Lucifer devoured the lobster whole, the bones of the creature crunching loudly which did create astounded looks from the people at the nearby tables. Alphar and Lucifer laughed again and ordered more Champagne.

"So what are you immediate plans Alphar?" Lucifer asked.

"Early this morning I employed a building company to repair the Church Of The Fallen, I will see that the old caretaker will oversee that…"

"You have been a 'busy bee' then" laughed Lucifer, "Let me know the cost and I will pay you my share."

"No need for that Lucifer, all I am concerned with is that they do an excellent job… yes, I have been busy I suppose, I did not, could not sleep" replied Alphar and this made Lucifer think about Mary Myers but he did not mention her, he was quite sure that Alphar was not that interested in his sex life.

"But getting back to your question Lucifer" Alphar continued, "I think that I may stay here awhile, certainly until the church is rebuilt and I have requested that the size of the church be much larger… the fate of mankind hung in the balance in that church and I think that its new status should reflect that."

"Most certainly, a good decision" agreed Lucifer.

"And you Lucifer, what will you do?"

Lucifer eased back in his chair and looked down at the outside pool. The sky was clear and he could see the hills of White Palms rising behind the pool. A solitary man was swimming in the pool toward a clothed man who was standing as if waiting for him. For a moment it reminded Lucifer of a David Hockney painting that he had seen and had been tempted to buy. The reflection of the water ripples caused by the man swimming and the Hockneyesque scene made him think of View Ness, his mansion in Scotland and his art collection there and the lady known as Elize who had looked after it for so many years… he suddenly felt sad.

"I… I am not really sure Alphar, I feel the need to reflect for some reason…"

"What we accomplished in the church will have surely have caused that… but wait, I seem to recall that that you said that you had met Yeshua before?"

Lucifer looked around the room which was sparsely populated, he was making sure that his words reached no mortal ears.

"Yes, I did meet him, long ago in the wilderness during his darkest of days… I saved him from a poisonous snake after Nameless had tempted him, I think Nameless sent the snake to kill him. I took him to the house of his mother Maryam where he recuperated from his ordeal."

"So the living of this world owes you more than they will ever know Lucifer."

"He was just a man I saved, I would have done the same for any other… but then I followed him and listened to his teachings and I began to wonder, I offered to save him from his crucifixion but he declined, I carved a large cross in the ground and demanded that this would be how he would be remembered and it became his symbol of life and I am very proud of that. At the time I raged at the Akhet but gradually I came to understand."

"It is the greatest story, the greatest sacrifice, turning the deadly cross of crucifixion into the symbol of everlasting life" added Alphar.

"Yes, he took the sins of mortals into himself that day and eventually the world realised this."

"But not Nameless."

"Well Nameless does now" laughed Lucifer and Alphar joined in with him.

"Amen to that."

INTRIGUING NEWS

Alphar suggested that they take afternoon refreshments by the pool and take in the refreshing breezes that were drifting in from sea. They sat at a secluded table at the end of the pool bar, quite near to the large television that was on the bar wall, it was showing Sky News. They were still drinking the best Champagne. Alphar had taken his jacket off and laid it over the back of his chair, Lucifer had loosened his white shirt, they looked like two businessmen relaxing after a meeting inside the hotel. The solitary man that Lucifer had watched swimming was now gone replaced by two young women who had definitely noticed Lucifer.

"I see that you are admiring the two young ladies Lucifer" smiled Alphar.

"It seems that we may have company for dinner tonight Alphar."

"Oh, I do not think that they are interested in me dear Lucifer."

"You underestimate yourself Alphar, many women are attracted by that rough unshaven look."

"It is not unshaven, it is how I prefer to look, similar to how I was in the beginning. I have always thought that I looked a little, how can I put it, scary by today's standards? But it is who I am, I have modified my facial features because the face of a man that is millions of years old may be a little too much for most people in this day and age."

Lucifer laughed, "Yes, and I think those two swimmers would probably agree with you."

"You give me the impression of an affable man Lucifer but I sense in truth that a lonely man might be hiding behind that façade?"

Lucifer became thoughtful, he was not expecting this honest observation from Alphar then he replied, "I have always wanted to enjoy life, in whatever form, whatever time. I take pleasure in women as often as I can… but yes, maybe you are right, though I have loved women throughout my earthly existence…"

Lucifer's gaze focussed on the two swimmers again who were now playfully splashing water on each other displaying their sensual shapely bodies.

Alphar's face became animated, "You must tell me about them sometime Lucifer, it would be a way to offload for you maybe?"

"Oh and is this now Doctor Alphar, the Caring Angel that speaks?"

Alphar smiled.

"We all need someone we can lean on dear Lucifer, even fallen angels like us."

"And you Alphar, have you ever 'offloaded' to anyone?"

Alphar smiled again, "I recently thought about publishing a book, an interview with a mortal maybe, though probably nobody would realise that it was actually fact not fiction."

"Like Interview With The Vampire?"

"What?"

"The book by Anne Rice."

Lucifer realised that Alphar was none the wiser, *Too much time in remote places?* he wondered then he said, "You could call the book Interview With The Angel or maybe The First Angel, I mean you were the first mortal to be recruited by the Akhet, sorry, the Clear Conscious were you not?"

"Yes… I think I was although I am not sure of this… it was such a long long time ago now."

And this time it was Alphar who was momentarily drifting away.

Then he suddenly snapped out of it and held Lucifer's hand while his mind sent information to Lucifer's mind…

This is how you can contact me Lucifer, any time you want, I value your friendship greatly my friend.

As I value yours dear Alphar. These are my contact details…

And Lucifer sent his personal contact information to Alphar.

"Then we will drink to that" replied Alphar and one again their glasses of Champagne clinked together in appreciation of each other.

Lucifer felt that he had now found a sincere genuine friend, one that he could really share his thoughts and life with and he was really pleased that he liked this ancient Angelic who was once known as Upright Man *or was it even before that?* and he smiled as he wondered what life was like millions of years ago. Lucifer decided that they should arrange to meet up when the Church Of The Fallen had been rebuilt and was about to mention this to Alphar when something on the large bar television caught his eye. It was still showing Sky News and it appeared to be showing a mobile phone video of a white marble-like figure that was floating, descending from the sky. The video was shaky and unclear as if something unnatural and criminal was occurring. Lucifer immediately thought of the vampiric Luxar Lu'na and how her skin turned hard and white in the sun but he was not sure if she had the power of flight. Lucifer immediately asked the barman to turn the volume up and he listened acutely to the rest of the broadcast.

It was a news report of strange happenings in an English coastal town, a female teenager that had disappeared, a missing boat owner and macabre deaths at a marina… then censored photographs of empty withered skins were shown and mentioned and Lucifer froze as the memory of Lanar's death at the hands of the creature Vaag suddenly flooded his mind, the image of the remains of her skin made him instantly feel sick

Lucifer stood up abruptly, sending his glass of Champagne crashing to the floor.

"I'm afraid that I must leave you dear Alphar, something urgent demands my immediate attention. But we will meet again at the soonest opportunity, you must come to Vew Ness and tell me more about your life."

Alphar was obviously very surprised by this and asked, "And where are you going Lucifer in such a strange and unexpected hurry?"

"A city in the North of England, a place called Sunderland."

The story of Lucif-er Heylel continues in Bloodlust and Lust For Life.

And in the memoirs of Alphar, The First Angel.

ACKNOWLEDGEMENTS

Many thanks to Robbie MacDonald for title page photograph.

1 - Chapter illustrations by Richard Valanga using Bing Image Creator.
2 - Google Translate and Search.
3 - Sgt. Pepper's Lonely Hearts Club, The Beatles.
4 - Sympathy For The Devil, The Rolling Stones.

Other books by Richard Valanga

RICHARD VALANGA
BLOODLUST

- The adult sequel to The Sunderland Vampire -

If you pick this up, you won't put it down!
Once I started, I couldn't stop reading, another excellent dark and brooding and a little bit sexy tale from Mr Valanga.
Julie Bramley - 5 Stars.

"Couldn't stop once I had started reading! Nearly made me late for work."
Julie Bramley.

"Getting engrossed in my book… Making the nightshift much more entertaining!!"

"It's such a great read… I only put it down when I absolutely had to!! Well done… I'm well and truly hooked!!"
Debbie Read - "Richard Valanga is a true talent."

RICHARD VALANGA
LUST FOR LIFE

The sequel to Bloodlust and The Sunderland Vampire

Where is the evil shape-shifting creature known as Vaag The Bone Drinker?
Why does Luxar 'vampire' Ella Newman need to find Vaag?
Heed the words of the angel Lucifer…
Dare thee try to resurrect?
Dare thee tempt the demons of the mind?
Dare thee tamper with life and death?
The end may not be the one thou seeks.

**A lust for life and a lust for death
The fate of one man lies in the love of others…**

RICHARD VALANGA
THE LAST ANGEL

When the unbelievable finally happens, who will be the one who will save us all?

Heaven is no more. All the Angelic have gone and the world is about to be consumed by a Dark Conscious, pure evil as old as time itself.

After thousands of years of exile, one of the banished Angelic finally returns to Earth.

Is he the last angel? Or are their others like him who will join him in the fight against the inevitable darkness that threatens the world of the living.

First reactions…

"I have just started reading The Last Angel **and I am totally gripped!**"

"Cracking!"

Fantastic tale of fallen angels
I literally devoured this book, I was hooked from the first chapter. Excellent story telling from an amazing author... new to me, but now I will be working my way through his entire library and looking forward to new releases.... amazing!
Debbie Read - 5 Stars.

"OMG!! Just finished The Last Angel. What a fabulous book!!!!!
It really is a great read, love the characters, the twist in their stories and the hint of sexiness."
Debbie Read

Best yet!
My husband read this book and has reported that it is his favourite by this author to date. Excellent work!
Miriam Smith - 5 stars.

"Just finished reading The Last Angel and I can safely say it's my favourite of your books so far."
John Smith.

"I loved it, really enjoyed it, made me think about the deeper aspects of good and evil. At one point during the first chapter I thought that I was not going to finish it because I am not a paranormal fan and I have never read a book like this before but then the end of Chapter One just hooked me and I just had to continue reading it to the end. How do you think of such things?"
Laura Appelby.

RICHARD VALANGA
THE SUNDERLAND VAMPIRE

Late at night, a man awakes in a Sunderland cemetery and is confused and alone. The man cannot remember what has happened and has no recollection of the events that have led him to such a cold and desolate place. Why was he there and more importantly... who was he?

It is not just his loss of memory that is worrying him though, it is the strange new urges that are calling to him from the surrounding darkness, unnatural thoughts that seem somehow familiar... and disturbing.

The Sunderland Vampire is a psychological paranormal mystery thriller and a ghostly gothic romance that ultimately leads back to the coastal town of Whitby.

'It oozes Anne Rice...'

'A great book! Loved it.'

'This is brilliant, wonderfully vivid, very detailed and sumptuous and a pleasure to read.'

'Thrilling and intriguing, I love this book!'

'Great writing... great work!'

<u>'Don't put this down - someone will steal it'</u>
'This handbag size novel **is a total treat to own**. I read it in one sitting then my daughter who has similar tastes as I do started reading it. **From the beginning it draws you in** and you will delight at music references throughout, Sea Breezes by Roxy Music a favourite. **My only request to the author is to write some more!'**

Engaging and haunting...
"The Sunderland Vampire" - Late at night, a man awakes in a Sunderland cemetery and is confused and alone. The man cannot remember what has happened and has no recollection of the events that have led him to such a cold and desolate place. Why was he there and more importantly... who was he? It is not just his loss of memory that is worrying him though, it is the strange new urges that are calling to him from the surrounding darkness, unnatural thoughts that seem somehow familiar... and disturbing.... -

I've never not enjoyed a novel by Sunderland born author Richard Valanga. **He never fails to deliver on giving the reader a truly ghostly paranormal experience with his supernatural writing talents. His flair with words is exceptional** and this psychological paranormal mystery thriller with a ghostly gothic romance leaps off the page with an engaging and haunting ambience.

A novella that packs a punch, "The Sunderland Vampire" is a perfect Halloween read (or for anytime of the year around a roaring fire late at night) and is suitable for readers of all ages.
#TheSunderlandVampire - 5 stars
Miriam Smith.

RICHARD VALANGA
THE WRONG REALITY

Running to save the life of his son, Ryan Walker and the Reverend Daniel McGovern are transported to another reality by an enigmatic blue ripple that suddenly appears on the Tyne Bridge.

For Walker, this reality provides everything he has ever desired except for the complications caused by the death of his ex-wife.

For the Reverend, the other reality is absolute Hell, a Hell that is tearing his vulnerable soul apart.

Murder, blackmail, dark eroticism and a dangerous religion threaten the sanity of the two men but there is a way back to their own reality, a possible window of opportunity that could enable them to return…

The problem is; will they realise this in time as both men are slowly being consumed by their alternate personalities.

'The author's talent for writing engaging tales of the paranormal is second to none.'

'The Wrong Reality for the real world…'
'Richard Valanga's **talented and imaginative** writing style is so suited to the supernatural genre and this together with a mix of horror and dark eroticism, **"The Wrong Reality" is proof of his superb eclectic ability to engage his readers in a truly alternative world.'**

'Excellent read; nostalgia, horror and mystery.'
'The whole theory of one's world being turned on its head is both fascinating and terrifying. **Richard has hit the mark once again**.'

'SUPERnatural - Another **thought provoking** novel from this North Eastern writer.'

'Not like run of the mill sci fi - Haven't read a lot of science fiction but this had a believable storyline, plausible characters, **couldn't put it down until I'd reached the end.'**

'A book to entertain and challenge you.'
An excellent read! An interesting book … it stays with you after you put it down. It starts like a British version of **Sartre's Roads to Freedom trilogy,** but veers off into something else a third of the way through, yet retains the existential thread. **A truly amazing book.**
A well constructed book in all ways. **I highly recommend it**, if you want a fantasy, sci-fi story that challenges you & asks deep questions. Lovely easy to read style, **he leads you deeper into the recesses of you mind than you planned to go.**

'Thought provoking and literally made me shudder in parts…'

RICHARD VALANGA
COLOSSEUM

In the theatre of death only evil reigns supreme.
During the Festival of Death in Rome, four American art students go missing. One of the students is eventually found dead, horribly mutilated as if by wild beasts inside the Colosseum

One year later, Nick Thorn is sent by the New Sanctuary to help the father of one of the missing students, a desperate man who is still looking for his daughter.

The New Sanctuary believes that Thorn has a psychic ability, a 'special gift' that could help him; Thorn however has always denied such a thing, claiming it to be pure nonsense and probably the product of an overactive imagination instigated by his drinking problem.

Shortly after Thorn arrives in Rome, the Festival of Death begins again and another of the missing students is gruesomely murdered. It is now a race against time to find the other two.

Can Thorn find and save the remaining two students or will Mania the Roman Goddess of Death succeed in devouring their souls and satisfy the blood lust of her followers?

Another five star novel from Sunderland born writer…

Whenever you pick up Sunderland born Richard Valanga's novels, you just know it's going to be **filled with his most vivid imaginations and his incredibly engaging storylines,** for which he has put his heart and soul into writing them.

His latest publication "Colosseum" is no exception, this time with a visit to the chilling and haunting atmospheric location of Rome.

"In the theatre of death only evil reigns supreme. During the Festival of Death in Rome, four American art students go missing. One of the students is eventually found dead, horribly mutilated as if by wild beasts inside the Colosseum. One year later, Nick Thorn is sent by the New Sanctuary to help the father of one of the missing students, a desperate man who is still looking for his daughter. The New Sanctuary believes that Thorn has a psychic ability, a 'special gift' that could help him. However, shortly after Thorn arrives in Rome, the Festival of Death begins again and another of the missing students is gruesomely murdered. It is now a race against time to find the other two. Can Thorn find and save the remaining two students or will Mania the Roman Goddess of Death succeed in devouring their souls and satisfy the blood lust of her followers?"

This story is quite blood thirsty, as you'd expect from the ancient gladiator days. The author has included some really spectacular graphic scenes during the Festival of Death, that really set the scene for the plot. I particularly liked the first person narrative from Nick, I found him a curious protagonist, hard drinking, heavy smoking, Robert Mitchum lookalike with a sardonic humour and a similarity to the detective Philip Marlowe and his fellow American dime heroes. His special ability with his physic dreamlike visions make him quite remarkable and the perfect detective to help find the missing students.

There is no denying Richard Valanga's talent for paranormal and horror thriller writing. His visions just keep getting stronger and stronger. "Colosseum" is his most commercial outing to date following on from some very personal and emotive novels and he's a writer I'm more than happy to continue to follow, in the future.

Excellent gripping novel - Amazon Review 26/11/2020

Great thriller!
When a number of students go missing in Rome and one of them is later found dead in the Colosseum, a man with supposed psychic abilities is sent to investigate what happened to the missing students.

He arrives just before the Festival of Death and when another of the missing students is discovered dead in a grisly manner, tension mounts. The race is on to find and rescue the other two students, assuming they're still alive. Were they kidnapped and killed by a secret Roman cult, and tortured by a sinister group of evildoers?
This is an excellent international thriller. Gripping and suspenseful. Highly recommended!

Stephen King meets James Herbert? Or Edgar Allen Poe.
Wow! What a story! Stephen King meets James Herbert! Maybe! A psychological tale with enough gore and horror to scare the living daylights out of you, yet **a plot to tease and intrigue you**, and characters you grow to really care about! **Well written, and excellently plotted**, this book cruises along at breakneck speed. Easy to read, very difficult to put down. **Highly recommended for those wanting a gripping, exciting story that stays with you**. This book needs a follow up …

RICHARD VALANGA
COMPLEX HEAVEN

Set in the North East of England, Complex Heaven is a psychological supernatural thriller that tells the story of a troubled soul tormented by the anguish of his distraught son. Called back from the Afterlife, father of two Richard; is concerned about the mental welfare of his youngest son JJ. There is a suspicion that somehow JJ is connected to the death of a young girl called Rose in Washington. The mystery however, is much more complicated as Richard finally confronts the evil that has been preying on his family for generations. A suffering that forces Richard back to the world of the living; where the answers to some of the darkest moments of his life are waiting.

'Complex and gripping.'
'I read this book in two sittings, very difficult to put it down. The characters are well developed and the plot twists and turns as it snakes to a dramatic conclusion. I heard through the grapevine that there is a sequel coming soon, it can't be too soon for me.' - **Mick Averre.**

'Brilliant, creepy and compelling!'
'I really enjoyed this **brilliant**, psychological supernatural book. **Totally unique** and wholly original I can't recommend this book enough!'

'**Emotional rollercoaster I want to ride again!**'
'When I started reading this book it brought forward so many emotions I had kept locked away. **It captured me right from the start and I couldn't put it down until I had finished!!** I would definitely recommend it.'

'**Gripping**'
'**I started reading the sample to this book and could not tear myself away**. I love the style, subject and setting. I have received my own copy of the book this morning and cannot wait to continue reading.'

'**A resonating read for fans of the paranormal. Excellent!**
'**Profoundly thought-provoking and so descriptive at times** I found myself there! An intense journey - but an enjoyable one. Would highly recommend.'

'**A gripping read.**' Complex Heaven is **imaginative and original in style and content. Definitely a must read.**'

RICHARD VALANGA
COMPLEX HELL

'It's present-day Sunderland and a mysterious manuscript is discovered in the house of an evil spirit, leading the unwary reader to a tale of the sixties in North East England, where not everything is quite as it seems. Forbidden love, loss and a lifetime of pure evil lie in store for whoever dares turn the ageing pages further. In Devils Wood House the memory of the missing girl, Rose, waits desperately. Unfortunately for her, time is not on her side. Can her soul be saved or will the child be lost forever?'

"Richard Valanga writes about the Afterlife like nobody else today, he's the 21st-century Dante of the North." - Tony Barrell, The Sunday Times

'Unique and interesting, thought-provoking, original and creative, it certainly is a tale that will stay in my mind.'

'Creepy paranormal read.'
'The author has a **wonderful and unique writing style** that draws you in instantly. "Complex Hell" is a wholly original take on the afterlife and quite believable too.'

'The author Richard Valanga writes like a poet and has a brilliant and impressive imagination to match.'

'A good read, good memories and pretty good musical taste…
Once again Richard **Valanga excels in not only scaring the reader to death, but evokes fond memories of a time when things were simpler**, when mobile phones and computers were still in the imagination of Science Fiction writers! I feel sure Mr Valanga actually uses the typewriter mentioned in the first chapter! A good read; good memories and pretty good musical taste for something undead. **Richard writes like a man possessed**...because I think he probably is!'

'A very good read.'
'This book was **a very good read, great concept**. Scary, but engaging; **I was compelled to keep reading.'**

RICHARDVALANGA

COMPLEX SHADOWS

Fleeing Devils Wood House in Washington with a car full of ill-gotten riches; a father and his son check into the Seaburn Hotel on the Sunderland coast.

With them is the father's old manuscript which is his account of what he experienced in the jungles of Burma during World War Two. Where there is war there is immense evil, a breeding ground for dark supernatural forces that once encountered will change your life forever.

This book is the third in the Complex Series and helps explain why one family becomes entangled with and haunted by the malevolent Dark Conscious.

'A great read!!'
'I really enjoyed reading this creepy, ghostly and at times scary book. You could truly feel how passionate the author was about his personal and emotional memories during the first half of the story. The whole storyline comes together flawlessly at the end and was certainly quite emotional. **Richard Valanga is a highly talented and imaginative author and I highly recommend this wholly original book**.....it really is a frightening thought that the dead do walk our streets!!'

'Richard Valanga's amazing book Complex Shadows is not for the weak- hearted.'

'The past can be intense and in this supernatural and extremely dark thriller that takes place in the north east of England (Sunderland to be exact) he adds more to this 'one of a kind' read that will have you captive from the start with great visions of the harshness and ugly events of Burma during World War Two to the Shadows of the Past which most of us can relate to.

The attention to detail in this fine piece of work sets this apart from a lot of supernatural and paranormal books I have read. If I was a betting man and with an outstanding Hollywood agent, **I could see this on the silver screen** with an outstanding soundtrack that will draw you into this fabulous read.'

RICHARD VALANGA
COMPLEX REALITY

This is the story of one family's unfortunate entanglement with the malicious evil force known as the Dark Conscious.

A paranormal journey that takes you from present day Sunderland back to the sixties and then even further back to the World War Two jungles of Burma and the horrific beginnings of the story.

Can this persistent deadly evil be defeated, can the reborn spirits of a man and his father finally triumph over the darkness that threatens them and achieve everlasting peace for their family?

"Richard Valanga writes about the Afterlife like nobody else today, he's the 21st – century Dante of the North."
- Tony Barrell, The Sunday Times.

A Great Read!
'A unique and intriguing supernatural tale that blends fact and fiction and leaves the reader questioning the eternal questions of life and death!'

"Fantastic, entertaining read."
"Absolutely loved this book. It hooks you in from the start, triggers your imagination and keeps you entertained with great references to north east locations throughout. Definitely recommend this book to anyone who enjoys science fiction, horror or just an entertaining read."

RICHARD VALANGA
BLIND VISION

To see the evil dead is a curse...

It begins with the Roman exploratore Stasius Tenebris and the Calicem Tenebris (the Dark Chalice) - a vessel of evil that is brought back to life years later by Ethan Chance, a young man who was cruelly blinded by falling into an ancient Roman well when he was nine.

Was it an accident or did the spirits in the well choose Ethan for a reason? ...the Calicem Tenebris restores his sight but at a price.

This is the story of the chalice and the village called Darwell and the dark fate awaiting its inhabitants at the Festival of Healing.

Can Ethan, his friends and a knight from the Crusades save the day or is Darwell doomed to forever serve those who worship Mars, the Roman God of War.

'Blindingly good book'
This is the second book by Richard Valanga I have read and it's even better than his first, Complex Heaven. **If, like me, you enjoy fantasy novels that you can't put down then this author is for you.**
- Mick Averre.

'Brilliant!'
'Although "Blind Vision" is primarily aimed at young adult readers I still thoroughly enjoyed this book, I was drawn into it from the very first page with **great characters and a truly intriguing dark supernatural story line**. Set in 2 time frames- present day and fantasy Roman/Crusaders the story comes together brilliantly in a very detailed and fascinating way.'

'Richard Valanga is a great writer who has a fantastic imagination and I would happily recommend "Blind Vision" to readers of any age - you won't be disappointed!'

'**The end is very exciting.** You can feel the tension in the air. You can't put the book down. You just want to read faster and faster to find out what's going to happen. It is absolutely amazing. **One of the best books I have ever read**.' – A Young Adult reader.

THE MUSIC OF FAMILY AND ME
a memoir
RICHARD VALANGA

Family were an English underground progressive rock band of the late sixties and early seventies. Brilliant, eclectic, original and unique are just some of the words that describe Family, a band fronted by the amazing singer songwriter called Roger Chapman who still continues to excite people today with his excellent solo career, check out his latest brilliant album called Life In The Pond.

In this memoir, I use the music of Family as a vehicle to journey back in time as I review each album and each song to see what memories they open up for me. I really hope that you enjoy this personal trip which I primarily wrote for my son James. For me, Family were the best, they produced music like no other, it is as simple as that.

revisit, review, recall

"I have to say **I feel humbled** in a big headed sort of way. Anyway, tell Richard it's great to read 50/100 pages of great reviews & **I appreciate it very much.** If he could send me some copies when published, I'll circulate to the people who I think & hopefully himself count. Again thanx very much, **a real honour**. Cheers, **Roger Chapman**."

"Cheers & must say **love the idea** as it also brings me back long forgotten memories good & bad. - **Roger Chapman**."

Wow!!! I am now starting the chapter about Family's 2nd LP, "Entertainment." What is so nice to read is the author's memories juxtapositioned next to his discussion of the music and the times in his life and world make this **such a warm, inviting reading experience**. This combination engages me on diferent levels. Even better, Richard Valanga's book causes me to reach for the CD'S that he is focussing on. Music is a universal language. So is the lexiconic message in words. **This gentleman does this exquisitely!!**
I would most highly recommend this book. Especially, if you loved the band Family and the music of Roger Chapman. (By the way, Roger's new CD, at 79 years young, **"Life in the Pond"** is also an incredible slick of **fabulous Music of the highest order**.)
David Freshman.

What a great book to read about the songs of **Family**, the British band. This band operated on so many different musical levels and styles! **Richard Valanga's work is so unique in that it juxtapositions his life and how the songs and music of Family made him feel.** This book is a fast read with **great insights** and defining understandings of the inner workings of the band and their music.
With **great details** explained by Mr. **Roger Chapman**, the lead singer/lyricist in the iconic band, the veracity and meanings become all the more **focussed and clear.**
A great book to have! Great work Mr. Valanga!
David Freshman.

I've had the privilege to read this before it went to print, and I have to say that **I am mightily impressed by this tome, to the extent that I couldn't put it down!**
This book is different from so many other Rock biographies in so much that it connects Valanga the writer to whatever he was doing at the time, and it does this in a song by song album way. So not only do you get a history of the writer as he came of age he carefully juxtaposes his

life with the music of Family as it came out of the gramophone round a friend's house, or the radio at work, or in concert in Sunderland - **quite clever really…**
Simon Boxall.

Great Book
It was about time someone wrote a book about Family! Along with the Beatles and Led Zeppelin they were one of the most influential in my career as a musician. It gives **a great insight into the band and it's music. Fantastic writing** from someone who undoubtably loved Family as much (if not more) as I do.
It's a must have for me!
Paul Thompson - Roxy Music.

A mixture of 'High Fidelity' and '31 Songs' THE MUSIC OF FAMILY AND ME is **a very readable tale of fandom, obsession and heartache.** It is a great example of what music means, not only for teenagers but to people of any age!
Marc Andelane.

A great read
Love this book. As a lifetime fan of Family it's great to relate back to the memories of the group and the legacy of the music. Richard used his memories of the group to paint a .picture of the albums and the live gigs I could easily relate to. **A lovely nostalgic trip back.**
Tony Upton.

Entertainment
Excellent read chronological review of the great band FAMILY. **Well done Richard** got me to play all the albums again. **Thank you.**
Eddy.

Excellent!
I **really enjoyed reading this book** and reminiscing about my favourite band and their songs.
Mr Paul D Barnett.

Great Family read
Richard **takes us through every album** release and I'm right there with him.
David Jeanes.

A **fantastic** read from one of the finest rock bands Britain produced.

John Atkinson.

Evocative Memoir of a Great Band
Never saw Family perform live since I was a USA midwestern boy/man. But **this personal memoir helps evoke what being there in the UK in those heady days would have felt like.**
Richard L Giovanoni.

A criminally neglected band from the 70s gets it due - 5 STARS
In the early 70s a friend from my high school years Mike Green came back from a hitch-hiking trip he made through England. As was common back in the day Mike and I talked music when we got together, specifically we talked about the music scene in England this time. Mike knew I loved the bands Yes and Jethro Tull, " Yeah, Yes and Tull are big in England like here in the States", he mentioned. He went on, "But you know what? There is a different scene going on in England than here." A band called the Move is big "over there" he told me and there is this other group that is bigger than all of these... Mike loans me a record by this band that goes by the name Family, the record is FEARLESS. I notice the album has this multi-leaf cover, that is pretty novel, and I take it home and put it on with no expectations (the best way there is to listen to a new record if you ask me) and no previous knowledge of the band. Putting side 2 on first (a habit of mine) Take Your Partners spills into my room from my console tv/ record player combo I had at the time. There is this squiggly, funky electronic intro first, then the percussion starts slowly kicking in and with the first minute of Take Your Partners my consciousness takes immediately to "something" in this music, others have called the experience the sound of surprise (always a good thing to adventurous listeners). It was playful, syncopated and very English in a way I had yet experienced at the time.

So it went over the years with each of their albums. Each one with a different vibe that drew me in in some way as Take Your Partners and the rest of FEARLESS had. I played Family to friends who came by my place, but I can't recall anyone being all that impressed with them back in the day. Undaunted and in some way emboldened it made their music more endearing to me, they became one of "my" bands.

Fast forward to almost 50 years later I come across the Facebook group Richard Valanga leads - **Family With Roger Chapman Appreciation Society. There I found the music I love by Family**, the solo music of Roger Chapman and other members of the band cast in a new light. **Here were droves of mostly folks from the British Isles who took for granted all along that Family was the greatest band ever.** I was like Dorothy landing in Oz. I love the insights into a favorite band of mine from fans who were boots on the ground back in the day. So many stories from the past as well as current heads ups to recent developments with the band and members. Not the least of which came from the current book's author Richard Valanga.

With this as a lead in I was all set for Richard's book THE MUSIC OF FAMILY AND ME.♥ **This is not Richard's first book and clearly is a labour of love.** The hours I shared with friends like Mike Green at the beginning of this review, hours talking about music come back in rich ways as **Richard shares his love for the music of Family. This was unexpectedly and especially endearing about this memoir.** Check it out. Doesn't matter if you are a die-hard fan or a complete and total novice like I was in 1972. Read the book and re-hear the music in tandem; or hear the music fresh to your ears and go the book for a clear perspective that Richard lends. **Either way this book is a winner.**
Jeff Gifford.

Like being in the pub with a friend…
Like the author I first saw Family back in 1971 and like the author my father fought at Kohima (one of the bloodiest battles of WW2). Back then, when your mate got a new album and before you got chance to get together to listen to it, erstwhile chum would describe the songs to you :) This review and recollections of Family's canon of music is like being down the pub with your friend talking about the latest music that you have heard. To be picky, the downside is that the book is self-published and suffers the vagaries of sending a file off for printing - no matter how hard you try the pagination etc is going to get a bit weird. But that is being picky. A great read… and if you are not familiar with Family then you should be… jazzy, rhythmically interesting, wonderful melodies and musicianship. In addition Roger Chapman wrote thoughtful well constructed lyrics. Live, they were on another planet...Chapman terrifying!
Kim38

A thoroughly good read
For someone like myself who like the author was an avid Family fan this is a must, the author blends his own experiences with his love of Family's music a time-line that I completely identified with. His description of every song is both illuminating and interesting and conveys perfectly the atmosphere of the time. I enjoyed every page.
Chris Longdon

RICHARD VALANGA
THE NEXT REALITY

To get to Heaven
You have to go through Hell

The Blue Ripple is an anomaly of nature that will transfer your mind to another reality.
A young man risks the Ripple to see the woman he had loved and had died in his reality.
The man is accidentally joined by investigator Nick Thorn in a strange twist of fate that makes them battle the dangers of a different world together.
Murder, abduction and dark eroticism await the two men in the deadly and vicious next reality.
Will love prevail?
Or was the journey a leap of faith too far?

5 Stars on Amazon.

RICHARD VALANGA
BLOOD MIRACLE

A theological mystery thriller.

A young man with amnesia finds himself in an isolated farmhouse during an unnatural heavy snowstorm. Where is he, who is he? Mysterious dreams, sudden hallucinations, enigmatic artworks, contemporary music, strange marble statues, compelling intriguing books, famous artists and an obsessive author become part of the metaphysical puzzle that builds in intensity day by day, threatening the young man's sanity as the answer to the mystery of who he is becomes increasingly crucial. Will Churchyard Farm experience a miracle; can the stranded, lost young man's sanity and his fragile soul be saved?

RICHARD VALANGA
DAY OF THE ROMAN

- The sequel to Blind Vision -

They all thought that the story of the Festival of Healing had been concluded.

But the shadow of evil is back in the northern town of Darwell, determined to find the Sword of Pluto, a sword that could determine the future of the world.

Ethan Chance is blind and has gone missing and his family and friends are worried. Ethan has a 'Blind Vision' that is capable of seeing pure evil and the living dead but now this power has mutated.

Where is Ethan and what is is his connection to the Sword of Pluto and the Shield of Saturn?

Can Ethan's friend, Adam Sunderland and an old Viking spirit called

Ragnar save Darwell once again from the threatening forces of the ancient Roman AGOTE, who want to send the world back in time?

RICHARD VALANGA
THE MUSIC OF ROXY MUSIC ENO AND ME
a memoir

Inspired by the critical success of my Music of Family memoir, I decided to continue with a Roxy Music Eno memoir which sort of made sense to my personal time-line, the inclusion of my formative art college years.

So I drifted back to those golden years aided by the incredible music of Roxy Music and Brian Eno which was a vehicle to re-ignite my memories, a key to unlock those dormant thoughts…

We cannot go back but we can remember, the what ifs, the if only's, the heartache and joys of a young life and I always needed something to get me through the dark times and music was that something, a shining light of hope that has never faded.

    Once again, this memoir is for my son James, a little insight into the life of his father when he was a young man so any unfavourable critical response to this book will mean absolutely nothing to me, all I can hope is that you do enjoy this memoir and I am sure that the music of Roxy Music and Eno will bring back memorable moments for you too.

    Viva Roxy, viva Eno!

"Thanks for the memories!"
"I picked up the Sunderland vampire's latest edition of him. Devoured it in two sittings and thoroughly enjoyed it. I was more interested in Richard's life than the Roxy/Eno bits, although I was obviously into those too. I figure there's a couple of years between us and NE common ground, so a lot of it felt really familiar - from the plastic Beatles wig to the strangeness of leaving hyem for college. Thank you for sharing your memories and helping me relive mine. X"

"If you were present at the time, a great read, and even if you weren't!"
"Brought back so many memories of an amazing time in the music world. If you're a Roxy Music fan this is a must have. I lived in London at the time but can relate to so much of what Richard writes about.
Great stuff and also fascinating insight to the authors life."

"Another rapid page turner from the 21st century master of thrillers/nostalgia."
"I loved the reviews of songs, and memories of the writers younger days, it made me think I'd been there although I'm a bit younger and located miles away."

RICHARD VALANGA
BLIND VISION/DAY OF THE ROMAN

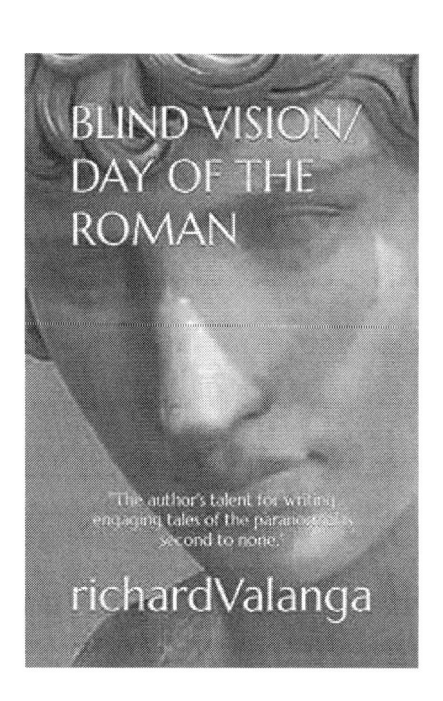

BLIND VISION

To see the evil dead is a curse...

It begins with the Roman exploratore Stasius Tenebris and the Calicem Tenebris (the Dark Chalice) - a vessel of evil that is brought back to life years later by Ethan Chance, a young man who was cruelly blinded by falling into an ancient Roman well when he was nine.

Was it an accident or did the spirits in the well choose Ethan for a reason? ...the Calicem Tenebris restores his sight but at a price.

This is the story of the chalice and the village called Darwell and the dark fate awaiting its inhabitants at the Festival of Healing.

Can Ethan, his friends and a knight from the Crusades save the day or is Darwell doomed to forever serve those who worship Mars, the Roman God of War.

DAY OF THE ROMAN

They all thought that the story of the Festival of Healing had been concluded.

But the shadow of evil is back in the northern town of Darwell, determined to find the Sword of Pluto, a sword that could determine the future of the world.

Ethan Chance is blind and has gone missing and his family and friends are worried. Ethan has a 'Blind Vision' that is capable of seeing pure evil and the living dead but now this power has mutated.

Where is Ethan and what is is his connection to the Sword of Pluto and the Shield of Saturn?

Can Ethan's friend, Adam Sunderland and an old Viking spirit called Ragnar save Darwell once again from the threatening forces of the ancient Roman AGOTE, who want to send the world back in time?

RICHARD VALANGA
THE BLUE RIPPLE

This book is The Wrong Reality and the sequel The Next Reality.

A metafictional sci-fi/paranormal/horror story about The Blue Ripple, a spacial anomaly that will send your mind back in time to another reality.

To get to Heaven, you have to go through Hell.

Which reality are you living in?